Calder
Promise

Calder
Promise

JANET DAILEY

KENSINGTON BOOKS
http://www.kensingtonbooks.com

KENSINGTON BOOKS are published by

Kensington Publishing Corp.
850 Third Avenue
New York, NY 10022

All Kensington titles, imprints and distributed lines are available at special quantity discounts for bulk purchases for sales promotion, premiums, fundraising, educational or institutional use.

Special book excerpts or customized printings can also be created to fit specific needs. For details, write or phone the office of the Kensington Special Sales Manager: Kensington Publishing Corp., 850 Third Avenue, New York, NY 10022. Attn. Special Sales Department. Phone: 1-800-221-2647.

Kensington and the K logo Reg. U.S. Pat. & TM Off.

Library of Congress Card Catalogue Number: 2003116198
ISBN 0-7582-0440-X

First Printing: July 2004
10 9 8 7 6 5 4 3 2 1

Printed in the United States of America

PART ONE

There's a promise in the wind,
A hint of devil-may-care,
A time for fun and frolic,
And a Calder wants her share.

Chapter One

The flattering glow of candlelight welcomed the arriving guests to the home of Count and Countess Valerie, a sixteenth-century palazzo on Rome's Capitoline Hill. Twenty-one-year-old Laura Calder ran an appreciative eye over the frescoes and friezes that adorned the walls and ceilings of one of the palazzo's many ballrooms, but her attention quickly reverted to her fellow guests.

Not all had gathered in the ballroom. Some, first-timers like herself, were being shown around the palazzo, a tour Laura had recently completed. Virtually all on hand were strangers to her, although Laura recognized several faces, identifying them from photographs she had seen in either the society or business pages. So far she had spotted an Italian film producer, a French dignitary, an American industrialist, a former British prime minister, a robed papal envoy, and a Pulitzer Prize–winning author.

Yet, surveying the throng of notables and glitterati, Laura was half-tempted to unleash a rather raucous "Yee-haw" just to watch the shock waves it would create among such a staid and dignified gathering. She smiled at the thought of all the raised eyebrows and down-the-nose looks that would be directed her way if she did. *Perhaps another time,* she decided.

"Excuse me—you there, young lady." Amongst the foreign chatter going on around Laura, the gruff and rather demanding male voice was too distinctively American with its trace of Texas twang not to immediately catch her attention.

When she looked around to locate its source in the acoustically poor ballroom, she spotted an older man in a wheelchair, positioned facing the doors that opened into the palazzo's inner courtyard. In a glance, she took in the grizzled silver of his hair, the harsh, age-lined gauntness of his face, and the thickness of his heavily muscled torso beneath the fine cut of his suit jacket, a thickness that was so at odds with the atrophied slenderness of his legs.

There was something vaguely familiar about his face, and about the fact that it belonged to a man in a wheelchair, but Laura couldn't make the connection to come up with his name. Belatedly she noticed that his hard, dark eyes had fastened their gaze on her.

"You there." He motioned to her, then paused and scowled uncertainly. "Do you speak English?"

Her mouth curved in an easy smile. "I do indeed."

"An American. Thank God," the man muttered, half under his breath, then broke eye contact with her and nodded toward the door. "Give me a hand with this door. I need some air."

Laura caught the note of frustration in his voice and guessed immediately that this was a man who loathed the idea that he required anyone's assistance. Just like her grandfather, it could make him very irritable.

Certain that he would find any verbal response from her irksome, Laura said nothing and simply crossed to the door. As she pushed it open, she noticed the raised threshold and knew it could pose a problem for him even though the wheelchair was motorized. Without a word, she passed him her beaded evening bag and stepped to the back of his chair. Gripping the handles, she gave it a push and a tilt and wheeled him into the inner courtyard.

With a touch of the controls, the man swung the chair toward her and ran an appraising eye over her, inspecting the sophisticated upsweep of her blond hair, the sculpted fineness of her features, the diamonds that dangled from her lobes, and the silken elegance of her gown, its rich chocolate color intensifying the deep, dark brown of her eyes that contrasted so with the gold of her hair.

"You're stronger than you look," he announced, making no effort to return her evening bag.

"I'll take that as a compliment." Laura allowed a small smile to play across her lips.

"What's your name?"

"Laura Calder."

"Calder, you say. Any relation to the Calders of Montana?" he asked, exhibiting a mild curiosity.

"Chase Calder is my grandfather," she confirmed, not at all surprised that he should know of her family. While the Calder name meant little in Europe, it was widely known at home.

"Your grandfather," he murmured and looked at her with new eyes. "You must be Jessy Calder's daughter, 'cause you certainly didn't get that blond hair from Chase." He shot a look toward the ballroom. "Is your mother here? I don't recall seeing her."

"No, I'm with Tara Calder. She's been like an aunt to me." She was deliberately offhand with her answer, skipping any specific response to a relationship that was difficult to explain, even though it had existed almost from the day she was born. Eyebrows were invariably raised when people learned that Tara Calder had been her father's first wife. Yet, in many ways Laura was closer to her than she was to her own mother.

"Tara," he thoughtfully repeated the name, then brightened in sudden recognition. "Of course. E.J. Dyson's daughter. I remember now; she was married to your father once." His eyes narrowed on her, an avidly interested gleam lighting them that Laura had seen in others when they made the same connection. "And you're here with her."

Laura was too used to fielding such remarks to be bothered by it. She handled it the way she always did, by altering ever so slightly the direction of the conversation.

"Yes. I graduated from college at midterm, but Tara insisted that my education wouldn't be complete without a tour of Europe."

He nodded, his expression taking on a faraway look. "Yes, that's the way it used to be done when a girl came of age. February in Switzerland, March in Greece or the Riviera, April in Paris, naturally, and . . ." He paused before concluding, "Italy in May."

"Something like that," Laura admitted, his guess at her itinerary coming close to accurate.

"Must be missing Montana about now," he surmised.

"I haven't really had time. There's been too much to do, to see, and to experience." And she was loving every moment of it. With his questions answered, it was her turn to ask some. "I'm sorry. I don't mean to appear rude, but—I know I should recognize you."

"I'm Max Rutledge."

"Of course." Everything clicked into place: Max Rutledge, the Texas rancher turned oilman, turned banker; a politically powerful mover and shaker behind the scenes, crippled in a car wreck that claimed his wife's life—and worth billions. "I've heard of you."

His chin lifted in measured challenge. "What have you heard?"

Laura knew instinctively that she was being tested. "I've heard that you have no patience with fools or liberal Democrats."

With a grin as big as Texas splitting his face, he settled back in his wheelchair and surveyed her with approval. "That's one and the same thing, isn't it?" The question at the end was purely rhetorical. "That answer was a bit cheeky. Kinda surprised me."

Laura smiled, certain now that she knew how to deal with him. "I imagine you are a lot like my grandfather. He can't stand it when people pull their punches because of who he is."

"I met your grandfather a couple times. It was some years

back, though," Max Rutledge recalled. "He struck me as a man who knows exactly what he wants. More important, he knows how to keep it." He studied her thoughtfully. "I get the feeling that some of that trait runs in you."

"You definitely have met my grandfather." Laura carefully avoided a direct response. It was something she had learned from her grandfather. Endless times he had told her never to brag about who she was or what she had, counseling her that if someone didn't know, he'd find out on his own soon enough. It was a lesson that had gone hand in glove with Tara's teaching that it was more important for Laura to make the *right* impression than a good one.

"So"—Max Rutledge dropped her evening bag onto his lap and clamped both hands on the armrests of his wheelchair—"are you enjoying this little do?"

"I am. Aren't you?" she countered.

He harrumphed ever so faintly, with a note of amusement. "Not really. For a man like me, trapped in this thing, I spend half the evening staring at buckles and bosoms."

Laura laughed, a spontaneous and natural reaction to his irreverent remark. She struggled to swallow it back, not wanting him to think she was laughing at his infirmity. But remnants of it bubbled in her voice when she said, "That offers a very different perspective on what it's like for you."

"It's a view that can have some eye-opening rewards on occasion," he declared with a naughty twinkle in his eyes.

"I can imagine—vividly." There was a movement in her side vision as one of the guests passed by the door, briefly blocking the light from the ballroom streaming into the courtyard. It suddenly occurred to her that Tara might be wondering where she was. For that matter, whoever came with Max Rutledge might be wondering the same thing about him. Laura was certain a man of his stature wouldn't have come alone. "Is there someone with you? I could—"

"Just my son."

Laura thought she detected a note of impatience, almost disgust, in his rather abrupt reply. "Boone—isn't that his name?" she recalled, unable to summon up much else about him except a vague memory that this most eligible bachelor from Texas had a bit of a reputation for playing the field.

"That's right. He's getting the grand tour of the palace."

Again she sensed an air of dissatisfaction and decided that Boone Rutledge wasn't a wise subject to pursue. "The view from the palazzo's rooftop garden is quite spectacular."

"So I hear. But these old palaces don't come equipped with elevators."

"I hadn't thought of that," Laura admitted with a touch of her mother's candor.

"No reason why you should," he replied and once more subjected her to the penetrating study of his gaze. "I like you. You'd make a good wife for my son."

She arched her eyebrows a little higher at his bold statement. "Thank you, but I think your son may have something to say about that."

A darkness gave his eyes a steely quality. "Not as much as you might think," he muttered and looked up when a tall, broad-shouldered figure filled the doorway and threw a shadow across them. "It's about time you showed up, Boone." Again his voice had that edge to it as if there was little about his son that pleased him. "I thought I would have to hold on to this lady's handbag all evening." He stretched out an arm, extending the beaded purse to Laura.

When she stepped forward to reclaim her bag, Boone Rutledge moved out of the doorway to approach them. Laura slid her glance over him, quick to notice the hint of curl in his dark hair, the hard and manly angles of his face, and the muscled trimness of his physique. When Boone added a sexy smile of greeting to the mix, the result was a package of raw virility that required only a black Stetson to complete the image of Texan manhood. It made her wonder if Max Rutledge had cut a similar figure when he was whole and in his prime.

"I'd like you to meet my son, Boone," Max said, beginning the introductions. "Boone, this is Laura Calder, Chase Calder's granddaughter."

"Chase Calder of the Triple C Ranch in Montana?" Boone glanced at his father for confirmation even as he reached out a hand to Laura in formal greeting.

"The same." Max nodded.

"I always meant to attend one of the Triple C's private livestock auctions. And now, meeting you, I really am sorry I haven't." He held her hand an instant longer than necessary, conveying his interest.

Laura didn't feign any false modesty. She was blond, built, and beautiful—and knew it. Dealing with a man's advances, whether wanted or otherwise, was one of the first things she had learned.

"In that case I'll make sure that you both receive a personal invitation to our next one." She made her smile warm enough to encourage his interest.

"If you do, you can count on me being there." His gaze locked on hers, the darkening light in his eyes adding an intimate message of his own. She recognized the signs of a man used to making easy conquests. Her own reaction was an instinctive desire to rise to the challenge of being the one who held the lead rope.

"Better bring your checkbook," she replied. "Once you see what the Triple C has to offer, you'll be glad to pay the high price."

Max Rutledge barked out a laugh. "By God, Boone, if you've got a brain in your hand, you'll marry this gal."

"Don't mind him," Boone said to Laura, a tiny flicker of irritation showing in his expression. "My father is a little brash, but he has good taste."

"But taste is always a matter of personal choice, isn't it?" Laura smiled to let Boone know she didn't take his father's comment at all seriously.

"You young people these days," Max grumbled, "you're a lotta talk and little action."

"Don't rush things, Max," Boone replied without pulling his gaze from Laura. "You don't want to scare her off."

"I have a feeling it would take a lot to scare this one," Max stated, sizing her up again with another sweeping look before firing a glare at his tall son. "And it sure as hell would take more than you."

A smile continued to curve Boone's mouth, but Laura observed the tightening of suppressed anger in it as he sliced a look at his father. "*You* could scare her, though. There aren't many women willing to tolerate meddling in-laws."

The friction between father and son was obvious, and Laura suspected it was long standing. Considering that her own relationship with her mother was far from perfect, Laura could sympathize with Boone.

Seeking to smooth away the awkwardness of the exchange and its undertones of bitterness, Laura issued a practiced laugh, a soft and tinkly sound, and sent a twinkling glance at Boone. "Ahh, isn't the generation gap a pain?"

Gone was that sexy flirting of a man who had made a habit of directing it at any attractive woman within range of his vision. In its place was a searing warmth that made Laura wonder if she was the first to ever be the recipient. She experienced a little surge of triumph as she felt him slipping around her finger.

"A royal pain," Boone agreed, regarding her with a new and more intimate interest.

Laura didn't need to glance at the man in the wheelchair to be aware that he was observing the two of them with a good deal of satisfaction.

"There you are, Laura,"

The femininely soft drawl was instantly familiar. Laura turned, watching as Tara Calder moved toward them with her typical gliding grace. She was struck again by the woman's incredible beauty, a beauty that was stunning and absolutely ageless. Tara's only concession to her advancing years was a dramatic streak of white in her otherwise midnight dark hair. Whether the streak was nature's doing or mere artifice, not even Laura knew.

"I looked everywhere for you. What on earth are you doing out—" Tara broke off the question the instant she noticed the wheelchair-bound man. "Max Rutledge. I don't believe it." Altering her course, she crossed to his side, first bending to air-kiss his cheeks, then crouching down next to him, the fullness of her gown's skirt poofing about her. "I certainly never expected to run across you here in Rome. I won't bother to ask how you are. You're looking as robust as ever."

"I look like hell, but you are still the most charming liar I have ever known," Max declared in a voice that was dry and mocking.

Tara laughed, low and musical, and briefly pressed a hand on his arm. "My daddy told me a long time ago that when you come across something sour, just pile on a lot of sugar." With a fluid move, she stood erect and turned to Boone. "My, but you have grown into a handsome rogue, Boone. How do you manage to put up with this grumpy old bear?"

"He doesn't have a choice," Max inserted, but Tara gave no sign that she had heard his somewhat caustic remark.

Boone dismissed her question with a noncommittal, "You can't pick your parents." He warmly clasped her hand, enveloping it in both of his. "You are as beautiful as ever, Tara."

"Thank you," she replied with a demure dip of her head, then withdrew her hand and divided her glance between father and son. "Tell me, how did the two of you manage to lure my ward into the courtyard?"

"Sheer luck, I think," Boone replied as he directed an intimate, warm look at Laura.

"I suspect the luck is all Laura's." Tara drifted closer to her self-proclaimed ward, then addressed Laura in pseudo-confiding manner. "You do realize that you are in the company of two of the world's most sought after bachelors, not to mention that you are practically neighbors—at least in a manner of speaking."

"Really?" Laura said with some surprise. "Do you own land in Montana?"

"Good Lord, no. It's too damned cold up there," Max stated with force.

"Actually," Tara began, "I was referring to the Rutledge family ranch. The Slash R can't be far from the old Calder homeplace in Texas that Chase bought from Hattie before they were married, and especially after he bought so much of the adjoining land." She looked to Max for confirmation.

"We have a boundary in common," he acknowledged.

"If I had known we had such attractive neighbors," Boone inserted, smiling at Laura, "I would have paid a visit long ago."

"Actually I've only been to the C Bar a couple of times, and that was when I was much younger," Laura said.

"Chase bought it for purely sentimental reasons," Tara recalled, "after learning that the C Bar was his grandfather's birthplace. For a good many years, he and Hattie used it as a winter retreat to escape the Montana cold, but I don't think he's been back since Hattie passed away five years ago. Truthfully, I don't think he's physically capable of making the trip any more. It's hardly surprising, considering Chase is in his eighties."

"If he ever decides he wants to sell the place, tell him to give me a call. It would be easy enough to incorporate the ranch into my spread," Max declared.

"I'll let him know," Laura promised, although she doubted her grandfather would be interested in selling.

Losing interest in the subject, Tara changed it. "So what brings you two to Rome? Is it a business or pleasure trip?"

"Business, of course," Max retorted. "And don't bother asking what kind. It's my business and none of Dy-Corp's."

"Now, Max," Tara said in a chiding tone. "You know I have nothing to do with running my daddy's corporation."

"Not officially," he agreed dryly, "but you know the right strings to yank when you want something done. There's a lot of truth in that old saying, the fruit never falls far from the tree.

You're E.J. Dyson's daughter, all right. Unfortunately, Boone is his mother's son—all looks and no brains. He'd rather play than work."

Boone smiled away the criticism. "It's always bothered him the way I manage to make time for a little pleasure on any business trip. And having two such beautiful women as dinner companions definitely makes this trip a pleasure." Even though he included Tara in his remark, his attention was centered on Laura.

"You're being too kind," she told him in mock protest.

"Kindness has nothing to do with it," Boone assured her.

"Speaking of dinner, when the hell are they going to serve it?" Max demanded in a sudden surge of impatience. "I suppose we'll have to wait until the middle of the damned night to eat."

The words were barely out of his mouth when the musical tinkle of a set of chimes drifted out from the ballroom. "You're in luck, Max," Tara said. "I believe that's the signal that dinner is served."

"High time, too," he muttered, as Boone moved to the back of his chair to assist him.

After reentering the ballroom, the foursome joined the flow of the other guests idly making their way to the hall. With the wheelchair rolling along under its own power, Boone left his father's side to join Laura.

"How long will you be staying in Rome?" he asked. "I don't believe you said."

"A day or two, at least. We've been toying with the idea of going to Tuscany for a few days, or maybe to the coast. We have a very flexible schedule, totally subject to the whim of the moment. And you, will you be staying long in Rome?"

"Unfortunately no. Just two more days here, then it's on to London."

"What a shame. England's on our list, but not until later."

"There's nothing to stop you from making more than one visit, is there?" Boone asked in light challenge. "You did say your schedule was subject to the whim of the moment."

"I did say that, didn't I?" The teasing smile she gave him was playfully noncommittal. With a man like Boone Rutledge, Laura suspected it would never be wise to seem too eager for his company.

"Yes, you did." He leaned fractionally closer, his voice lowering to a volume intended for her hearing alone. "I can promise you dinner, alone, at an intimate little restaurant I know with a great view of the Thames."

As they reached the wide doorway into the hall, Laura threw him a laughing look. "Ahh, but can you promise me a misty London fog—" She suddenly collided hard with another guest, the sudden impact surprising a small outcry from her. A pair of hands gripped her upper arms, preventing Laura from being knocked completely off balance. She couldn't say how, but she knew in that instant they didn't belong to Boone.

"Hey, watch where you're going." Boone's indignant voice came from very near.

"I'm sorry. Did I hurt you?"

It was the second voice, male and distinctively British in its accent, that prompted Laura to lift her head. "No. I . . ." The words died in her throat when she found herself face to face with a fair-haired stranger with hazel eyes, flecked with beguiling glints of gold. The air between them seemed suddenly charged with a white hot current of electricity. Laura felt the tingle of it through her entire body, snatching at her breath and scrambling her pulse.

Something flickered across the stranger's lean, angular features, erasing the look of concern and replacing it with a deep, heady warmth.

"Hel-lo," he said, giving each syllable a dazed and dazzled emphasis.

"What happened, Laura? Did you forget to look where you were going?" The familiarity of Tara's affectionately chiding voice provided the right touch of normalcy.

Laura seized on it while she struggled to collect her composure. "I'm afraid I did. I was talking to Boone and—" she paused a beat to glance again at the stranger, stunned to discover how rattled she felt. It was a totally alien sensation. She couldn't remember a time when she hadn't felt in control of herself and a situation. "And I walked straight into you. I'm sorry."

"No apologies necessary," the man assured her while his gaze made a curious and vaguely puzzled study of her face. "The fault was equally mine." He cocked his head to one side, the puzzled look deepening in his expression. "I know this is awfully trite, but haven't we met before?"

Laura shook her head. "No. I'm certain I would have remembered if we had." She was positive of that.

"Obviously you remind me of someone else then," he said, easily shrugging off the thought. "In any case, I hope you are none the worse for the collision, Ms.—" He paused expectantly, waiting for Laura to supply her name.

The old ploy was almost a relief. "Laura Calder. And this is my aunt, Tara Calder," she said, rather than going into a lengthy explanation of their exact relationship.

"My pleasure, ma'am," he murmured to Tara, acknowledging her with the smallest of bows.

"And perhaps you already know Max Rutledge and his son, Boone." Laura belatedly included the two men.

"I know *of* them." He nodded to Max.

When he turned to the younger man, Boone extended a hand, giving him a look of hard challenge. "And you are?"

"Sebastian Dunshill," the man replied.

"Dunshill," Tara repeated with sudden and heightened interest. "Are you any relation to the earl of Crawford, by chance?"

"I do have a nodding acquaintance with him." His mouth curved in an easy smile as he switched his attention to Tara. "Do you know him?"

"Unfortunately no," Tara admitted, then drew in a breath and sent a glittering look at Laura, barely able to contain her excitement. "Although a century ago the Calder family was well acquainted with a certain Lady Crawford."

"Really. And how's that?" With freshened curiosity, Sebastian Dunshill turned to Laura for an explanation.

An awareness of him continued to tingle through her. Only now Laura was beginning to enjoy it.

"It's a long and rather involved story," Laura warned. "After all this time, it's difficult to know how much is fact, how much is myth, and how much is embellishment of either one."

"Since we have a fairly long walk ahead of us to the dining hall, why don't you start with the facts?" Sebastian suggested and deftly tucked her hand under his arm, turning her to follow the other guests.

Laura could feel Boone's anger over the way he had been supplanted, but she didn't really care. She had too much confidence in her ability to smooth any of Boone's ruffled feathers.

"The facts." She pretended to give them some thought while her sidelong glance traveled over Sebastian Dunshill's profile, noting the faint smattering of freckles on his fair skin and the hint of copper lights in his very light brown hair.

Despite the presence of freckles, there was nothing boyish about him. He was definitely a man fully grown, thirty-something she suspected, with a very definite continental air about him. He didn't exude virility the way Boone Rutledge did; his air of masculinity had a smooth and polished edge to it.

"I suppose I should begin by explaining that back in the latter part of the 1870s, my great-great-grandfather Benteen Calder established the family ranch in Montana."

"Your family owns a cattle ranch?" He glanced her way, interest and curiosity mixing in his look.

"A very large one."

"How many acres do you have? I don't mean to sound nosy, but those of us on this side of the Atlantic harbor a secret fascination with the scope and scale of your American West."

"So I've learned. But truthfully we don't usually measure in acres. We talk about sections," Laura explained. "The Triple C has more than one hundred and fifty sections within its boundary fence."

"You'll have to educate me," he said with a touch of amusement. "How large is a section?"

"One square mile, or six hundred and forty acres."

After a quick mental calculation, Sebastian gave her a suitably impressed look. "That's nearly a million acres. And I thought all the large western ranches were in Texas, not Montana."

"Not all." She smiled. "Anyway, according to early ranch records, there are numerous business transactions listed that indicate Lady Crawford was a party to them. Many of them involved government contracts for the purchase of beef. It appears that my great-great-grandfather paid her a finder's fee, I suppose you would call it—an arrangement that was clearly lucrative for both of them."

"The earl of Crawford wasn't named as a party in any of this, then," Sebastian surmised.

"No. In fact, the family stories that were passed down always said she was widowed."

"Interesting. As I recall," he began with a faint frown of concentration, "the seventh earl of Crawford was married to an American. They had no children, which meant the title passed to the son of his younger brother." He stopped abruptly and swung toward Laura, running a fast look over her face. "That's it! I know why you looked so familiar. You bear a striking resemblance to the portrait of Lady Elaine that hangs in the manor's upper hall."

"Did you hear that, Tara?" Laura turned in amazement to the older woman.

"I certainly did." With a look of triumph in her midnight dark eyes, Tara momentarily clutched at Laura's arm, an exuberant smile curving her red lips. "I knew it. I knew it all along."

"Knew what?" A disgruntled Max Rutledge rolled his chair forward, forcing his way into their circle. But Boone stood back, eyeing the Englishman with a barely veiled glare. "What's all this hooha about?"

"Yes, I'm curious, too," Sebastian inserted.

"Well . . ." Laura paused, trying to decide how to frame her answer. "According to Calder legend, Benteen's mother ran off with another man when he was a small boy. If the man's name was known, I've never heard it mentioned. He was always referred to as a remittance man, which, as I understand, was a term used to describe a younger, and frequently ne'er-do-well, son of wealthy Europeans, often titled."

Sebastian nodded, following her line of thought to its logical conclusion. "And you suspect your ancestor ran off with the man who became the seventh earl of Crawford."

"Actually, Tara is the one who came up with that theory after she found some old photographs."

Taking Laura's cue, Tara explained, "Back when I was married to Laura's father, I was rummaging through an old trunk in the attic and came across the tintype of a young woman. At that time, the housekeeper, who had been born and raised on the ranch, told me it was a picture of Madelaine Calder, the mother of Chase Benteen Calder. I'm not sure, but I think that was the first time I heard the story about her abandoning her husband and young son to run off with another man. Needless to say, I was a bit intrigued by this slightly scandalous bit of family history. And I became more intrigued when I happened to lay the tintype next to a photograph taken of Lady Crawford. Granted, one was a picture of a woman perhaps in her early twenties, and the woman in the other photo was easily in her sixties. Still, it was impossible to discount the many physical similarities the two shared, not to mention that the young woman had been called Madelaine and the older one was known as Elaine. I just couldn't believe it was nothing more than a series of amazing coincidences. I've always suspected they were pictures of the same woman, but I have never been able to prove it."

"And if you could, what would that accomplish?" Max challenged, clearly finding little of importance in the issue.

"Now, Max," Tara chided lightly, "you of all people should know that sometimes there is immense satisfaction to be gained from finding out you were right about something all along."

Max harrumphed but didn't disagree with her response. Boone remained a silent observer. Something about the way he looked at Sebastian Dunshill spoke of his instant dislike of the man.

"You say there's a portrait of Lady Elaine displayed at the earl of Crawford's home," Tara said, addressing the remark to Sebastian.

"Indeed there is. A splendid one."

"I'd love to see it sometime." Her comment had an idle, offhand ring to it. Laura suspected she was the only one who knew the delivery was deliberately calculated to achieve results.

"If you intend to visit England in the near future, perhaps I can obtain an invitation for you." Sebastian's glance included Laura.

"As matter of fact, we have talked about flying to London," Laura admitted and slid a glance at Boone, subtlety letting him know that she hadn't forgotten his dinner invitation. His expression immediately warmed to her.

A liveried servant approached the group, bowed respectfully to Sebastian and addressed him in Italian. Sebastian responded in kind, then explained to the others, "We are to be escorted to the dining hall where the other guests are being seated."

"Let's quit dawdling and go." With a flick of a switch, Max sent his wheelchair rolling forward.

When they arrived at the banquet hall, the Rutledges were directed to the upper end of the table. Boone had barely taken his seat when Max demanded in a low, gravelly voice, "Where's that gal sitting? Not next to that Englishman, I hope."

"No. He's seated to the left of the *contessa*. Laura and Tara are closer to the middle section."

"Good," Max muttered and nodded curtly to the gentleman

seated opposite from him. Then he addressed his son. "Why'd you let that damned Englishman monopolize the conversation like that? You let him snatch her right from under your nose and never said a word."

"Just what is it you think I should have done?" Boone countered in a voice of tightly controlled anger.

"Good God, do I have to tell you everything to do?" Max shot him a look of disgust. "All you had to do was speak up. Instead you stood there and pouted like some kid that had his new toy taken from him. I swear, sometimes I think the only thing you have for a spine is a wishbone."

"For your information, Laura has agreed to meet me in London for dinner later this week," Boone murmured tightly.

"She said that." Max stared at him with a mixture of surprise and skepticism.

"Yes. I plan on talking to her after dinner to settle on an exact date and time."

"See that you do."

"You are actually serious about wanting me to marry her, aren't you?" Boone realized.

"You're damned right I am," Max stated. "I hadn't talked to her two minutes before I knew she had more sand in her little finger than you have in your whole body. It's not likely that any of it will rub off on you, but there's a damned good chance your kids will have it. And that's just about all I've got to look forward to."

Boone held his tongue with an effort and fought the urge to wad up his linen napkin and shove it down the old man's throat.

The multiple-course meal was followed by a private recital performed by a well-known Belgian pianist. It was well after midnight when Laura and Tara emerged from the palazzo and climbed into their hired car.

"What a marvelous party," Tara declared as she absently adjusted the folds of her satin evening wrap. "And so full of surprises, too. First running into the Rutledges—" She broke off the rest of that thought to glance curiously at Laura. "Which reminds me, I noticed that Boone cornered you after the piano recital. What did he want?"

"For me to fly to London and have dinner with him later this week."

"How wonderful. It's little more than a two-hour flight from here. We can arrive in the early afternoon, which will give you plenty of time to get ready," she stated, as always taking charge. "First thing in the morning, I'll notify our pilot of our plans and arrange for reservations at Claridges. Or would you rather stay at the Lanesborough?"

"You're assuming that I accepted the invitation," Laura replied lightly.

Tara gave her a startled look. "You did, didn't you?"

"You sound so shocked." Laura couldn't help but laugh. "Have you suddenly decided to become a matchmaker?"

"Hardly," Tara scoffed. "Actually, I was thinking that a quick trip to England would provide the perfect opportunity to see if Mr. Dunshill could arrange for us to view the portrait of Lady Crawford. Did you speak to him at all after dinner?"

"No." Laura was a bit confused by the disappointment she felt over that. Several times she had caught Sebastian Dunshill looking her way, but he'd made no effort to seek her out. That failure prompted Laura to dig in her heels and refuse to make the next move. Laura knew her pride had been stung. Men had always pursued her.

"Neither did I," Tara admitted. "I'll call the *contessa* in the morning and find out where he's staying. Or . . . do I need to bother?" She glanced expectantly at Laura. "Did you accept Boone's dinner invitation or not?"

"Actually, I told him I would call him tomorrow after I talked to you. So my answer was a tentative 'yes.' "

"You don't sound very enthusiastic." Tara continued to study her. "I had the impression earlier that you found him attractive."

"I do. In fact, I'm looking forward to having dinner with him."

"I shouldn't wonder. Boone Rutledge is unquestionably a rogue. In the last few years, he's gained the reputation of playing the field, although I suspect Max might be the cause for that," Tara added thoughtfully.

It was the kind of remark guaranteed to pique Laura's curiosity. "Why do you say that?"

"I suppose because Max has been so openly critical of nearly every woman Boone has seen. And when Max doesn't like someone, he can make things very uncomfortable for Boone, and painfully humiliating for the object of his scorn." She sent Laura a smiling look of approval. "Fortunately, that's something you don't have to be concerned about. In one short meeting you managed to completely captivate Max. What exactly did you say to him before I arrived?"

Laura smiled, feeling just a bit smug. "The kind of things you taught me. Something respectful yet laced with a careful touch of sass."

Tara's soft laugh was rich with amusement. "I should have guessed you would instantly pick up on that. Above all else, Max Rutledge despises weakness." She ran a thoughtful glance over Laura. "You have an innate ability to make a quick read of a person. It's quite likely a knack you inherited from Chase. It certainly can't be taught—not by me or anyone else."

"I'll take your word for it." Laura idly watched the other traffic zipping through the streets.

"It could prove to be an invaluable asset to the Rutledges," Tara mused. "Max doesn't do as much business entertaining as he should. You could easily change that, though. And the education you could obtain in the machinations of big business would be priceless."

"Matchmaking again?" Laura teased.

"No, merely fantasizing. And perhaps doing a bit of reminiscing, too," she added with a hint of melancholy in her voice. "I always knew your father and I together could achieve great things. There really wasn't any limit to the possibilities we had. I confess, when I imagine you and Boone together, I see a bit of Ty and me. Heaven knows, you are too much like me to ever be content merely becoming some man's wife and the mother of his children. Obviously, you can always have a career of your own, completely separate from whatever your husband may do. But it can be infinitely more stimulating when the two are combined."

Laura listened, aware that there was invariably wisdom in Tara's counsel. But this time Tara's words seemed only to remind her how unsettled her future was. Sooner or later, this tour of Europe would come to a close, and she had yet to decide what she wanted to do with the rest of her life. The income from her trust fund meant she didn't have any financial concerns. At the same time, Laura knew she wouldn't be satisfied for long flitting from one party scene to another. A tension wound through her, making her edgy and restless.

When the car rolled to a stop in front of their hotel, Laura swung her legs out of the car before the doorman had her door fully opened. Ignoring his outstretched hand, she climbed out of the car unassisted and waited by the steps for Tara to join her. She watched with impatience while Tara paused to rearrange the drape of her satin stole.

Headlights caught Laura in their wide beams as a low-slung convertible halted behind their hired car, the sound of its motor reducing to a powerful purr. Laura glanced at the red Porsche, welcoming the distraction of its arrival. An instant later she had her first clear look at the driver's face when he agilely levered himself out of the car. A deep, heady satisfaction quivered through her at the sight of Sebastian Dunshill.

Chapter Two

Without bothering to open the door, Sebastian vaulted from the sports car and approached them with a long-striding walk. All that edgy frustration that had darkened Laura's mood vanished under the warm regard of his hazel eyes.

"Mr. Dunshill, this is a surprise," Tara greeted him, then tilted her head at a curious angle. "Are you staying at the Hassler, too?"

"Not at all. I came to give you this." He held out a folded slip of paper to them. "When Bianca told me you had left, I realized I had failed to let you know how to contact me when you come to England."

"We would have tracked you down somehow," Laura assured him, a knowing smile dimpling the corners of her mouth as she took the paper from him and slipped it into her evening bag. "But this makes it easier. You see, Tara and I just decided to fly to London at the end of the week."

"You have? Wonderful," Sebastian replied with an easy show of pleasure. "Give me a call after you arrive, and we'll settle on a time to view the portrait."

"We'll do that," Laura promised. "We're both curious to see it."

"Indeed we are," Tara agreed, but at the moment her interest was on something else. "You must have known the *contessa* for a long time to be on a first-name basis with her."

"I've known her most of my life," Sebastian replied. "She and my mother are third cousins." Without giving Tara a chance to question him further about his connection to the countess, he changed the subject. "You two aren't calling it an evening already, are you? Rome is just coming alive at this hour."

"If that's an invitation to show me some of the nightlife, I accept," Laura declared with unabashed boldness and threw a brief look at Tara. "You don't mind, do you, Tara? I've been a dignified lady all evening. Now I'm ready to let my hair down and do something improper."

"Not too improper, I hope," Tara admonished lightly. "You two go and have fun. I'll see you in the morning."

Laura turned expectantly to Sebastian, an alluring sparkle in her brown eyes. "Well? Was it an invitation or not?"

"It was." An answering light danced in his own eyes. "If I seem at a slight loss for words, you must forgive me. I thought it would require a great deal more persuasion."

She laughed. "You thought wrong."

"To my everlasting delight," he said and ushered her to his car. After Laura was comfortably settled in the front passenger seat, Sebastian made his way around the hood and slid behind the wheel. Hands on the steering wheel, he asked, "Which nightspots would you prefer—something secluded and romantic, or loud and crowded?"

"Let's start with loud and crowded," Laura stated.

"Loud and crowded it is." The powerful engine roared to life.

As the Porsche accelerated away from the hotel, Laura threw Tara a parting wave and reached up to pull the pins that secured her long blond hair in its confining style. Sebastian darted her a sideways glance when she tossed her head to shake her hair loose.

"You were serious about letting your hair down, weren't you?" An amused smile tugged at a corner of his mouth.

"I'm a firm believer that when you ride in a convertible, you have to let your hair down so the wind can blow through it. It's part of the experience." Laura turned her face into the motion-generated breeze. "A little faster, if you please."

Chuckling softly, Sebastian stepped on the accelerator and the sports car increased its speed. At a reckless pace, they zipped along the busy city streets, darting in and around slower vehicles, careening around corners with tires squealing.

"You're going to get a ticket," Laura warned with laughter in her voice. "You didn't even slow up at that last light."

"One of the first things you have to learn about driving in Rome: motorists tend to regard traffic signs as mere suggestions. So, when in Rome . . ." he reminded her of the oft quoted phrase without bothering to finish it, an impish twinkle in his eyes.

Her throaty laugh was hearty and full. "I knew the moment I saw you behind the wheel of this Porsche, you weren't some stuffy Englishman."

"I hope you haven't made the erroneous assumption that it's mine," he warned. "I merely borrowed it from Bianca."

"I'll bet you had a choice, though."

"As a matter of fact, I did." Sebastian paused to glance her way. "Something told me you might favor a sports car."

"You have sound instincts."

The car picked up more speed along a straight stretch, and Laura surrendered to the freshened wind, enjoying the feel of it whipping through her hair. It reminded her of the many times she had galloped her horse across the rolling range of her Montana home just to feel that exhilarating rush of air against her face.

"I take it you found Bianca's dinner party a bit dull," Sebastian remarked.

Laura dragged a tendril of hair off her cheek and hooked it behind her ear. "Only toward the last. It's a failing of mine," she stated without a trace of repentance. "At times, I'm easily bored."

"It happens to all of us, especially when we've had a surfeit of elegant soirees."

She threw her head back and laughed. "Is that ever the truth. It's been almost nonstop since we arrived in Europe. Which proves it is possible to have too much of a good thing."

But as her glance skimmed his leanly chiseled profile, she became aware again of that little buzz of excitement she felt in his presence, and doubted that it would be possible to have too much of Sebastian Dunshill.

"It's definitely possible to have too much of formal affairs." His voice was laced with humor.

The smile drew her attention to the manly construction of his lips. From there it was an easy step to wonder what his kiss would be like. Laura was conscious of her pulse quickening in anticipation of that moment. She had no doubt at all that it would come, whether at his instigation or hers.

She was almost sorry when they arrived at a nightclub on the edges of Rome's city center. A part of her wanted to continue the car ride, just the two of them. Then the loud, driving beat of a bass drum reached out from the club and caught her up in its primitive spell.

"You asked for loud and crowded," Sebastian reminded her as they entered, greeted by blaring music and a din of laughing, chattering voices.

"It's wonderful." Laura declared, already feeling the need to move with the music's contagious beat.

After a discreet slipping of bills, a waiter led them through the crush of people to a small table near the dance floor. The waiter lingered long enough to take their drink order: a glass of white wine for Laura and a gin and tonic for Sebastian. One song had barely ended before the band struck up another.

"So, do you samba?" Sebastian asked.

"Absolutely." Taking his hand, Laura rose from her chair. The firm pressure of that hand on her waist, guiding her to the dance floor, started her pulse racing. "I never expected to hear Latin music in Rome," she said when he turned her into his arms.

"It's currently riding another wave of popularity here in Europe."

"I'm glad." The blatant sensuality of it suited her mood perfectly.

But they hadn't taken more than a dozen steps before Laura found her movements restricted by her gown's long, pencil-slim skirt, making it difficult to throw herself into the music as she wanted to do.

She stopped dancing. "Let me have your tie."

"My tie?" Sebastian drew his head back in mild bewilderment.

"That's right." She proceeded to hitch her skirt up until the hem was above her knees. "I need it for a belt."

Amused, he unknotted the tie and pulled it from around his neck.

Holding her skirt at the desired height, Laura instructed, "Tie it around my waist."

When Sebastian bent to the task, he brought his head closer to her, close enough that she could make out the shape of some of the faint freckles on his face. With each breath she inhaled the heady, masculine scent of his cologne. She discovered that nearly everything about him stimulated her.

When he tied the first knot to secure the makeshift belt around her waist, Laura cautioned, "Make sure it's tight," and she pressed a finger in the center of the first knot, holding it in place while he made the second one. The intimacy of having him fix her clothes brought its own brand of stimulation to the moment, adding to her high awareness of him.

Finishing the task, he straightened. "That should do it."

Laura placed a hand on his shoulder. "Let's try it again, shall we?"

In answer, he slid his fingers between those of her free hand and fitted his other hand to the curve of her hip bone directly below her newly belted waist. Without hesitation, Sebastian guided her into the samba's opening steps.

The passionate music throbbed around them. The samba's emphasis on eye contact and impression of isolation, along with its exaggerated hip movements, made it an innately sensual dance, but in Sebastian's arms, it took on an added quality of sexiness that Laura hadn't experienced before. And she realized that in the past she had always danced to the music, but not really *with* her partner. The connection she felt with this man, something that was more than merely physical, gave a new dimension to the moment. She felt alive as a woman.

They stayed on the dance floor for song after song, returning to their table only once to take a quick sip of their drinks. As another song drew to a close, Laura leaned into Sebastian's chest, unwilling to break the closeness. She felt the heaviness of his breathing and the hard beat of his pulse, matching her own. The solidness of him made her feel deliciously weak.

Tilting her head back, she looked up into his downturned face and lifted a hand to touch the sheen of perspiration across his upper lip. "It seems we're both working up a sweat," Laura murmured, conscious of her own flushed skin and the pounding of blood through her veins.

"It would be a shame to cool off now." His words were accompanied by a suggestive look that made everything inside her leap. Just then the band struck up another tune. Hearing it, Sebastian smiled. "I thought they were never going to play something slow."

Before Laura had a chance to register the tempo of the music, he had molded her to his length, releasing her hand to circle both arms around her to keep her close. Glorying in the sensations of this new contact, Laura slid her hands behind his neck and let her fingers slide into his light red-brown hair. The scent and feel of him was all around her.

As they swayed together with the music, their feet barely moving, her body felt liquid—and molten. He nuzzled the side of her neck and the sensitive hollow behind her ear, sending little shivers of excitement quivering through her.

Passivity was something totally alien to her nature, making it impossible for Laura to allow him to make all the moves. She turned her head, seeking and finding those masculine lips that were creating so much havoc.

It was no tentative first kiss they shared, but one that was hot and tonguing in its demands. It shook Laura to her toes. She felt herself being pulled into the heat of it without first deciding if it was what she wanted. She was scared and excited by the power of it.

Sebastian was the first to break it off, dragging his mouth from hers in obvious reluctance. She saw the quick delving of his gaze, and realized, with much satisfaction, that he had been shaken by the kiss, too.

"Do you always kiss strange men like that?" he asked with a teasing lightness that gained her instant approval.

"No, but I'll bet that you kiss all strange women that way," she retorted, recovering some sense of control while still thrilling to the disturbance within.

"None have ever been quite like this," Sebastian assured her in a dry voice.

"That's good to know," she murmured and stroked a hand along the strong cut of his jawline.

As the last note of the song faded away, a voice came through the sound system, speaking in Italian. At its conclusion, Sebastian glanced at Laura, regret twisting the line of his mouth. "It's closing time."

She released a mock sigh. "And we were just getting warmed up."

"Shall we go back to the table and finish our drinks?"

The prospect of spending the next twenty minutes sitting and sipping sounded much too mundane for Laura, especially now when she was on such a sensual high. "Why bother?" she countered with an elegant little shrug of her shoulders. "By now the wine's flat. Let's just leave."

"As you wish." Sebastian inclined his head in acceptance of her decision and guided her out of the club into the refreshing coolness of a Roman night.

With his tie still belted around her waist, Laura climbed into the low-slung sports car, her movements unhampered by the gown's slim skirt

As they pulled away from the club area, Laura felt exactly like a cat, alive to the night and purring with the possibilities. She lifted the weight of her hair off her sweaty neck and let the cooling wind dry it.

"Back to the hotel, is it?" Sebastian asked with a side glance.

"Not yet." She kicked off her shoes and wiggled her stockinged toes. "That fountain. The one you throw coins in. Let's go there. I definitely don't want this to be my last visit to Rome."

"One Trevi Fountain coming up." Leaning forward, Sebastian peered at an upcoming street sign, slowed the Porsche, and turned the corner. "Feet hurt after all our dancing?" he asked, noting her shoeless feet.

Staring down, Laura wiggled her toes some more. "They don't hurt at all. They just want some freedom. To borrow that corny phrase from *My Fair Lady,* I could have danced all night."

With the Latin music still playing in her head, Laura raised her hands and snapped her fingers to the imaginary tune, moving her shoulders and torso to its rhythm while she da-da-dahed out a mambo beat. Halfway through the song, she remembered.

"Your tie. I forgot to give it back." Her arms came down, and she worked to loosen the double knot.

She had the first one undone when they arrived at the plaza. She finished the second as Sebastian opened the passenger door for her. Without bothering to put her heels on, Laura swung her legs out of the car and caught hold of Sebastian's outstretched hand.

He glanced at the sheer stockings covering her feet. "You'll ruin your stockings."

"I have more," she replied with unconcern and stepped out of the car, the hem of her long gown falling to brush the tops of her feet. "Your tie, sir."

Rising on her tiptoes, she draped it around his neck and hung on to the two ends, giving them a pull to bring his head down, needing to taste the heat of his kiss again. Obliging her, he arched her into him and claimed her lips with bold sensuality. The invasion of his tongue brought with it the taste of gin and the essence of something else. Everything quickened and rose, her pulse rocketing, sending her blood running sweet and fast.

Laura was conscious of hands shaping her more fully against him, increasing the intimacy of his kiss. She strained closer to him, pushed by the building pressure inside. Passion was something she had always known she possessed, but the feeling had never been this intense.

Momentarily unnerved by it, Laura pulled away and ducked under his arm. At a half-run and half-walk, she crossed to the fountain's perimeter wall, secretly glad that only she knew how shaky her legs felt. Several seconds passed before she heard the scuff of Sebastian's shoes on the concrete, signaling his approach. He halted on her left and faced the massive fountain. Her whole body tingled with an awareness of him.

"If that's the way you thank someone for the loan of an item, remind me to loan you something else." His voice had a disturbed huskiness about it.

She laughed, mostly because she didn't completely trust her voice yet, and focused on the artfully lit statue of a sea god aboard his shell-shaped chariot being pulled by spirited horses.

"Is he Neptune or Poseidon?" Laura asked in a deliberate change of subject. "I can never remember which is Greek and which is Roman."

"Neptune."

"Neptune," she repeated as if that would somehow help her to remember, and slipped her evening bag's gold chain off her shoulder, then opened the beaded purse to search its contents. "Will paper money do, or does it have to be a coin?"

"The legend has always referred to a coin."

"In that case . . ." Laura snapped her purse shut and held out a hand, palm up. "I'll have to borrow something else from you. One coin, please."

His mouth slanted in amusement as he dug in a pants pocket and came out with a coin. "Here you go." He dropped it in her palm.

Her fingers curled over it as Laura turned toward the semicircular expanse of water. "Here's to my return visit to Rome." Leaning across the wall, she pitched the coin far into the pool. It hit the water with a faint plop. Small concentric waves radiated out from its landing point. Satisfied, Laura straightened away from the wall. "Now my return is guaranteed."

"I wouldn't be so sure of that," Sebastian cautioned on a teasing note.

"Why not?" She tilted her chin in challenge while a smile played with the corners of her mouth.

"I'm not sure it works with a borrowed coin."

"*Now* you tell me!" In a mock huff, she turned her back on the fountain and began gathering up her long skirt.

"What are you doing?" A curious frown flickered over his smooth forehead.

"I'm going to go get it, of course," Laura replied, then paused to cock her head at him, holding her skirt almost up to her hips. "You surely don't think that I throw away money for nothing, do you?"

"No. I . . ." Sebastian faltered at the sight of the shapely length of leg she had exposed.

"Good, because I don't." The material went higher, revealing the lower curve of a cheek. Abruptly she let go of it. "Oh no, you don't. Turn around." She waggled a finger in a turning motion. After a second's hesitation, Sebastian pivoted so his back faced her, his mind still replaying that tantalizing image of womanly flesh. "No peeking, either."

"So you expect me to cover my eyes as well?"

"If you want." There was laughter in her voice.

An instant later his imagination ran wild when he heard the

gliding whisper of a zipper. The sound was followed by the rustle of material.

"You will tell me when I can look, won't you?" The want was strong in him, but he was willing to play along with her game for the time being.

Her answer was a laugh, alluringly low and rich with amusement, the kind of laugh that said she knew the things that were in his mind.

With the fading of her laughter, only faint sounds came from behind him, too indistinct to tell him what she was doing. His impatience grew in direct proportion to his curiosity.

A loud splash came from the reflecting pool. Sebastian spun in its general direction. His eyes fell immediately on the nude female wading through the water away from him. He let his gaze travel over her bare shoulders and follow the ribbon of her spine down to the rounded curves of her bare cheeks. With her tawny blond hair tumbling about her shoulders in artfully wild disarray, she looked like some goddess, with a shape as flawless as her smooth skin.

Desire surged through him. He struggled to find his voice. Needing her to turn around, he called out, "You could be arrested."

She threw him a laughing glance over her shoulder and kept wading closer to the statuary. "Don't tell me it's illegal to retrieve a coin?"

"Not necessary for retrieving a coin, but for your attire—or lack thereof."

"Don't be silly." She crouched down into the water and began feeling around the bottom. "Any Italian gendarme who might happen along would be as delighted to see me as you are."

Amused by her logic, Sebastian could only smile. This woman not only aroused him, she completely intrigued him. The Laura Calder he met at the dinner party had been all elegance and class, a master of the social repartee required at such gatherings, always careful to be no more than discreetly flirtatious, never overly assertive in seeking center stage. In short, she had seemed no different than dozens of other society types he knew.

The woman in the Porsche had come across as the ultimate party girl, out for a good time and wanting nothing more than to dance the hours away. Sebastian knew more than a few of those.

And the naked woman playing about in the reflecting pool had all the earmarks of some madcap heiress, always out to do the outrageous and unexpected. An heiress, she definitely was. According to Bianca, Laura was not only the daughter of a wealthy ranching dynasty, she also had a sizable trust fund of her own.

Yet the madcap heiress didn't quite ring true, either. The ones he knew would have been cavorting about the pool, splashing and squealing in their invariably desperate bid for attention. But there was Laura Calder, naked as the day she was born, calmly and systematically searching the pool bottom for that coin.

And there was the matter of the clothes. Laura hadn't left hers puddled on the sidewalk in careless disregard. Her chocolate silk gown, its Armani label partially visible, was carefully and neatly draped across the fountain wall, along with her stockings, a skimpy lace bra and undies.

No, Laura Calder was unlike any other woman in his experience. Certainly he knew of none who possessed that curious blend of elegance and earthiness.

In the reflecting pool, Laura stood up and turned to hold a coin to the light, showing him the classic purity of her profile. After a close examination of the coin, she looked his way.

"This must be it," she declared and lifted one bare shoulder in a vague shrug. "It's the only British coin I could find."

The search over, she started back, and Sebastian was treated to his first frontal view, softly lit by the glow from the statuary lighting. Her breasts were round and firm, perfectly shaped, her waist slenderly concave, and there was a suitable roundness to her hips. With the sheen of moisture on her skin giving it the look of marble, Sebastian was reminded of Botticelli's famous painting of

Venus. His gaze drifted downward to the vee of her pelvic area and the curly mat of pubic hair that proved Laura Calder was a natural blonde.

Stunning, that's what she was, so incredibly beautiful that she took his breath away and ignited an ache in his loins. Sebastian clamped his teeth together to shut off the groan that threatened to rise in his throat.

"I'm going to need your help getting out of here," she informed him with an air of absolute unconcern. "Over there would be easiest, I think." She gestured to a section of the pool near the massive statue some distance from him.

Her words were full of common sense that sliced easily through his lusty thoughts. Sebastian muttered under his breath, strictly for his own hearing, "Better get a grip on yourself, old boy." Louder, he replied, "Be right there."

With more reluctance that he cared to acknowledge, he turned away from the fountain and loped back to the Porsche. Trying to be as levelheaded as she appeared, he popped open the trunk and removed a blanket robe that was always stashed in the boot.

She was waiting for him when he arrived at the designated spot.

"Here." She stretched out a hand to him, the coin held between two fingers. "Better take this before I accidentally drop it."

He took the coin from her and slipped it in his pocket, then reached down and caught hold of her hand. Her skin was wet and icy cool to the touch. Sebastian waited while she found a toehold. At a signaling nod from her, he hauled her out of the pool. She stumbled and fell against him.

Automatically his arms went around her to catch and steady her. A dozen impressions registered at once: the slippery wetness of her skin and the roundness of her breasts pressed against his chest; the clean scent of her hair and the faint smell of chlorine; and the look of almost rapturous relief in her upturned face.

"Lord, but you feel warm." Her voice had a slight quiver to it that seemed to echo the first shivers that trembled through her.

"And you are cold and wet," Sebastian declared.

She laughed in her throat. "I know. They really should heat that pool."

"I doubt if the Italians thought it would be used for a late-night dip," Sebastian chided dryly.

"They should have." Her reply was accompanied by an exaggerated shudder.

The temptation was there to use his body to thoroughly warm her. With more than a degree of regret, Sebastian lifted the folded blanket robe off the wall with one hand while continuing to hold Laura close.

"It's a bloody shame to do this." He shook out the folds and draped the blanket around her shoulders, drawing it together in front.

Laura caught hold of the edges and pulled them snugly across her front, overlapping the edges. "And here I thought you'd put your jacket around me. This is much better." Even as she shivered, there was laughter dancing in her eyes when she glanced up at him. "I didn't expect you to be so practical."

"Bianca is the practical one. Truthfully, I have never understood why she keeps a blanket robe in the boot. And I am certainly not going to question it now. Come on." He wrapped a steering arm around her and guided her toward the Porsche. "Let's get you in the car."

Halfway there Laura halted. "My clothes." Careful not to loosen the blanket, she stuck out one finger and pointed in their direction.

When Sebastian went to fetch them, Laura continued to the car and waited by the passenger side.

"I feel like one of my uncle's relatives," she said as he opened the door for her.

"Beg pardon?"

Seeing his puzzled look, Laura explained, "Logan is part Sioux Indian and the local sheriff."

An eyebrow arched in amusement. "You clearly have a colorful family tree."

"And you haven't even heard the stories about my sod-busting great-grandmother or the one about my father being born out of wedlock," Laura teased, holding tight to the blanket as she climbed into the car.

"As I said, colorful." A small smile crooked his mouth. After she was comfortably ensconced in the seat, he deposited the bundle of clothes on her lap. "Shall I put the top up?"

Laura shook her head. "Don't bother. The hotel isn't very far from here."

Chapter Three

To Laura's amusement, the doorman's expression didn't so much as flicker when she stuck a high-heeled foot out of the Porsche and stood up, swaddled Indian-style in a blanket while clutching her evening clothes. She waited by the hotel steps for Sebastian to join her, head up and the slightest hint of a naughty smile touching the corners of her lips.

She tipped her head to him. "You are coming in with me, aren't you? I may need your assistance with little things like doors and elevator buttons."

"Of course." His smile was quick and warm, his eyes echoing the sparkle of amusement in her own. Turning to the doorman, he handed him the car keys and some folded bills, then swung back to Laura and escorted her up the hotel steps.

"I hope you were generous with your tip."

"I was," Sebastian assured her.

"Good. The man was the absolute epitome of tact. For all the notice he took of my clothes, I could have been wearing a mink. I considered giving him a quick flash, but he didn't seem to be interested."

Sebastian reached ahead of her and opened the door. "Perhaps he's gay."

"A gay Italian." Laura released a soft, incredulous laugh. "That sounds like an oxymoron."

"It does, rather." He guided her to the elevators and pushed the button to summon one. Almost instantly a set of doors glided open with a faint whoosh.

Laura entered the elevator car ahead of him and began the awkward task of searching through the folded clothes for her purse while still maintaining an adequate grip on the blanket. Giving up, she turned to Sebastian. "Find my evening bag, will you? It has my room key in it. And I certainly don't want to wake up Tara."

"Do you share a room with your aunt?" In quick order, Sebastian located her beaded bag and extracted the computerized room key from it.

"No. We have separate suites. And Tara isn't actually my aunt," Laura declared on a breezily offhand note. "I just call her that to avoid lengthy explanations. Technically we aren't related at all."

"How's that?" He eyed her curiously.

"Tara was my father's first wife. Several years after their divorce, he married my mother. That's when Trey and I entered the picture."

"Trey is your brother," Sebastian guessed.

"My twin. He favors the Calder side of the family—tall and big-shouldered, with dark hair and dark eyes; hard, angular features. While I—"

"Take after your great-great-grandmother," he inserted.

"Who may or may not also be Lady Elaine," Laura finished.

Sebastian smiled at that and returned to the original subject as the elevator doors opened on the designated floor. "So you are traveling with your father's ex. That's a bit unusual."

Laura laughed at the understatement. "Over the years it has

raised more than a few eyebrows." She exited the elevator and added over her shoulder, "Tara definitely isn't popular with the rest of my family or anyone else on the ranch, for that matter. My grandfather is convinced she is a horrible influence on me. My mother has never actually said so, but I know she agrees. I think she long ago reconciled herself to the fact that I am my own person."

"That"—his mouth curved wryly—"is very obvious." He inserted the room card into the slot, waited for the light, and opened the door, then stepped back to admit her.

Laura sailed past him into the suite, paused long enough to deposit her bundle of clothes on the sofa's damask-covered cushion, then walked straight to the steps that led to a private terrace without ever once glancing back at him.

After an instant's hesitation Sebastian returned the room card to her purse, entered the suite, and closed the door behind him. By the time he crossed the room, Laura had already disappeared onto the terrace. He left her evening bag with her clothes and followed her outside.

She stood at the outer wall, gazing into the night, indifferent to the terrace's spectacular view of the Spanish Steps and the sprawl of Via Conditti.

He wandered over to the wall and briefly surveyed the view. A smattering of stars dusted the sky, their light dimmed by the city's bright glow. The view of the city and its landmarks was a familiar one, though the same couldn't be said about the woman beside him.

Angling his head in her direction, he let his glance run over her and studied the play of light and shadow on her face, accenting the high, strong line of her cheekbones and marble perfection of her skin. The night gave a silvery sheen to her hair, lightening the color of that glorious blond mane tumbling about her shoulders.

At that moment she had the cool, untouchable look of a goddess, beyond the reach of any mere mortal. But Sebastian knew she had but to turn those sultry dark eyes on him and the impression would change to that of a siren, tantalizing in her beauty, with glistening lips promising rapture.

He smiled inwardly at such fanciful thoughts while simultaneously aware that there was more than a little truth in them. Just being near her aroused all his male instincts. Sebastian suspected he was in danger of completely losing his head over this woman. But that only seemed to add some spice.

"You seem to be in deep thought," he observed, seeking to pull her attention back to him.

She drew in a long breath and released it in a slow and soft exhalation. "I guess I was." A small curve lifted the corners of her mouth.

"What could possibly require such heavy contemplation at this late hour?" he asked in mild jest.

"The future," Laura replied without any hesitation and continued to face the city. "I have some important decisions that I need to make."

"Such as?" Sebastian prompted, determined to engage her attention.

With a slight toss of her head, she turned at right angles to face him and leaned a hip against the terrace wall. "Oh, very important things," she assured him in mock earnestness and dipped her chin, her head cocking in a pose that was provocative and alluring. "Whether to travel the world or rule it, whether to feed the starving children in Africa or . . . go to bed with you."

Heat surged through him with rocketing force. Desire was a hard, stony ache in his loins that somehow managed to thicken his voice. "Personally, I am highly in favor of the latter."

Her smile widened, Cheshire-like. She moved toward him, maintaining her hold on the blanket edges as she opened her arms, the material winging from them in a gesture that reminded him of an exotic butterfly emerging from its chrysalis. But his view of her body was brief as she curved her arms around his neck, wrapping him inside the blanket with her.

Head back and lips parted, she challenged huskily, "Show me."

His hands had already moved around the bareness of her waist to mold her more firmly against him. This time her skin was hot to the touch, but just as silky smooth as before.

Before he could take possession of her mouth, she began eating at his lips, taking playful bites of them with her teeth. In all such previous occasions, Sebastian had been the one doing the seducing. But Laura was the aggressive one now. Something told him that was a dangerous precedent. Seeking to claim the initiative, he scooped her off her feet and swung her toward the suite entrance.

Laughter gurgled in her throat. "How masterful," she purred and stroked a hand along his jaw before sliding her fingers into his hair.

"I assure you I am well-equipped for the role," he murmured, matching the racy lightness of her tone.

His response surprised a laugh from her, and her dark eyes took a new measure of him, a suggestive gleam in their depths. "Is that boast or brag?"

"I'll let you be the judge of that." He negotiated the steps into the suite's sitting room.

"That will be my pleasure," she informed him as her fingers found the top button of his shirt.

"Indeed it will."

"Have you always been so confident of your prowess in bed?" she teased while her fingers continued to undo more buttons.

"I have never heard a single complaint." He carried her through the sitting room into the suite's sumptuous bedroom.

"Ah, but men never do—not if a woman is smart. The male ego tends to be much too fragile."

Control: he could sense her subtle attempt to exert it again. "And I have never met a woman willing to concede that she might be a disappointment in the bedroom."

He stopped near the bed. A single lamp burned on the bedside table, throwing a pool of light over the downturned bedcovers. He let her feet sink to the floor while keeping an arm around her.

The blanket fell away, only a corner of it caught by his encircling arm.

"That's hitting a bit below the belt, isn't it?" she challenged lightly while her hands glided down the opened front of his shirt, halting when they reached the waistband of his slacks.

"But that's often what happens when Mars and Venus collide."

"But what a magnificent collision it can be," she murmured, her dark eyes shining with promise.

"Indeed," Sebastian agreed and stayed her attempt to unfasten his trousers, catching hold of her hands and pulling them away despite the hot and hungry part of him that was eager for her to continue. "But you are rushing things." He set her away from him and made a quick, appreciative skim of her uptilted breasts, slender waist and curved hips. "We men tend to be dreadful creatures of habit." He steered her toward the bed, maintaining discreet pressure until the back of her knees made contact with the mattress. Then he gave her a little push that forced her to sit down. All the while she watched with intense curiosity and interest. "Each of us has our own particular routine when it comes to disrobing. Some prefer to start at the bottom and remove their shoes first. Others begin with the tie."

"You have a head start there." She reclined onto the bed with languorous ease, bending one leg over the other to show him the full rounded curve of her cheek bottom.

"And I have been remiss in not thanking you for that before now." Which was the truth. There was hardly a part of him that didn't feel thick and rigidly swollen. Sebastian doubted that in his present condition his fingers could have managed the intricacies of unknotting a tie or unbuttoning his shirt. Clamping down on a very primitive urge to rip off his clothes and join her on that bed, he pulled the tie from around his neck, striving for a leisurely air that he was far from feeling. "Myself, I do a combination of top and bottom." He draped the tie across the overstuffed armrest of a nearby chair and shrugged out of his suit jacket. "After the tie, comes the jacket." After making a show of precisely folding it, he laid it on the chair. "Then the shirt." He pulled the tails loose from his pants and proceeded to remove it as well, conscious all the while of her avid gaze.

Again, he was anything but casual about the way he arranged it on the chair. At that point he paused and faced her once more. Her eyes made a greedy, almost tactile inspection of the muscled width of his chest and shoulders, taking special note of the curly mat of auburn chest hair.

"This is where I reverse the procedure and begin from the bottom." He sat down on the edge of the cushioned seat, careful not to muss the clothes already there, and began removing his shoes. After he had arranged them neatly side by side next to the chair, he peeled off his socks, shook them out, and laid them precisely one on top of the other.

"First the top, then the bottom. The middle must be next," she declared, her dark eyes agleam with anticipation.

"An astute deduction." He smiled lazily as he stood up, unzipped his trousers, and stepped out of them. Wearing only his briefs, he folded the dress pants together, leg crease against leg crease, draped them over their suit jacket, and gripped the elastic waist of his lone remaining garment. "Last, but far from least, I remove my briefs." As he stripped them off, he turned his back to the bed and fixed them on the chair with the rest of the clothes.

"Thus the deed is done," he announced, squaring around to face her once more, quick to notice the way her gaze instantly zeroed in on his erection.

After a moment's pause, she lifted her glance to his face. "Are you quite sure you're British and not Greek?"

"Quite sure." He arched an eyebrow in silent question.

"You look like Adonis." Her voice, like the smoldering heat of her gaze, had the breathiness of arousal.

"That's a relief." A smile twitched the corners of his mouth. "For a moment I thought you were going to compare me with Michelangelo's young David, able to show off only big hands."

Her head fell back against the pillow as she broke into laughter. Sebastian took advantage of her distraction to climb into bed with her, stretching out on the inside, keeping her in the lamp's pooling light. Quick to recover, she rolled toward him and arched her body closer, her hands reaching to spread her fingers over his chest and the mat of hair on his chest.

"I understand," he began in a voice husky with suppressed desire, "that lovemaking techniques may vary from man to man as well. Some"—with his fingertips, he brushed wayward strands of hair off her cheek—"start at the top."

Featherlight in his pressure, he nuzzled the corner of her eye and the prominent ridge of her cheekbone, followed the curve of her cheek to the corner of her lips, and rubbed his mouth over them, exploring their shape and softness. When he felt her straining toward him, inviting his full possession, he took a couple of tasting kisses, lipping their moist softness, then backtracked along the sculpted line of her jaw to her ear.

He took his time tracing the outline of its delicate shell with his tongue, nibbling at her lobe and nuzzling the sensitive hollow behind it. An involuntary quiver traveled through her when he located her particular erotic spot. He went back to ignite it again and again, taking satisfaction in the faint, animal sounds of pleasure and need that came from her throat.

All the while her hands moved over his back and shoulders, her fingers flexing and curling, while his own made long, slow strokes down her spine and up the side of her waist, allowing his thumb to only occasionally brush the outer curve of her breast. Yet, ever so gradually, he worked his way down, abandoning the erotic spot by her ear and transferring his attention to the arcing curve of her throat and the hollow at its base.

When his hand at last cupped the underside of her breast, her body arched in anticipation. Its firm roundness was nearly his undoing. Even as his thumb circled its peak, feeling it grow hard under his stimulation, he struggled to keep control. Drawn by its irresistible lure, his mouth began a slow foray to it. Upon arrival, his tongue encircled her button-hard nipple, and she breathed in sharply in reaction.

She dug her fingers into his hair, applying downward pressure. His mouth opened on her breast, drawing its nipple inside. Conscious as he was of her every response, he knew the exact moment when her inner thighs tightened and her hips writhed slightly in an attempt to ease the building pressure. Heat flamed through him. He knew he could easily take her over the brink right now. But it was too soon.

While he still could, Sebastian pulled away and worked to even his breathing. His glance lingered on her parted lips, then lifted to her dark eyes, heavy-lidded with desire.

"And, of course," He ran a hand down her leg, letting his gaze follow it, "there are those who prefer to start at the bottom."

As he shifted to focus his attention on her feet, she murmured, "God, but you are a horrible tease." Mixed in with her frustrated tone was amusement and a touch of curiosity.

The narrow heel, the delicate arch, the ball of her foot, and each individual toe, his mouth wandered over all of them before it began the upward journey to her slender ankle and the curve of her calf.

As he nuzzled the back of her knee, the bedside telephone rang. "Feel free to answer that," he told her while lightly rubbing his mouth along her inner thigh.

"Oh no, I'm not," Laura rejected his suggestion out of hand, unwilling to allow anything to intrude on this new, exciting seduction and the desire that swirled around her. "It's probably a wrong number. If not, they can leave a message."

"Whatever you say," he murmured, continuing his leisurely ascent.

She dug her nails into the bedsheet, gripped by an ache that was more intense than any she had ever known. His teasing foreplay was fast becoming more than she could stand.

In a voice tight and throbbing with that need, she said, "I have one question."

"What's that?" His mouth brushed across her pubic hair onto her lower stomach, his moist breath warming her skin that already felt feverishly hot. The intimate touch only intensified the powerful need. Her voice shook with it. "When do we . . . meet in the middle?"

"Do you think it's time?" Sebastian countered on a dryly teasing note.

"Past time." Laura replied with impatience, aware she had never before been aroused like this—not with this driving need to possess and be possessed. In open demand, she reached for him. "No more."

Hot with his own throbbing need, Sebastian needed no second urging and levered himself up and onto her. The driving pressure of his claiming kiss forced her lips apart even as his hand slipped under her, lifting her hips, arching in eagerness for his entry.

When he slid into the tight opening, her astonished groan of pleasure nearly had him exploding on contact. For a moment he went rigid to check it. She shifted under him in grinding urgency.

Exerting every ounce of control he could summon, he gripped her hips and held them still as he moved slowly against them. But the pressure grew. Soon she was all motion under him, her tongue pushing into his mouth to make demands from him. He drove into her, letting the thing that rocked them both take over. The tempo increased, sensation kicking through them in a golden and violent storm.

The lingering dampness of perspiration clung to her skin as Laura lay, arms and legs still tangled with Sebastian, her body tingling with those delicious aftershocks. She had never felt so gloriously spent or so incredibly energized in her life.

Reaching up, she lifted a lock of auburn hair off his forehead and idly curled it around her finger. "You lied to me."

"When was that?" His head faced hers on the pillow, his mouth quirking in a lazy smile.

"When you claimed to be Sebastian Dunshill. That's merely an identity you have assumed."

"Really? And just how did you come to that conclusion?" Amusement gleamed in his eyes.

"I deduced it." Laura replied, stretching and curling catlike against him. "You have such a mastery of the art of lovemaking, it's obvious that you must be James Bond in disguise." The impossibly beautiful thrill she had felt still flowed through her. Lying there beside him, Laura had a moment's regret that he hadn't been her first man—although her mind told her it was best that he hadn't been or she might have become his slave.

"I hate to disillusion you, but 0-0-7 I am not."

"What a pity," she declared and released an exaggerated sigh.

"It is, isn't it?" he murmured and bent his head to nuzzle the rounded point of her shoulder. "How did I overlook such a delectable shoulder?"

She felt that familiar shiver of pleasure dance over her skin and closed her eyes to focus solely on the sensation. "You seem to be making up for—" She broke off the sentence, startled by a sudden series of hard, insistent raps. It took her a full second to realize that someone was knocking on the door to her suite.

The sharp *rap, rap, rap* was repeated again. This time followed by a muffled female voice calling, "Laura, are you in there?"

"It's Tara," she murmured in recognition, unable to recall a single other time when Tara had knocked on her door in the middle of the night. "I'd better see what she wants."

Laura quickly untangled herself from Sebastian and rolled out of bed. On her way out of the room, she grabbed the robe the night maid had left lying on a corner of the bed and pulled it on.

"Just a minute," she called when the rapping came again. Hurriedly she knotted the sash and pulled the door open.

"You are here," Tara stated the obvious as her glance made a rapid survey of Laura's tousled appearance. "I'm sorry to waken you, but your brother just called my room."

"Trey?" Laura said with some surprise. "Why did he call you?"

"Evidently he has been trying to reach you, but you haven't answered your phone, so he called to see if I knew where you were," Tara explained. "He wants you to call him right away. He said it was important, but he wouldn't tell me why." Which clearly irritated her.

Laura dismissed the possibility his reason was anything earth-shaking. "Knowing Trey, he probably took first place at some roping contest. I might as well call him, though. Thanks," she said and closed the door before Tara could invite herself in. As she started back to the bedroom, the telephone rang. Laura picked up the extension in the sitting room. "Hello."

"Where the hell have you been?" Trey's familiar voice responded. "I've been trying to reach you for over an hour. I couldn't even get you on your cell phone."

"I didn't take it with me tonight." Aware that Trey had absolutely no understanding of fashion, Laura didn't even attempt to explain that the cell phone added too much bulk to her evening bag, ruining its line. "Why are you calling at this hour? Do you have any idea what time it is here?"

"I don't know. Maybe two or three o'clock." His tone made it clear that he didn't know and didn't care. He had something else on his mind. "Mom will call you tomorrow, I imagine, but . . ."

He paused, and in that hesitation, Laura knew immediately that something bad happened. "Trey, what's wrong? It's Granddad, isn't it," she guessed, tension knotting her stomach muscles.

"No. No, he's fine. It's Quint," he said, referring to their older cousin, Quint Echohawk, who had followed in his father's footsteps and become a Treasury agent right out of college.

"What about Quint?" She clutched the receiver a little tighter, bracing herself for bad news.

"He got shot in the leg. It broke one of the bones." After a barely perceptible pause, Trey added, "He's going to be worthless as a team-roping partner for a while."

Laura sensed his attempt to make light of the incident, but she knew this had hit him hard. He and Quint had always been as close as brothers. Taking Trey's cue, Laura searched for a light retort.

"What do you want to bet that when they hauled him off in the ambulance, the only thing he wanted to know was whether they got the bad guys."

"Yeah, that would be Quint," Trey agreed with a smile in his voice. "He always wants to finish anything he starts. It makes him real mule-headed sometimes."

"Where is he now?" She heard faint stirrings of movement coming from the bedroom.

"In a Detroit hospital."

"Aunt Cat must be worried sick about him."

"She and Logan took off about an hour ago to fly there. According to Logan, Quint and his partner had gone to a farmhouse, following a lead they had on some guy suspected of illegally selling firearms. I guess they no more than got out of the car when somebody in the house opened fire on them."

"At least he's going to be all right." Laura chose to dwell on the positive aspect.

"Yeah." But the flatness of his voice revealed the apparent lack of comfort he took in that.

Sebastian emerged from the bedroom, fully clothed. "Just a sec," Laura said into the phone and promptly covered the mouthpiece with her hand. "It's my brother," she said to Sebastian as he moved toward her.

"I suspected as much," he murmured and caught her chin between his thumb and forefinger, lifting it to press on a warm kiss on her lips. "See you in England," he said and crossed to the door.

The life seemed to go out of the room when he went, leaving it feeling empty and alien—something Laura had never experienced before. Suddenly she was very, very glad Trey was on the other end of the phone.

"Sorry," she said into it.

"I guess Tara was there," Trey guessed. "I should have known she'd hang around to find out why I was calling."

Laura chose not to correct him. "Phone calls in the middle of the night generally bring bad news. Where's Mother?"

"She and Laredo went into town for supper. Did I tell you Harry's is up for sale?" Harry's was the sole eating and drinking establishment in the small town of Blue Moon, located some fifty miles from the headquarters of the Triple C Ranch.

"I can't imagine anyone buying that old place." Laura sank onto a nearby chair and curled her legs under her, oddly eager to hear a bit of local gossip; gossip she wouldn't have cared a whit about an hour ago.

"Neither can I," Trey agreed. "Ever since Dy-Corp shut down the coal mine, Blue Moon has practically become a ghost town." They talked a while longer, with Trey filling her in on the latest happenings in and around the ranch. "When are you coming home, Laura?" he asked at last.

"Not for a while yet. We're flying to England the end of this week." Laura smiled, anticipating seeing Sebastian again and launched into an explanation of meeting Sebastian, his acquaintance with the earl of Crawford and subsequent invitation to visit the manor house.

Trey's only reply to that was, "You will be home in time for the big horse sale the first of June, won't you? Mom's counting on you to help with it."

"I'd forgotten all about it." The sale marked only the second time horses bred on the ranch had been sold separately from the biennial livestock auction. Just like the livestock auction, the horse sale was as much a large-scale social event as it was an auction. And the lone bright spot in the usual monotony of ranch life, as far as Laura was concerned. "I'll be home in time for that," she promised.

After an exchange of good-byes, Trey hung up and rocked back in an oversized swivel chair behind the den's massive desk, his thoughts still troubled by the news about Quint. His glance drifted idly to the wide sweep of horns mounted above the fireplace's mantelpiece.

The sound of shuffling footsteps pulled his attention from the old stone fireplace and swung it toward the den's open door into the hall as his grandfather, Chase Calder, paused outside it. Age had stooped his tall frame and turned his dark hair an iron gray. There was a sagging of the skin across his hard and angular features, the cracked and weathered texture of it resembling old saddle leather. At first glance, his grandfather looked every bit of his eighty-plus years, but there was a vitality burning in his dark eyes that couldn't be ignored.

"I thought I heard you talking to your mother," Chase stated as if in explanation for his presence.

"No, I just got off the phone with Laura." Trey gripped the armrest and pushed out of the chair, driven by a restless feeling that demanded movement. "I called to let her know about Quint."

"Is she coming home?"

"No. She's flying to London at the end of the week." Trey moved out from behind the desk and crossed to the door.

"London," Chase repeated in disgust. "It's high time she quit gallivanting all over Europe and came home. This is where she belongs."

Trey stopped in front of him. In Chase's younger days, the two men would have stood eye to eye. But Trey was a good inch taller than Chase now. Despite the stark age differences, the family resemblance was strong.

"No, Gramps, she doesn't. I don't know where Laura belongs, but it isn't here." Trey had never felt more certain of that than he did at that moment, and he couldn't say why.

Chapter Four

Clouds drifted through the blue sky that arched over the sprawl of metropolitan London. A river bus plowed through the murky waters of the Thames past the famed Savoy Hotel. But Max Rutledge took no notice of the fine spring afternoon or the expansive views of the river his suite in the Savoy provided. He was too preoccupied by the latest batch of reports that had been forwarded to him.

Distracted as he was, he was slow to register the initial click of the door latch. Not until he heard the door close did he become aware of someone entering in the room. With a swing of his massive shoulder, he glanced toward the door, his gaze lighting on his tall son, dressed in sweats, a towel draped around his neck, and a lingering sheen of perspiration on his face that said, as much as his dress, that he had come straight from a vigorous workout at the hotel's health club.

As usual, Max wasted no time with preliminaries. "I thought you told me that Calder girl was staying at Claridges."

Boone Rutgledge hesitated a split second. "That's what she indicated to me before we left Rome." He caught up a corner of the towel and mopped his cheek and jaw with it.

"Well, she's not. She called an hour ago to say that they're at the Lanesborough on Hyde Park Corner.

"Obviously, there was a change of plans," Boone stated with unconcern and crossed to a phone.

"What are you doing now?" Max demanded.

"I'm just calling to confirm that I'll pick her up at eight this evening." He picked up the receiver.

"Don't bother. She's not there." Max pivoted his wheelchair around to face him. "She said she was going downstairs for tea."

Boone set the phone back on its cradle. "In that case, I'll shower and call her later."

Max snorted in disgust. "You're always letting grass grow under your feet. What's wrong with going over there and joining her for tea? It's not like you're going to spend the rest of the afternoon working. You never do a damned thing unless I tell you. Just once I wish you'd take some initiative yourself."

Boone glared at him for a long, stiff second, then pivoted on his heel and crossed to one of the suite's adjoining bedrooms, the one that he had claimed as his own.

Thick traffic swirled around the busy Hyde Park corner, but little of its noise invaded the Lanesborough's Library Bar, where afternoon tea was being served. Laura paid little attention to the hushed conversations taking place around her as she took a sip of the Earl Grey tea in her Royal Worcester cup.

"Did you speak to Sebastian?" Tara deftly added a dollop of clotted cream to her scone.

"No, I had to leave messages for both Sebastian and Boone." Laura returned her cup to its saucer and used the serving tongs to remove a petit four from its tray. "I let the desk know that we'd be in here if either of them called."

"Good." Tara nodded in approval and took a delicate bite of her scone and chewed it thoughtfully. "As I recall, Crawford Hall is somewhere in the Cotswolds. I shouldn't think it would be much more than a two-hour drive from London. I wonder if there's a suitable inn nearby where we could spend the night. It would be too much to hope that we might actually be invited to stay at the manor."

Where they might stay was of little interest to Laura. "I'm looking forward to seeing that portrait of Lady Elaine." But not nearly as much as she was anticipating Sebastian's company.

"I'm half-tempted to hire a genealogist to track down any documentation that may exist on both Lady Elaine and Madelaine Calder just to see if we can prove our suspicions," Tara remarked idly.

"I don't know what it would accomplish," Laura said with a shrugging lift of her shoulders.

"You haven't lived with the question as long as I have, or you would understand how satisfying it can be to at last have the definitive answer." Tara lifted her cup and carried it to her lips. "How's Quint doing? Did you speak to your mother?"

Laura nodded that she had. "He came through the surgery on his leg with flying colors. Logan flew back home, but Aunt Cat is staying until Quint's released from the hospital. Mom said that other than having a pin in his leg he'll be as good as new in a few weeks."

"That's good to hear. I know how worried Cat must have been about him."

A man entered the Library Bar, coming within range of her peripheral vision. When he paused beneath the Empire-style chandelier, its light reflected off the deep copper lights in his hair. The hue was much too familiar for Laura to ignore. With a turn of her head, she saw Sebastian making a scan of the room's patrons, and her pulse quickened.

Before she could lift a hand to draw his attention, he spotted the two of them seated by a window. With an easy masculine grace, he crossed to their table.

"I see you two ladies are enjoying one of our quaint British customs," he said in greeting.

"When in Rome," Laura quipped, her thoughts racing back to the night they had spent together, the memory fresh and stimulating.

"Indeed." His glance said that he knew exactly what she was thinking.

"We were just talking about you," Tara declared.

"All good, I hope."

"Naturally." Tara smiled in reassurance. "You will join us for some tea, won't you?"

"It would be my pleasure," he said and signaled to one of the staff, who quickly added a chair to the table, followed by a third place setting. Hitching up his trousers, he took a seat. "Your flight from Rome was uneventful, I trust."

"It was." Doing the honors, Tara poured tea into a cup for him.

"So . . ." Laura settled back in her chair, letting her gaze run over his smoothly hewn features, their aristocratic lines so at odds with the smattering of freckles on his fair skin. "Were you able to wangle an invitation for us to see the portrait?"

"Better than that," He paused to stir a spoonful of sugar into his tea, "I come with an invitation to stay the night at Crawford Hall."

"That's amazing," Tara murmured, then explained, "Laura and I were just discussing whether we should make the drive back to London or find lodging in the area. Obviously that is no longer an issue. We accept the earl's gracious offer of hospitality with pleasure."

"Will you be spending the night as well?" Laura asked with more than a little interest.

"I will," he confirmed.

"Wonderful," Laura murmured, her interest in this excursion to the English countryside growing with each passing moment. It definitely promised something more diverting than an inspection of Lady Elaine's portrait.

"You have no idea how much I'm looking forward to this, Mr. Dunshill," Tara inserted.

"Sebastian, please," he insisted.

"Sebastian," she repeated in easy familiarity. "Is there anything special in the way of dress we should bring with us?"

"Life is fairly informal at Crawford Hall. Although if you have some riding clothes, you might want to bring them along," he replied. "A morning canter across our English hills can be an excellent way to start the day. I expect they will seem quite tame to you, considering that you were raised on the wild western plains." He addressed the latter remark to Laura.

"It's also a reason why civilized scenery might be a bit more appealing to me," she replied.

"There's certainly a plentitude of civilized scenery in the vicinity of Crawford Hall." Sebastian sipped his tea. "Have you ever ridden English style before?"

"I have," Laura confirmed. "In fact, I prefer it—much to my family's horror."

"Is that ever the truth," Tara declared. "Do you remember the time you tried to put one of the ranch horses over a homemade jump, Laura? You couldn't have been much more than fourteen or fifteen. Your grandfather almost had apoplexy. He and your mother were positively furious with me when I went out and bought you a show jumper, then hired a riding instructor."

"Actually I don't think my mother minded all that much. I think she was just relieved that I hadn't decided to climb on the back of a Brahma bull the way Trey did at a local rodeo." Turning her attention to Sebastian, she said, "Over the years, my brother and I have managed to contribute more than a few gray hairs to our mother's head. We each have a bit of the daredevil in us."

"Really," Sebastian murmured, eyes dancing. "I never would have guessed that about you."

"The truth is out, then." A knowing smile curved her mouth as she brimmed with the certainty that he was remembering when she had ventured nude into the Trevi Fountain.

With all her attention wrapped up in Sebastian, Laura never noticed the tall dark-haired man approaching their table until he stopped by her chair. "I was told at the desk I could find you in here."

She looked up with a start, her glance quickly taking in the man's familiar features, full of rough and raw masculinity. "Boone," she said in surprise that quickly gave way to pleasure. "Your father must have given you my message."

"He did." He flashed her a broad smile. "Rather than call you back, I decided to come over myself and find out if you can be ready about eight for our big night on the town." Without waiting to be asked, he pulled up a vacant chair and sat down at the table.

"Eight o'clock will be perfect," Laura replied.

As the tardy waiter hurried over to their table, Tara inquired, "Would you like some tea, Boone?"

"No, thanks." He dismissed the waiter with a curt shake of his head. "The only tea I drink is the kind we serve in Texas—sweet and on ice." His glance drifted to Sebastian, as if only then taking notice of his presence.

"You remember Sebastian Dunshill, don't you, Boone?" Tara said, supplying the name on the off chance he had forgotten it. "We met at the *contessa's* party in Rome."

"I remember," he said and acknowledged him with a brief nod that was neither friendly nor unfriendly.

"Sebastian just brought us an invitation to spend the weekend at Crawford Hall," Laura explained.

"Are you going?" Boone asked and continued without waiting for her answer. "I was going to suggest we fly up to Newmarket and take in a horse race."

"I wish I'd known." Laura gave him a look of regret, tempered with a smile. "But Tara and I can hardly pass up the chance to have a firsthand look at the portrait of Lady Crawford that hangs in the hall. She has been the subject of much speculation in our family for too many years."

Boone lounged back in the chair, hooking an arm over the corner of its backrest. "This is the first time I've ever been turned down in favor of a painting." But his broad Texas smile didn't reveal any signs of rejection. "Now you've got me curious about it. It must be something special."

"We think it will be," Tara replied. "Which is why we are so anxious to see it."

"When are you leaving?" Boone divided his glance between Laura and Tara. On the surface, the tone of his question seemed to be one of idle curiosity, but his attention to their answer was a bit too sharp.

"Actually"—it was Sebastian who spoke up first—"they are expected for dinner tomorrow evening. I was about to suggest making a leisurely afternoon drive of it. I thought I could pick you up around two," he said to Laura, "stop for tea along the way, and still arrive in ample time for dinner."

"I have a better idea." Boone's broad smile never wavered as he pinned his gaze on Sebastian, the subtle challenge in it obvious to everyone. "I'll take them instead. It'll give me a chance to get a peek at this painting myself."

Laura watched Sebastian, intensely curious to see how he would handle this gauntlet Boone had thrown down.

"There's no need for that," Sebastian began in smooth dismissal, "as I'll be making the drive myself tomorrow—"

"But I have a Daimler limousine at my disposal," Boone interrupted. "I think you'll agree it would be much more comfortable for the ladies to ride in it than in an ordinary car."

During the briefest of pauses, Sebastian studied his adversary with a sizing glance, then smiled lazily. "Since you seem so determined to make the drive, why don't I arrange for you to spend the weekend at Crawford Hall as well."

The invitation was the last thing Laura had expected from Sebastian. Most women in her shoes would have found the prospect of having both men under the same roof to be an awkward situation. Laura regarded it as a challenge. And she thrived on challenges.

"I'd love to spend the weekend in the country with Laura if you're sure our host wouldn't object," Boone replied.

"His philosophy tends to be 'the more, the merrier' or something like that," Sebastian stated with a droll smile.

"Will Max be joining us as well?" Tara asked with sudden curiosity, then glanced at Sebastian in quick apology. "I'm sorry. I shouldn't have presumed to include him. Besides, if Crawford Hall is typical of most old homes, it isn't exactly wheelchair-friendly."

"Crawford Hall happens to be an exception, then, thanks to an ancestor who was similarly handicapped in his later years," Sebastian explained. "So there are suitable accommodations for your father if he should wish to come."

"I believe he's already made other plans, but I'll ask him," Boone replied.

"Do that," Sebastian said with an aristocratic nod.

"I will." Boone gripped the arms of his chair and pushed out of the seat, rising to his feet. "I'll let you all get back to your tea. Pick you up at eight," he said to Laura, then winked. "And bring your appetite. Don't waste it all on those sweets." He gestured to the petit four on her plate and left the table.

Laura watched him exit the room before she brought her attention back to the table. "This should be a very entertaining weekend, don't you think?" Her smile was wide and full of amusement.

Boone slammed into the suite and threw a glance around the sitting room that never even paused on his father. "Where the hell is Edwards?" he demanded, referring to his father's personal secretary and chief assistant.

"He went to FedEx those documents back to the States. Why?" Max's frown was sharp with suspicion. "What's happened? Did that girl break her date with you?"

"No." Boone strode across the room, jerking loose the knot of his tie as he went. "As a matter of fact, we have been invited to spend the weekend in the country with her and Tara Calder." He snatched up the telephone receiver and punched out a series of numbers. "I want to place an order," he said into the phone.

"I don't understand." Max wheeled his chair over to the desk where Boone stood. "What do you want with Edwards?"

Ignoring the question, Boone continued his conversation with the unknown party. "I want a room full of orchids delivered to Ms. Laura Calder's suite at the Lanesborough. No, wait," he said on second thought. "Make that one exotic and absolutely perfect orchid. On the card, simply put, 'See you at eight,' and sign it 'Boone.' Make sure it's delivered immediately. I want it in her suite when she returns."

When he hung up, Max pounded the arm of his wheelchair. "Dammit, are you going to answer my questions? I want to know what the hell is going on."

Boone looked at him, his lips drawn back in an expression that was more snarl than smile. "Did I forget to mention that the weekend invitation came from that Englishman, Sebastian Dunshill?"

"Dunshill." Some of the anger went out of Max's voice as his mind grabbed hold of the news and ran with it, exploring its many ramifications.

The door to the suite opened and J.D. Edwards walked in. He was short and stout and all Texan, as evidenced by the bolo tie and pointed-toe cowboy boots he wore with his business suit.

"It's about time you got back," Boone said with impatience. "Find out everything there is to know about a man named Sebastian Dunshill. And I mean everything," he snapped. "And I want it yesterday."

"Well, well, well," Max murmured, fairly beaming in approval. "You do know how to take the initiative."

But Boone was too angry to notice his father's reaction as he stalked into his room.

*   *   *

With the setting of the sun, a gossamer-thin fog drifted through the London streets. It veiled the glow from the lampposts along the street outside the restaurant.

Laura was oblivious to the fog and the night-darkened view from their window table. The whole of her attention was on her dinner companion, Boone Rutledge. She doubted that anyone could have looked more out of place amidst the restaurant's marble and gold Louis XVI decor than this big and brawny dark-haired Texan. Yet its fussily feminine perfection served only to accent his blatant good looks and raw virility. His bold maleness was like a powerful magnet, irresistible in its attraction.

She watched him cut into his steak while she idly toyed with her plate of veal and lobster in a seafood sauce atop a bed of tender vegetable noodles.

"So, tell me," Boone began in a conversational tone, "have you always been interested in tracing your family tree?"

"Hardly," she replied in amused denial.

"Really?" His thick black eyebrows lifted in mild surprise. "You seemed so interested in this portrait that I figured it must be a hobby of yours."

"Truthfully, Tara is more interested in seeing it than I am. Which isn't to say I don't have some curiosity about it, because I do," Laura admitted. "But if I never had the opportunity, I wouldn't cry over it."

"A lot of people these days have become obsessed with uncovering their roots," Boone commented. "A few years ago my father hired some guy to trace back our family tree. He was convinced we were related to one of the defenders of the Alamo," Boone recalled with a smile. "You should have seen my father's face when he learned that the only famous ancestor we had was the outlaw John Wesley Hardin."

"John Wesley Hardin? You're kidding!" Laura all but hooted with laughter

" 'Fraid not. Needless to say, he fired the researcher on the spot."

"He must have been furious."

"Believe me, he was roaring louder than a Texas tornado. It didn't help that I suggested he might have come by his skill in business honestly—he had merely found a bloodless way to do it, first snuffing out his competition, then taking over its assets."

"Something tells me that didn't make you very popular with him."

"He did a bit more roaring," Boone admitted, his grin broadening.

"I can imagine," she said, then added thoughtfully. "I suspect, though, that Max welcomes any excuse to roar."

"And he does bite as well," Boone warned.

The remark reminded her of the many stories she'd heard about her own Calder family. On occasion they had been known to bite, too.

"He wouldn't have become what he is today if he didn't," she said realistically. "Just the same, I like your father. I'm glad he's going to join us this weekend."

"He likes you, too." His glance traveled over the golden sheen of her hair, its loose waves framing a face that was classic in its beauty. "He usually doesn't have much time for the opposite sex, but he's really taken with you. Exactly how did you manage that? I could use some lessons."

For all the jest in his tone, Laura suspected he was half serious. "My way probably wouldn't work for you." She laid down her silverware and reached for her wineglass, using those few seconds to think through the rest of her answer. "You and my brother Trey are in somewhat similar positions. Both of you are being groomed to take over the family business. I don't have any of that pressure. The only expectations my family has for me are negative ones— you know, don't get into trouble, don't become involved with drugs—that sort of thing. It leaves me amazingly free." She took a sip of her wine as if to punctuate the thought. "My brother, on the other hand, if he makes even one small mistake, everyone seems to come down harder on him than they would on anyone else. Not

out of cruelty, but because of the role he'll have to fill one day."
She tilted her glass toward him. "I suspect it's the same for you
with your father."

"I suppose that's true." He was deliberately offhand even
though he knew her summation was right on the nose. It was the
first time he could recall anyone ever demonstrating an understanding of his situation. In one way, it touched something deep
inside him. But in another, it made him uncomfortable.

"I remember my brother said to me one time, 'You know, Sis,' "
Laura switched to an imitation of a man's voice, 'the worst thing
about it is you've got to take their guff and keep your mouth shut
when you really want to knock their heads off.'"

"I've been there a time or two," Boone agreed wryly.

"I think that's why Trey took up rodeoing in college. It's his
way of rebelling a little—and blowing off some steam at the same
time." She studied him over the rim of her wineglass, a knowing
gleam in her dark eyes. "So what's your form of release from the
pressure? Fast cars or fast women? I'd bet it's the latter, considering your reputation for playing the field."

He was much more comfortable with this kind of conversation,
and it showed. "You know what they say about safety in numbers."

"Variety is the spice of life and all that," she teased. "You
sound like me—easily bored."

It was not the response he had expected. In the past when he
had made similar comments, the response had invariably included
a subtle lecture on the benefits and joys of monogamous relation-
ships.

Even now, a part of him was skeptical of her reply. At the same
time, though, he had to acknowledge that it rang true. And it
stung a little that she didn't seem to be interested in "catching"
him. Simultaneously Boone realized that Laura Calder would not
be an easy conquest. He'd never had to work to get a woman before.

And it was that thought that prompted him to say, "Tonight,

sitting here with you, I'm not all that interested in the variety that's out there when you play the field."

"Now that sounds like a line," Laura chided lightly.

"With other women, it would be," Boone admitted. "With you, I'm really not sure."

"In that case, I'll take it as a high compliment. Thank you," she said with an accepting dip of her head, her eyes alive to him in a way they hadn't been before. It was a look he was determined to keep there.

Following dinner Boone instructed the chauffeur to take them to one of London's many gaming establishments. Laura eyed him curiously. "Don't you have to be a member to go there?"

"I am," he stated.

"Do you enjoy gaming?" she wondered.

"Don't you?" he countered, flashing her a smile that was reckless and sexy.

The London casino had none of the Vegas clamor of slot-machine bells and clattering coins. Here the gambling was limited to table games—blackjack, poker, roulette, and craps. It was an atmosphere that would have been sedately British except for all the shouts and excited chatter that came from the crowded craps table.

Boone guided her toward it. "Have you ever played craps before?"

"Once or twice," she said, but the twinkle in her eyes indicated a greater familiarity with the game than that.

"In that case, you'll need a stake." He pressed a stack of tokens into her palm.

"There's really no need. I can afford to buy my own," she reminded him.

"I know. But tonight's my treat," he said with a smile and shouldered his way to the table, urged on by half a dozen excited bettors.

The feverish contagion of the scene had quickened Laura's pulse. The pace of the game was swift, almost nonstop. The only pauses came when the shooters shook the dice, sometimes muttering under their breath and sometimes calling for the needed point. Almost the instant the dice came to rest, the losing bets were raked in and the winners paid out amidst a mix of groans, the occasional curse, and a rare few triumphant outcries.

Through sheer good fortune, Laura managed to double her stack of chips, but Boone was on a hot streak, the stacks growing in front of him with each roll of the dice.

"You're bringing me luck," he said when the winnings from another bet were pushed his way.

"Of course." Laura flashed him a smile of absolute certainty.

"Let's keep it that way," he signaled to the dealer his intention to cash in.

She glanced at him in surprise. "I didn't expect you to quit while you were ahead."

He grinned. "That's how you walk away a winner."

"True." Laughing she gathered up her own chips, counted out the stake he'd given her, and gave them back to him. "This is yours, I believe." The rest she collected and dropped inside her black silk evening bag. As they moved away from the table, she released a long breath, conscious of her heart rate slowing to something closer to normal. "What an adrenaline rush," she declared. "It could so easily become addictive."

"And it does for some people." He ran his gaze over her upturned face, noting the lingering flush of excitement and finding something addictive in its look. "Want to try your luck at the blackjack tables."

She glanced in their direction and shook her head. "No, it looks much too tame. But I could go for something tall and cold. How about—" The rest of her question was never finished as she was sideswiped by a casino patron, the impact knocking her off balance and sending her stumbling against Boone.

"So sorry, miss," the man declared, instantly contrite, his voice slurring and his hands catching at her in an effort to steady her. "I wasn't watching where I was going. My wife's always warning me about that."

"I'm fine. Really," Laura insisted as he continued to hover over her, close enough that the sourness of his whiskey breath fanned her.

"Are you sure now?" he persisted.

"Positive." She wanted nothing more than for the man to leave, but he didn't seem to get the message. She suddenly sensed Boone moving away from her. Temper flaring that he would abandon her, Laura turned after him.

"No, you don't, buster." Boone growled directly behind her.

At almost the same instant, Laura felt a pull on the shoulder strap of her evening bag. When she glanced down she was stunned to see a man's hand inside it and Boone's clasping the man's wrist in a viselike grip.

"Stop that man!" Boone barked the order.

With a start, Laura realized he was referring to the man who had bumped into her. Turning, she saw the culprit scurrying away, moving with a haste that included no signs of drunkenness. She understood in an instant that the two had been working as a team, the first to distract her while the second pilfered her purse.

Action erupted behind her as the second man took a swing at Boone and jerked his hand out of her purse. The man struggled frantically to break free. From the outset it was obvious that he was no match for the younger and much stronger Boone.

An actual fight was something Laura had never witnessed. On rare occasions at the ranch she'd seen the aftermath of scraped knuckles, cut lips, bruises, and even a black eye a time or two, but she'd never been present when a fight occurred until now.

Within seconds, it seemed, Boone had subdued the man, holding him in a paralyzing headlock, his arm twisted high behind his back as the casino's security staff converged on the scene.

As brief as the incident had been, Laura had felt all of its heat and heart-pounding fury. She was conscious of the blood rushing through her system in a kind of savage high that simultaneously frightened and thrilled her.

Casino security were quick to take custody of the would-be thief from Boone, and Laura watched the violence ebb from him. Its passing was accompanied by a series of actions, beginning with a big shrug of his shoulders to correct the lay of his suit jacket, followed by a stretch of the neck and a quick adjusting of his tie to center it once again. Then his glance made a sweep of the gathering of onlookers, more as if to challenge any other takers than to search for danger.

When his glance finally stopped on her, his dark eyes still had a trace of battle glitter in them. It was that element of the primitive that Laura found fascinating.

But neither was given an opportunity to converse as security escorted them off the gaming floor to an inner office. There questions were asked, and events described. It was all repeated again when the police arrived and took their statements.

Nearly an hour later Boone and Laura climbed into the rear of the waiting limousine, apologies from casino management still echoing in their ears.

"At last that's over," Boone declared on a heavy sigh and settled back in the cushioned seat. "I had hoped to show you an evening to remember, but that wasn't what I had in mind."

The limousine passed by a streetlight, the streaming flood of light briefly revealing a tiny smear of blood at the corner of his lips. Laura removed the precisely folded handkerchief from the breast pocket of his suit and used a corner of it to dab away the touch of blood.

"My hero," she murmured with a lightly teasing smile. Boone smiled back, but she noticed the secretly pleased look he wore that she had called him that even in jest. "Have I said 'thank you' yet for preventing that man from absconding with my winnings?"

"I don't think you have." His eyes had an expectant gleam.

"Thank you," she murmured and leaned into him, covering his mouth in a nuzzling but brief kiss.

Before she could draw back, Boone hooked an arm around her waist to keep her against his chest. "You're more than welcome." His voice was husky.

His hand came up and cupped the back of her head, pulling her lips back to him. His mouth came down in a driving, delving kiss full of male aggression that made no attempt to conceal his desire behind finesse. A part of her gloried in its primitive heat, but her head warned her against letting it continue.

With a degree of regret, she flattened a hand against his chest and pushed back, dipping her head to pull in a breath that his kiss had denied her. His hands tightened on her in an attempt to draw her back, but Laura managed to maintain a small distance.

Peering at him through the top of her lashes, she murmured between deep breaths, "You do know the quick way to start a fire, don't you?"

"I had help," he reminded her.

Sensing his advantage, Boone again attempted to eliminate the space that separated. This time Laura laid two fingers on his lips.

"I think we both know where another kiss would lead," she told him without any trace of false primness. "And I don't know you that well—yet."

He hesitated, gauging the firmness of her refusal, then loosened his hold on her. "That's the most promising 'no' I've ever heard from a woman."

Laura moved out of his arms and sat back in the seat. "I'm surprised any woman has told you 'no' before." She removed a small mirror and a tube of lipstick from her purse and set about applying a fresh coat to her lips.

"There haven't been many," Boone admitted, aware that he'd seen only a rare few of them a second or third time, and lately, none at all.

"That's what I thought." Her sideways glance was bright with amusement. With her lips a shiny peach color once again, she capped the tube and returned both mirror and lipstick to her purse. "Quick, torrid affairs can be fun. But sometimes a person can get burned by them. And it isn't going to be me. You need to know that." She paused to meet his gaze. "So if you want to change your mind and forget about taking me to the country this weekend, there'll be no hard feelings at all."

He believed her. That knowledge made him all the more determined to possess her, even though there was a part of him that realized he was taking the risk of being possessed by her. Something told him that wouldn't be a bad thing.

"I'll pick you up at two—as we agreed earlier."

The slow and obviously pleased smile she gave him seemed to assure him that anything he gave up would be worth it.

Chapter Five

The stately Daimler limousine cruised along the rural highway
that wound its way through the rolling hills of the Cotswolds.
Spring had worked its magic on the land, greening its pastures and
turning its trees into thickly leafed canopies.

The scenery was the quintessence of the English countryside,
picturesque and quaint, but Max Rutledge had absolutely no interest in it or the easy chatter between Laura and Tara.
Impatiently he flipped on the intercom.

Rudely ignoring the chauffeur, he addressed his words to the
man riding in the front passenger seat, Harold Barnett, his personal valet who also doubled as his private nurse. "Dammit,
Harold, how much farther is it to this place? I thought we were
supposed to be there by now."

"Honestly, Max, you are really a poor traveler," Tara chided
with easy familiarity. "You know as well as I do that the chauffeur
told us that we should be there between four and five, depending
on the traffic. It's only half past four now."

"Then we should be there, shouldn't we?" Max said and glow-
ered.

"Excuse me, sir." The valet's tenor voice came over the intercom speaker. "But it appears the entrance to the estate is just ahead of us."

"About time," Max grumbled and for the first time took an interest in the view outside his window.

"The batteries on his cell phone went dead about seventy miles ago," Boone inserted his own explanation for his father's impatience.

"I'd like to know why you packed yours in your suitcase," Max threw him a glare. "You're supposed to carry the damn thing."

"I didn't see the need. You had yours," Boone replied.

"Both of you, stop bickering." Laura smiled to take any sting from her admonishment. "You're worse than a pair of old maids."

Max opened his mouth to make a hot retort, then looked at Laura, checked it, and offered her a rare smile instead. "Maybe it comes from a lack of having the civilizing influence of a female in our lives."

"And this weekend you're going to have the company of two. We'll see how much it improves your disposition," Laura declared impishly.

Max nudged Boone's arm and nodded in Laura's direction. "This one's got a brain. She'll keep you on your toes."

Laura laughed. "I can't imagine any man being on his toes unless it's Barishnikov."

The slowing of the limousine as it approached the entrance to the country estate brought a natural end to the exchange, their attention shifting to their destination. A pair of wrought-iron gates stood open. A narrow lane curved away from it, lined with towering oaks that obscured the view. Leaning closer to the window, Laura waited for her first glimpse of the house, feeling a kind of building suspense.

"It's a damned long driveway," Max grumbled.

"Not really. If it's a long driveway you want, come to the Triple

C. Ours is forty miles long." Laura informed him, amusement in her smile.

The lane made a sweeping turn, and the centuries-old manor house suddenly stood before them, a towering two-and-a-half stories, with rambling wings and a scattering of gables. Bathed in the yellowing light of the late-afternoon sun, its native limestone had a golden glow to it despite the weathering by time and the elements.

A castle it wasn't, but the scale of Crawford Hall was on the grand side. It could have been imposing, even intimidating, except for the thick vines that climbed over the exterior wall of one wing, providing a subtly homey touch.

The limousine rolled to a stop near the recessed front entrance. Moving with a practiced swiftness that showed no haste, the chauffeur exited the car and came around to open the passenger side door.

Tara was the first to emerge. While she waited for the others, she lifted her gaze to survey the old manor house. When Laura joined her, Tara murmured, "It reminds me of some aristocratic dowager, a radiant beauty in her day but a bit worse for wear now."

Not quite as critical, Laura said, "It still has a certain charm about it."

"Charming is not an adjective that should be applied to a titled estate." Tara was firm in that opinion.

"This dowager merely needs a face-lift," Laura stated with a wickedly teasing smile.

"How true," Tara murmured, fully aware that her own looks were due in no small part to the skill of a surgeon.

Both women were careful to ignore the continued activity on the other side of the limousine. Max's valet had retrieved the wheelchair from the trunk and with Boone's assistance was transferring Max from the car to the chair.

"I wonder where our host is?" Tara mused aloud.

"Be honest," Laura chided. "Aren't you also wondering just a little bit about how old he is and whether there is a current Lady Crawford or not?"

Tara laughed, and there was a slightly girlish sound to it. "Maybe just a little," she admitted.

The whirr of the wheelchair motor signaled the approach of the rest of their party. Laura turned as Max rolled out from behind the car.

"How come you two are still standing here?" he demanded, then motioned Boone toward the recessed entrance. "Go let them know we're here."

As Boone started toward the oversized door, it opened, and Sebastian stepped out, looking every inch the country gentleman in a tweed jacket with leather patches on the elbows.

"I see you arrived in good order," he said in greeting. "You had a pleasant journey, I hope."

"We did," Laura confirmed, feeling that familiar tingle of attraction when his gaze met hers.

"That's a matter of opinion," Max grumbled.

"Now, Max," Laura began in light reprimand and left it at that when she noticed the sharp way he was studying Sebastian. There was something in his look that said he had the man's number. It gave her pause.

If Tara observed his expression, she gave no sign of it. "Shall we go in?" she said to Sebastian. "I'm eager to meet our host."

Sebastian hesitated. "I fear I have a confession to make."

"He's not home," Tara guessed at once, disappointment clouding her expression.

"Oh, he's home," Sebastian assured her. "But I misled you a bit in Rome when I claimed a nodding acquaintance with the current earl of Crawford. Strictly speaking, it was the truth. I merely neglected to mention that I am the earl of Crawford."

Laura realized at once that this was what Max had known. It would have been like him to check out his host before he arrived.

She laughed, and there was a touch of relief in it that Max's knowledge had turned out to be something so innocent.

"Why didn't you tell us?" Amusement riddled her voice, removing any demand from it.

Sebastian's smile had a wry twist to it. "I expect the position is new enough that I'm not completely comfortable with it."

Tara regarded him with utter amazement. "Your announcement has been such a surprise that the proper way to address you has completely flown from my mind. Is it 'Your Lordship'?"

"Sebastian will do," he replied.

"That's good to hear," Boone stated, "considering our country successfully fought a war to rid ourselves of such pointless necessities."

Laura noticed the hard gleam of challenge in Boone's eyes and knew he regarded Sebastian as a rival. With some justification, she was forced to admit.

"Ah yes, the rebellion of the colonies," Sebastian murmured with a touch of drollery. "Fortunately, that war was over some time ago." He extended a hand. "Welcome to Crawford Hall, Mr. Rutledge."

"Thank you." Boone briefly grasped his hand, his fingers automatically tightening in a show of strength.

If Sebastian felt any pain, he didn't show it, and he turned to Max, again offering his hand. "And I welcome you as well, Mr. Rutledge."

"Better make it Max." He released Sebastian's hand almost before his fingers closed around it. "It will be too confusing this weekend if you persist in calling us both Mr. Rutledge. First names will be easier."

"I agree." Sebastian nodded, then swept all of them with a glance. "Why don't we go inside and I'll show you to your rooms? No doubt you would welcome the opportunity to freshen up after your drive. Ladies." He gestured for Laura and Tara to lead the way, then addressed Max. "As you will note, the steps have a side ramp that will accommodate your wheelchair. I'll have my man Grizwold see that your luggage is delivered to your rooms."

Once inside, Laura managed no more than a quick glance around the stone-floored entryway with its heavy woodwork before her attention was claimed by a young, ruddy-cheeked man, not much more than thirty, clad in a dark suit and tie.

"Good afternoon, ladies." He greeted them with a half-bow, his smile pleasant but reserved.

"You must be Grizwold," Laura guessed.

"Indeed I am," he acknowledged, all but clicking his heels.

"I assume you are the butler," she further surmised.

"I have been trained as one," he stated as the rest of the party arrived in the entrance hall.

"Here at Crawford Hall, Grizwold's duties tend to go beyond the scope of a butler," Sebastian inserted, making it clear he had overheard part of their conversation. "Obviously we no longer have the large staff that once ran the place. But you may be interested to know that he represents the fifth generation of Grizwolds to work here.

"It sounds like the Triple C," Laura remarked, shooting a quick glance at Tara, then explaining, "Most of the people who work at the ranch today are descendants of the original ranch hands."

"And the tradition continues," Sebastian murmured on a thoughtful note, then pulled himself back to the present. "I promised to direct you to your rooms. Grizwold, will you show Mr. Rutledge to the lift? It's an old and noisy contraption," he said to Max, "but I assure you it is in excellent working order."

"This way, sir." Grizwold gestured to a wide hall, one of several that branched off the entryway.

Manipulating the control stick, Max sent the chair rolling in that direction, trailed by his burly valet.

"We'll take the stairs," Sebastian said and led the way to the massive staircase that swept up to the second floor. Built of oak, it had been darkly stained, and time had deepened its color to a blacker shade of brown.

Laura trailed a hold along the railing, its wood satin-smooth to the touch, evidence of the many hands that had made use of its support over the years. As she climbed the steps, she lifted her gaze to the smattering of old tapestries and gilt-framed paintings that adorned the walls of the second-floor landing.

"The house is much larger than it appeared from the outside," Tara remarked. "When was it built?"

"Which part?" Sebastian countered. "The original structure was built in the seventeenth century. Over the years several additions have been made to it. It's been remodeled and renovated more times than I can count. Which is why you'll find a hodge-podge of architectural styles in evidence, not to mention a jumble of rooms." He motioned to a spacious hall off the upper landing. "You'll be staying in the guest wing, an eighteenth-century contribution."

"Will there be other guests here this weekend?" Laura wondered.

"Not guests, although my sister Helen intends to join us for dinner this evening. I thought it proper to even out the numbers," Sebastian explained with a hint of amusement in his glance.

"Is your sister married?" Laura stole a glance at Boone to catch his reaction to the news.

"Divorced," Sebastian replied as there arose a loud clatter and groan from somewhere within the walls. "The lift," he said in explanation. "I did warn you it was noisy."

An Oriental rug ran the length of the hall, leaving only the outer edges of the hardwood floor exposed to view. There was a well-worn path down the center of it, an indication of the traffic it had seen.

Sebastian paused in front of the second door on the right side and turned to Boone. "Here is your room. Your father will be occupying the next guest suite. The adjoining servant's quarters should be suitable for his valet." He turned the ornate brass knob and gave the door a push, opening it for Boone's admission. "I hope it will be satisfactory." After nodding to Boone, he switched his attention to Laura. "You'll have the room across the hall."

"Knock on my door when you're ready to go down," Boone told her, pausing by the door to his room.

"I will," Laura promised as she moved toward her own. Her glance landed on a small brass frame affixed to her door, a twin to the one she had noticed on Boone's door. "What's this for, Sebastian?"

A smile deepened the corners of his mouth. "How quick you are to notice one of Crawford Hall's former customs. A rather naughty one, I might add."

Her interest caught, she tipped her head at a curious angle. "Naughty? How?"

"It goes back to the days when it was considered uncivilized for husbands and wives to share the same bedroom. As you can see, this brass frame has a slot that allows you to insert a card identifying the occupant of the room. Obviously it prevents some- one from entering the wrong bedroom, but it was also useful for"—he paused in emphasis—"amorous purposes, proper or not. As the French would say, *chacun a sa chacune,* which translates more or less to 'each man to each woman.' "

The gleam in his eyes had her pulse quickening. "Fascinating," she murmured, her own libido stimulated by the subject matter.

"As a footnote, I might also mention that there is some indica- tion that installation of the cardholders occurred around the time that your Lady Elaine lived here. However, it's difficult to say whether they were installed at her direction."

A soft laugh rolled from Laura's throat. "Something tells me I would have liked that woman." She started into the room, then paused, giving him an over-the-shoulder look, one hand on the door. "By the way, does Crawford Hall have any resident ghosts?"

That lazily sexy smile curved his mouth again. "If it does, I've never met them. Why do you ask?"

She arched one eyebrow at him, an expression that was both subtly provocative and suggestive. "I was just wondering whether I might have any surprise visitors tonight."

"One never knows, does one?" There was something delightfully wicked in his expression. Desire fluttered in her stomach in response to it. "Your luggage will be up directly. Drinks will be served in the library around seven. Someone will be about to show you the way."

"Drinks at seven. I'll be there."

The elevator clanked to a stop, and the doors clattered open, signaling Max's arrival on the second floor as Laura entered her assigned bedroom.

An ornately carved four-poster bed dominated the spacious room, one of several furniture pieces that looked to be from another century. On the opposite side of the room, chairs and a cushioned settee were grouped around the fireplace, flanked by bookshelves. Laura wandered over to idly peruse the titles.

As promised, her luggage was delivered within minutes, accompanied by a motherly gray-haired maid named Maude who'd come to assist with the unpacking and press any items that required it. All was handled in short order, leaving Laura ample time to shower and change before dinner.

Twenty minutes later she emerged from the private bath clad in a kimono-style silk robe and busily toweling the worst of the wetness from her hair. She noticed the tea service that now occupied a table in the sitting area and realized the maid must have brought it in while she was in the shower.

As she crossed to it, she caught the sound of an arriving vehicle. Having already ascertained that her bedroom occupied the front side of the manor house, Laura indulged her curiosity and detoured to the nearest window. When she looked out, she saw a compact sedan park near the front entrance. A woman climbed out of the driver's side. One look at her flaming red hair and Laura knew she was looking at Sebastian's sister.

The mantel clock in the library chimed. Sebastian glanced at it, noting the time was half past six o'clock, and splashed some tonic in the glass with his freshly poured gin. From the hallway came the sound of approaching footsteps. Recognizing that quick-striding walk, Sebastian poured a second drink. With one in each hand, he turned as his sister Helen swept into the library.

"Is that for me? Jolly good." She all but snatched the drink from his hand. "You have no idea how much I need this. I almost had Grizwold fetch one to my room." She took a healthy sip of it. "Mmm, delicious," she declared, then paused, her brown eyes opening wide. "Grizzy did tell you I arrived, didn't he? I instructed him to inform you. I dashed straight to my room so I could tidy up before your guests caught a glimpse. They are here, aren't they?"

"They came about half past four or thereabouts," Sebastian confirmed.

"That's good." She sank into a leather armchair and reclined against its thickly cushioned back with a kind of graceful exhaustion. "I had the most bloody awful day. Two of my workers didn't show up this morning, leaving me dreadfully shorthanded. And I had these two huge trees that absolutely had to be planted. It took all of us to do it. The instant the last one was in place, I dashed to my car and flew here, so you can imagine the state I was in when I arrived. My blouse, my trousers, I had smudges of dirt everywhere. I certainly wasn't a fit sight to be seen by your guests."

Sebastian listened without interrupting. Helen, his junior by two years, always had a tendency to babble nonstop when she was nervous. And her day had obviously been a stressful one.

"I noticed when I drove in that the grounds looked immaculately groomed," she rattled on. "I must remember to compliment Leslie and his crew on a job well done. I had hoped to arrive early enough to inspect everything, but that simply wasn't to be. Although I did notice there were no flowers in the front urns. That needs to be rectified. I hope your guests didn't remark on it."

"I doubt they noticed." Sebastian idly swirled the gin and tonic in his glass, then lifted the glass to her in an affectionate salute. "Thank you for the use of your crew in tidying up the grounds. I was remiss in not saying that before now."

"It's important that the old place look prosperous even if it isn't. If not for your guests, then for . . ." She paused, her glance flying to him, her eyes dark with worry. "It is so utterly awful that you have been put in such a difficult position. Losing Charlie and Sarah—and the children, too—it was so dreadfully painful. And now for you to be faced with this . . ."

"No one ever claimed that the fates are kind, Helen," he said in a voice that was gentle and resigned to the situation.

"They have been horribly unkind to this family," she declared and took a quick swallow of her drink, then looked at him again with quiet concern. "Are you quite certain you want to go through with this? Isn't there some other way?"

"Believe me, I have explored every possible alternative." He smiled to deflect her concern.

A heavy sigh slipped from her. "Naturally you have," she acknowledged and went quiet for a moment, then sat forward, clasping her drink in both hands, an earnestness in her posture. "I love this old place as much as you do, Sebastian, but I can't bear the thought of you being unhappy the rest of your life."

His smile widened. "You haven't met her." He raised a finger. "Let me correct that. You have seen her before."

"When?" Skepticism riddled her question.

"Every time you looked at that painting." He pointed to a portrait, one of several that hung on the only wall in the room with shelves.

Swiveling in her seat, Helen glanced at the wall, then sharply back at Sebastian. "Are you referring to the portrait of Lady Elaine?"

He nodded. "In many respects the resemblance is almost uncanny." The distant clatter of the elevator coming to life made its way into the library. "I believe our guests are about to descend on us."

Helen gave no sign that she had heard either his remark or the ancient elevator. Her attention had returned to the portrait of an elegantly gowned woman somewhere in her early thirties.

She turned to Sebastian with a frown. "Wasn't it Lady Elaine who was an American?"

"As I recall, yes."

She cast another considering glance at the painting. "She was quite beautiful."

"So is Laura Calder," he stated and added with a remembering smile. "She is also intelligent and audaciously charming."

Her head lifted in sharpened attention as she gave him the look of a sister who well understood her older brother. "Do I detect a note of interest on a personal level?"

"You do," Sebastian confirmed, aware of the chatter of voices that grew steadily closer.

"That's reassuring." Her smile showed a new ease with the situation. "Perhaps this will work satisfactorily after all."

"You speak as if it is all but accomplished. It isn't," he said and paused for effect. "I have a rival."

"Ah." She relaxed against the chair back. "Is this the reason you were so insistent that I be present this weekend? You invited him as well, didn't you? And you want me to keep him—shall we say—otherwise occupied?"

"Yes, yes, and yes," he admitted, eyes twinkling.

"What a devilishly clever strategy," Helen declared with an approving smile. "Beat the opposition by never giving him an opportunity to win."

"Desperate situations require desperate measures," Sebastian replied on a slightly serious note as the sound of voices mingled with the footsteps in the outer hall. He raised his glass in a toasting gesture. "Wish me luck."

In an athletically fluid motion, Helen rose from the armchair and crossed the distance between them to clink glasses. "Only good luck," she said. "This family has already had its share of bad."

As they took a sip of their drinks, the butler Grizwold appeared in the open doorway, paused, and made a sweeping gesture, signaling his charges to precede him into the room. Brother and sister turned as one to greet their arriving guests.

Max Rutledge was the first to roll into the library, with Tara walking beside his wheelchair. Sebastian's glance skipped over them to Laura, elegantly stunning in a dress of raw silk that flattered her feminine curves. The only sour note was the sight of her on Boone Rutledge's arm, laughing up at him in that seductively provocative way she had. Sebastian felt the stirrings of possessiveness. The heat of his feelings took him aback.

After the obligatory introductions were completed, Grizwold unobtrusively determined the drink preferences of the rest of the party. The entire time, Helen had difficulty taking her eyes off Laura.

"I didn't entirely believe you, Sebastian," she said, sliding him a quick glance. "But it is true. The resemblance is quite amazing."

"Shortly before you joined us," Sebastian explained to Laura, "I had remarked to my sister that your likeness to Lady Elaine was so striking that one would almost think that you are a reincarnation of her."

"Where is the portrait?" Laura asked. "I for one am curious to see it."

"Directly behind you, on the wall." Taking her by the arm, Sebastian turned her toward it, effectively separating her from Boone.

Laura's gaze went unerringly to the painting. Even she was surprised by the resemblance that went beyond merely sharing the same hair and eye color. It was like looking at her mirror image, the same high cheekbones, straight nose, cleanly angled jaw, even the same enigmatic smile curving femininely lush lips.

"It's almost eerie," Laura marveled.

"I never dreamt the resemblance would be so strong," Tara declared. "It has to be more than a coincidence that Laura is virtually a replica of both Lady Crawford and Madelaine Calder. They had to be the same woman."

"It would seem so," Sebastian agreed, standing just behind Laura's right shoulder. He tipped his head in her direction. "Now here you are, Laura, standing in Crawford Hall just as your ancestor may have done all those years ago. It almost makes one believe in destiny."

"It does, doesn't it?" she said thoughtfully, then slid a backward glance at him, a provocative gleam in her dark eyes. "Although I'm here merely as a guest, while this was Lady Elaine's home."

"True," Sebastian conceded with a slight smile. "Though it does make one wonder if you aren't meant to follow in her footsteps."

"I'll have to think about that," Laura replied coyly, intrigued by the possibility yet too wise to commit herself to anything.

Oblivious to their conversation, Tara continued her study of the portrait. "Do you realize, Laura, that if your hair was styled like hers, you would look identical?"

"You know, you could be right." Boone's voice intruded as he moved to Laura's side.

As if prompted by Tara's remark, he tunneled a hand under her hair and lifted its loose length up and away from her face, holding it in a rough semblance of the ringletted style worn by the woman in the painting.

"You really could be her double, Laura," Boone stated.

"I could, couldn't I?" Her chin came up a little higher, echoing the proud tilt the artist had captured on canvas.

Max Rutledge rolled his chair forward to join them. "How much is that painting worth, Sebastian?"

His shoulders lifted in a vague shrug. "The work is by an obscure artist, so its value is mainly sentimental."

"Name your price and I'll pay it," Max stated, making it clear he was accustomed to getting what he wanted.

Sebastian deflected the offer with a smooth smile. "That is extremely generous of you, but as I said, its value is sentimental. I wouldn't consider taking advantage of a guest in such a manner."

"I'm not going to try to talk you into it. But the offer stands if you should change your mind in the future," Max replied, choosing not to make an issue of it, for the time being at least. Instead he shifted his attention to Boone and Laura. "I rather fancy the idea of that painting hanging above the fireplace in our living room back home, don't you, Boone? 'Course I'd gladly settle for having the real McCoy instead."

Laura shook her head at him in mock exasperation. "Max, I know you are used to controlling everything. But you remind me of a trick horse in those old western movies, always nudging the cowboy into the girl's arms. Stop nudging."

"What's wrong with helping things along a little?" Max argued. "After all, you're the one who claimed Boone was your hero."

"He is my hero." Laura slanted Boone a look that was half-teasing and half-serious.

"Your hero?" Sebastian's eyebrow arched in sharp challenge.

His reaction briefly startled her, then realization dawned. "Of course, you don't know anything about the incident last night," she said and proceeded to tell both Sebastian and his sister about the attempted theft of her casino winnings that Boone had thwarted.

When she finished, Helen gazed at Boone with frank admiration. "How astute of you to notice what was going on and catch the man in the act. He must have been desperate to escape, yet you managed to subdue him. How very brave of you."

"I didn't do anything that someone else wouldn't have done in my place," Boone stated with an easy modesty.

"I disagree," Helen protested with vigor. "Most of the men I know would never have observed the theft in process. And the few who might have noticed would likely have shouted an alarm. I can't think of any who would have actually struggled with the thief, let alone come out the victor. Have you had training for such situations? In the armed forces, perhaps?"

"Most men raised in Texas have found themselves in a fight or two somewhere along the line. That's just the way it is." His big shoulders lifted in a dismissive shrug.

"That's one thing I could always say about Boone—he's handy with his fists," Max declared, rearing back his head to gaze up at his son with approval. "He wasn't much more than fifteen when one of the ranch hands started hazing him. Boone didn't take it too kindly and proceeded to make his feelings known. Needless to say, that cowboy got his walking papers—along with a busted nose and a black eye. You didn't suffer anything worse than a cut lip, did you, Boone?"

"That and a bruise or two," Boone replied. "But that was a long time ago."

"How fascinating," Helen murmured, all her attention centered on Boone. "Do forgive me for being so curious, but I can't help wondering what prompted you to be suspicious. Casinos are often crowded. It isn't at all uncommon to be jostled by another patron."

Watching her, Sebastian couldn't help smiling to himself. Rare was the person who didn't enjoy talking about himself, and his sister had a natural flair for encouraging an individual to do just that.

With Boone otherwise occupied by Helen, his way was now clear with Laura. He took advantage of it. "I am relieved to learn that you are none the worse for your adventurous evening." He kept his voice low, strictly for Laura's hearing, to avoid attracting the attention of others to their conversation.

"Thanks to my knight coming to my rescue," Laura replied easily, her glance centering on Boone.

Sebastian flicked a glance at his rival. "I can't say that his armor is all that shiny."

She laughed softly. "I don't know of many cowboys who are polished."

"The son of Max Rutledge is a bit more than a cowboy," he corrected dryly.

"They're both cut from the same cloth, and it's a rough one," Laura stated with the certainty of one who had been born and raised with their kind.

"But you are different. You are silk, not denim." As expected, his remark drew the fullness of her attention.

Laura was quick to recognize the veiled attempt to persuade her that she didn't belong with the likes of Boone Rutledge. But what Sebastian didn't realize was that a daring woman would have no qualms at all about pairing silk with denim.

Tara joined them, preventing any further opportunity for private conversation. Within minutes the butler informed Sebastian that dinner was ready.

"That was a damned fine meal, Dunshill," Max declared as they all took their coffee in the manor's sitting room. "A helluva lot better than most of the tasteless food I've had since we've been here."

"I'm pleased you enjoyed it," Sebastian replied with a host's easy pride.

Coffee cup in hand, Boone wandered over to the room's elaborate marble fireplace. Laura covertly kept an eye on him, noting the air of restlessness about him and recalling how quiet he had been during dinner.

"No offense to tonight's meal," Max began in preface, "but if you want to taste some really good cooking, you'll have to come to Texas."

Boone spoke up, "Don't mind my father. A week away from home is about all he can handle before his mouth gets to watering for some of that down-home Texas food." His gaze fastened on Laura with riveting intensity, making it almost impossible to look away even if that had been her wish. "Ever had *cabrito*, Laura?"

"No. But I've heard it's good."

Max snorted at that. "Good! It's a helluva lot better than good. *Cabrito* is the best-tasting food you'll ever have."

"*Cabrito* is a specialty of the Slash R," Boone stated, referring to the Rutledge home ranch. "You'll have to come to the ranch sometime and we'll fix it for you." There was an invitation in his dark eyes that went beyond his words.

"Are you extending a formal invitation for me to come?" With lips in a playful curve, Laura cocked her head at him, her own dark eyes alight to the look in his.

"I am," Boone confirmed, smiling back.

"In that case"—rising, Laura took her cup and made a leisurely stroll to his side—"I just might take you up on it."

"Please excuse my ignorance," Helen inserted, "but I have never heard of *cabrito*. What is it?"

"You may not want to know," Tara warned.

But Max didn't give her a chance to retract her question. "It's a kid. After you've dressed it out, you bury it in a pit full of embers and roast it slow all night."

"A kid," Helen repeated with a slightly horrified expression.

"A young goat," Tara was quick to explain.

"Oh," Helen said. "For a moment I thought—never mind what I thought," she added with a self-conscious laugh.

But it was obvious to everyone what she had thought, which gave them all a good chuckle—and led to a discussion of more exotic fare that could be found on foreign menus.

Food wasn't a topic that particularly interested Laura. She let her attention wander to the ornate design of the marble fireplace.

"It's beautiful, isn't it?" she remarked idly, touching the smooth, cool stone.

Boone made a disinterested sound of agreement. "An old house like this, I'll bet it's cold and drafty in here come wintertime."

Laura sensed at once that his remark was more than idle observation. "Why would you think about that?" she asked in light challenge.

His expression was serious, with just a touch of irritation and uncertainty flickering in the depths of his eyes. "You wouldn't be the first woman who could get caught up in the idea of marrying into the titled nobility." He injected a trace of sarcasm in the latter phrase. "The reality usually turns out to be a lot less appealing."

He almost sounded jealous, but Laura suspected that Boone was the kind of man who hated losing above all else—even if he didn't particularly want the prize. His highly competitive nature was one of the things that attracted her to him.

"You surprise me, Boone. Brotherly sounding advice isn't something I expected to hear from you," Laura replied, her smile lightly mocking him. "But I wouldn't worry if I were you. As you can see, both my feet are planted firmly on the floor. No one has swept me off them. At least not yet," she teased.

"Dammit, I'm serious," His low-voiced retort rumbled with impatience.

"Are you?" Laura countered, giving his statement another meaning. "I'm not sure about that yet."

He drew his head back, a wariness leaping into his eyes. "What's this? A game of hard-to-get?"

"You misunderstand." She lightly ran her fingertips under the lapel of his suit jacket. "I'm not really hard to get, but I am very hard to keep." Laura caught the startled look that flashed into his expression as she turned back to face the others.

At that moment, Tara spoke. "I'm really curious to see the rest of the house. Would it be rude of me to ask if you could give us a tour, Sebastian?"

His attention was on Laura, and she knew that he had noticed her talking to Boone. With an effort he shifted his focus to Tara.

"Not at all," he replied, smoothly gracious. "We could go now if you like."

"Wonderful." Tara immediately returned her nearly empty coffee cup to its saucer and stood.

"You can count me out," Max stated. "I'll go up to my room instead. I've got some papers to go over. Touring houses is women's stuff, anyway." He pivoted his wheelchair around and pointed it toward the doorway. It started forward, then stopped as he fired a look at Tara. "If it isn't late when you come up, stop by my room. There's something of mutual interest I'd like to talk to you about."

The request caught Tara off guard, which showed in her failure to immediately respond. "Of course, I will," she said, recovering her aplomb. "And I doubt I'll stay up very late."

"Good," Max said with an emphatic nod, and the motorized wheelchair carried him out of the room.

With eyebrows raised, Tara glanced at Laura. "It obviously must be business. I doubt if it's anything serious." She lifted her shoulders in an eloquent shrug of unconcern and looked to Sebastian. "Shall we begin our tour?"

"By all means," Sebastian agreed. "The small sitting room is just across the hall. We might as well begin there."

After the somewhat stiff formality of the main sitting room, the smaller one had a definitely cozy and more casual air. With its eclectic mix of furniture styles, patterns, and colors, and an artful scattering of unrelated objects, it was a room that made no pretense about its purpose: to be a comfortable spot for the family to gather.

From there it was on to the music room, with its collection of instruments that had all been played by one member of the family or another. Tara took a turn at the grand piano and pronounced it in need of a tuning.

A ballroom took up much of the west wing's first floor. It was essentially bare of furnishing except for a few chairs hugging the wall, and its air had that stale, musty smell of a room that had been unused for years. Sebastian explained that he had been a lad of nine the last time the family had entertained on such a grand scale.

In addition to the library, there was a gentleman's study for conducting the estate business and an east-facing morning room for breakfast. Sebastian showed them another room that he said his mother had used as her office. Then he opened a double set of doors that admitted them to a game room, complete with card table, dartboard on the wall, and billiard table. Boone gravitated immediately toward the latter.

"This is a beautiful table." He ran a hand over the smooth slate top, then stepped back to give it an overall look and glanced at Sebastian. "Do you play pool?"

Helen laughed at his question. "Billiards is a passion with the whole Dunshill family."

"Do you play, too?" Boone frowned, not entirely certain what she meant.

"I do," she said with a proud and smiling lift of her head. "In fact, I even won one of our family tournaments a few years ago."

"Quite a few years ago," Sebastian inserted dryly.

"How about we have a game?" Boone suggested, a challenge in his eyes.

Not immediately answering, Sebastian turned to Laura. "Do you play billiards?"

"I have played, but my skill is strictly that of an amateur," she admitted without apology.

Helen promptly spoke. "We could play partners, Sebastian, and she can be on your team."

The implication that Sebastian was that good was not lost on Boone. Laura caught it, too. "I'm game if you are," she told Sebastian

"Why not?" He seemed amused at the prospect of the two of them against the world.

Laura sensed Boone's displeasure with the arrangement. But she also knew his combative nature wouldn't allow him to pass up the opportunity to compete head to head with Sebastian.

"I'll rack 'em up," he said and laid the triangle on the table, then set about collecting the billiard balls.

"As interesting as the outcome of this game might be," Tara

said, "I think I'll leave you all here and go see what Max wants to talk to me about. Have fun." She lifted a hand in farewell and exited the room.

"You'll need a cue stick." Sebastian guided Laura to the rack, surveyed the selection, then cast an assessing eye over her and picked one. "This should do." He passed it to her, a slightly conspiratorial air to his smile. "With any luck, you won't have to use it."

"Don't count on it," Boone stated with the easy confidence of a man certain of his skill at the game.

With the first scattering strike of the billiard balls, there was an electric feel to the air. It tingled through Laura, quickening all her senses and making her aware of the sizzling undercurrents.

She eyed the two combatants, each a contrast to the other in his approach. Boone was focused and intense, while Sebastian was calm and unconcerned. She was a little surprised that she could be attracted to two such different men. Sebastian was not only sexually attractive, but he also made her laugh. Boone, on the other hand, excited her in a different way, bringing a rush of some powerful, primitive emotion she hadn't been able to identify. As far as she was concerned, it was too soon to say which one would come out on top, regardless of this pool game.

Just then Sebastian made a particularly difficult shot, and Helen groaned. "He's going to beat us." Her low murmur was laced with defeat.

"No, he isn't," Boone stated, a determined set to his jaw. "We'll win. One way or another."

Helen glanced at him, slightly aghast. "You wouldn't cheat, would you?"

Boone flicked a glance her way. "I thought you said you had your own business."

"I do." She gave him a startled look that said more loudly than words that she didn't understand what one had to do with the other.

"Then you shouldn't have to ask." Boone picked up the chalk

cube and rubbed it on the end of his cue stick as Laura bit back a smile. There wasn't any doubt that Boone was the son of Max Rutledge by more than just blood.

A floorboard squeaked beneath the carpeted runner as Tara made her way along the second-floor hall. Her mind ran through a half dozen business events that might have prompted Max to feel he should alert her to them. Considering Max was the type who usually kept any such knowledge to himself, especially if it gave him an advantage over the competition—and Dy-Corp's many fossil-fuel interests certainly put her in that category—none of the possibilities seemed logical.

Pausing outside the door to his room, she lightly rapped twice. "It's Tara, Max." The only response was a muffled sound of footsteps from inside. Seconds later the door swung open, and Max's valet stepped back to admit her.

"Mr. Rutledge is expecting you."

"Come in, Tara," Max called and rolled into view. "Have a seat." He waved a hand to the grouping of chairs in the room's sitting area, then glanced pointedly at the burly Barnett. "That'll be all for now."

As the man withdrew to an adjoining room and closed the connecting door, Tara crossed to one of the chairs and gracefully sank into it. But Max didn't immediately join her. Instead he wheeled his chair over to a centuries-old secretariat, sifted through some folders in his opened briefcase on its top, and removed one.

"What is this mysterious business you wanted to discuss with me?" Tara asked, all smiles and bright-eyed southern charm.

"There really isn't anything mysterious about it." With a soft whirr, the wheelchair glided over to her chair. Max handed her the folder from his lap. "See for yourself."

"What's this?" Tara searched his face, seeking some hint about its contents, as she flipped it open.

"I did some checking on our host before we came. It makes for some interesting reading."

"That wasn't very polite," she said in mild rebuke.

"But it's smart. Read it."

Tara ran another glance over his closed expression, then made a quick scan of the contents and went back to the first sheet to make a more thorough study. When she finished, she closed the folder and handed it back to him, her own expression as bland as his.

"You're right. It was interesting reading," she confirmed.

"You need to talk to Laura. I'd do it myself, but it's better if it comes from you. After all, she wouldn't be the first woman to be taken in by someone with a title."

"We don't know whether Laura is even thinking along those lines," Tara pointed out.

"You'll never convince me that he invited her here this weekend just so she could see that portrait. And if you believe it, you're not as smart as I think you are."

Tara made no comment to that. "I'll speak to her," she said and stood up. "Like you, I would rather play it safe than be sorry."

Chapter Six

Boone's arm was hooked around her waist, keeping her firmly against his side as they climbed the stairs to their rooms. Conscious of her hip rubbing against his thigh with each step, Laura stole a glance at his face, noting the faintly smug curve to his mouth.

"You certainly seem rather pleased with yourself," she observed.

"Why shouldn't I be?" He smiled down on her. "After all, I did win."

"So you did," Laura agreed easily. "Although having me for a partner meant that Sebastian was obliged to play with something of a handicap." It was a mischievous perversity that prompted her to argue Sebastian's side.

But Boone seemed to sense that and didn't rise to the bait. "Did you expect me to play with one hand tied behind my back to make up for it?"

She released a breathy laugh and shook her head. "Not you. You'll make use of every advantage you can."

"Wouldn't you?" he countered.

"Probably," Laura admitted as they reached the top of the steps.

"Damn right you would," Boone stated. "Like me, you play to win or you don't play."

"Is that right?" she challenged playfully as they continued along the hall toward her room.

"You know it is," he replied. "But I don't expect you to admit it."

Inwardly Laura acknowledged that truth about herself. To her thinking, it didn't make sense to undertake something unless it was with the intention of succeeding.

When they arrived at the door to her room, she turned toward him and leaned back against the jamb, tilting her face up to him. "I suppose as the victor you intend to claim the spoils." There was an instant darkening of his eyes, desire heating them. When he made that initial move to claim the invitation from her lips, Laura added, "And I warn you, I am spoiled."

In answer, his mouth came down to claim her lips in a driving kiss that was rough with need. Laura absorbed its bruising force, so stimulated by its pent-up hunger that her own blood suddenly ran sweet and fast. His arm circled her waist to arch her against his length, leaving her in no doubt as to the extent of his arousal.

Unexpectedly, he dragged his mouth from hers and bowed his head for an instant. There was a piercing blackness to his eyes when he finally met her curious gaze.

"Sometimes I think you're trying to spoil me for anyone else." The roughness of his voice made it a kind of accusation.

Those were heady words. Laura was careful not to show how welcome they were as she crossed her hands behind his neck and let her fingers idly toy with his close-cropped hair. "Could I do that?"

He looked at her for a long second. "I'm beginning to think you can."

It was such a grudging admission she had to smile. "Being

spoiled can have its own rewards." Rising up on tiptoes, she pressed a quick, warm kiss on his lips and immediately drew back before he could make more of it, and reached behind her to turn the doorknob. "Good night. I'll see you in the morning."

She left him standing there, stunned by suddenness of her escape, and slipped inside the room, quickly closing the door behind her and leaning against it, savoring the satisfaction of the moment. After a short pause, she heard the sound of his footsteps moving away. She hadn't been sure he would leave, and waited a beat to make certain he wasn't coming back, then pushed away from the door.

Laura hadn't taken two steps into the room when some inner sense warned her she wasn't alone. Muscles tensing in vague alarm, she turned and made a visual sweep of the room. The search halted. For a startled instant, she simply stared at Sebastian, stretched out on her bed, reclining against its pillows.

"What are you doing in here?" she asked, wavering between shock and amusement.

"You did mention earlier that you wondered whether you would be having a surprise visitor," Sebastian reminded her and uncrossed his legs to swing them off the bed and stand up. "I didn't want to disappoint you."

Amusement reigned as she shook her head and sighed.

"But how did you get in here? I just left you downstairs."

His expression was one of mock consternation. "I must have neglected to mention on the tour that Crawford Hall, like other old manors, contains secret passageways. How remiss of me."

"Secret passageways. Where?" Her curiosity aroused, she looked about the room.

Sebastian clucked his tongue in reproach. "If I told you, it wouldn't be secret anymore, now would it?"

"Stop being so mysterious." Her smile chided him even as her pulse fluttered at his sauntering approach. "Tell me."

Pausing in front of her, he released an exaggerated sigh. "Very well, if you insist. You happen to be standing in one of the older sections of Crawford Hall. This room was in fact the master bedroom—"

Laura interrupted, "Which goes back to the days when husbands and wives didn't sleep together."

"You remembered," he said with a nod of approval.

"My retention level is very high." At the moment, it was their night in Rome she was remembering, especially his unique style of lovemaking. It had her heart beating a little faster.

"That's good to know." Something in his look suggested he was remembering, too. "But as I was saying, one of my long-ago ancestors apparently had a dislike for wasted steps. Hence he had the architect include a hidden staircase in his design, linking the master bedroom and the library."

Laura made another quick scan of the room and guessed, "The bookshelves flanking the fireplace—one of them is the door."

"The one on the right," Sebastian confirmed.

"That hidden staircase wouldn't have anything to do with your reason for selecting this room for me, would it?" She eyed him with the full expectation that his answer would be in the affirmative.

Sebastian chose to neither confirm nor deny that. "It does facilitate privacy for late-night visits. Don't you agree?" He stood close but made no move to touch her. His failure to touch her only served to make her doubly aware of the scant inches that separated them.

"Do you make a habit of assigning your female guests to this room?" she challenged.

"Only the very attractive ones." He trailed his fingertips along the shoulder seam of her dress, following its line to the curve of her neck. Her skin tingled under the lightness of the contact. It was as if every inch of her body became sensitized.

"Why does that not surprise me?" Laura murmured, aware that her voice had become breathy.

"Aren't you going to ask how many women have occupied this

room before you?" His fingertips lightly explored the pulsing vein in her neck, following it to the lobe of her ear.

She had a catlike urge to rub her cheek against his palm to encourage the fullness of his caress. "How many?" She all but purred the question.

"As it happens, you're the first."

"You don't really expect me to believe that, do you?" She showed her skepticism.

"If you'll recall, I did say I put only the very attractive ones in this room—and you are the first who qualified."

"Flatterer," she chided, her eyelids fluttering half-closed as his fingers made a slow track up to her cheekbone and down her cheek to the corner of her lips.

"It's no flattery. You are incredibly beautiful," Sebastian stated, then added in a musing tone. "Perhaps the portrait is to blame for it, but I have the distinct feeling that you have always been a part of my life. It's difficult to believe we met only a few nights ago in Rome."

"But it was a very memorable night." Laura was conscious of her whole body straining toward him, wanting his touch. When his fingertips lightly brushed over the curve of her lower lip, need trembled through her. "Do you always tantalize a girl like this?" she said in protest.

"Considering you just came from another man's arms, I thought you might need time to adjust to the idea of going into another's," he replied smoothly.

"Were you watching us through some secret peephole?" In truth, she was more amused than outraged at the possibility.

"No." His mouth crooked. "It's much more elementary than that. Standing this close, I can smell his cologne on your skin. It has a heavy citrusy scent that's a bit overpowering."

A smile grooved little dimples in her cheeks. "Your middle name must be Sherlock. Sebastian Sherlock Dunshill."

"It definitely has a ring to it."

"Indeed it does," Laura agreed and tipped her head in an age-old invitation. "In case you're wondering, I have adjusted to the idea. Will you kiss me now?"

"With pleasure." But it was nothing he rushed as his mouth made a slow descent to her lips and moved over them in a sensual delving of their softness.

It was a lazy heat that started low and gradually engulfed her. His arms encircled her, his hands molding her to his shape, demonstrating how perfectly a man and woman could fit together. When his hand cupped the underside of her breast, desire swelled within her.

All the while there was the magic of his drugging kisses—on her lips, her neck, her cheek, and back to her lips again. Laura had a rational moment to marvel that lovemaking could be so beautiful. Beautiful and rapturous, without haste or demand, just an endless giving of pleasure. She only knew she never wanted it to end.

The light *tap-tap-tap* at her door barely registered. Then Tara's muffled voice intruded. "Laura. It's Tara. May I come in?"

The request was immediately followed by a turning of the doorknob. Sebastian's hands gripped her shoulders and set her away from him as the door swung open and Tara walked in.

For a split second Tara froze at the sight of him. "Sebastian. I didn't know you were here." Her voice was unexpectedly cool with challenge. It matched the tilt of her chin and the veiled censure in her gaze.

"I came by to see if Laura wanted to go for a morning canter tomorrow," he explained with a smoothness that Laura wanted to applaud.

There was no doubt in her mind that she looked as if she had just been thoroughly kissed, which she had. And she wasn't the least bit embarrassed about it.

"Naturally I told him he could count on me," Laura said. "Would you like to ride along, Tara?"

"I'll see how I feel in the morning," she replied, effectively dismissing the topic as she once again fixed her dark gaze on Sebastian. "I need to speak to Laura. Would you mind?"

"Not at all," he assured her and glanced at Laura. "Good night"

"Good night. I'll see you in the morning," she said with regret.

"In your riding clothes," Sebastian added, throwing her a smile before nodding to Tara and moving past her into the hall.

With deliberation, Tara closed the door behind him, paused, then turned to face Laura, her expression one of thoughtful study. Laura sensed at once that something was wrong. It put her on guard. Disguising her unrest with an air of normalcy, she walked over to Tara and turned, presenting her back. "Unzip me, will you?"

After a slight hesitation, Tara lowered the zipper, and Laura moved away, stepping out of the dress as she went. Clad only in her slip and underclothes, she crossed to the bed and slipped off her shoes.

"You said you needed to talk to me," she prompted when Tara remained silent. "Did my mother call?"

"No. As far as I know, everything is fine there. I need to speak to you about something else." Tara moved into the room and walked directly toward the cozy sitting area. "Let's sit down over here."

"This sounds serious," Laura remarked in a deliberately light tone, noting that Tara seemed uncertain about how to bring up the subject she wanted to discuss.

"I don't know whether 'serious' is the particular word I would use. But I do think it could be important." Tara sat down in one of the plumply cushioned armchairs and waited for Laura to join her.

Laura curled up in a twin to it. "Important how?"

"That remains to be seen," Tara replied, hedging again. "You see, some information has come to my attention."

Suddenly several seemingly unrelated items solidified into one in Laura's mind. "If I had to guess, I'd say that Max is the source of your information."

Surprise flickered ever so briefly in Tara's expression at the astuteness of Laura's statement. It was quickly followed by a look of admiration and approval.

"As a matter of fact, he is," Tara admitted. "Obviously I haven't had an opportunity to verify anything he told me. At the same time, I have no reason to believe it isn't true."

Something else clicked into place. "It's about Sebastian, isn't it? I remember that Max didn't look at all surprised when Sebastian told us he was the current earl of Crawford."

"Really? I didn't notice." Nor was it of much interest to Tara at the moment. "It seems that Sebastian inherited the title after his older brother was killed in a plane crash this past winter. At the time, there was already a sizable mortgage on the property, a debt incurred by his brother in order to raise sufficient money to pay the taxes that came due when he inherited the title from their father. Sebastian is now facing a similar tax obligation—and few ways to satisfy it. Unless he can lay his hands on a very large sum of money in a very short period of time, it is likely he will have to sell all, or a major portion, of the estate to satisfy it."

Laura absorbed the sobering information without comment. She knew there was more, or Tara wouldn't be having this conversation with her.

"To be honest, Laura," Tara sat forward, clasping her hands together in an earnest pose, "Max thinks it's possible that Sebastian might be desperate enough to marry someone—anyone—with money. And he's concerned that Sebastian might have set his sights on you."

"What do *you* think?" Laura asked, stalling for time while she tried to understand her own reaction to the information.

"I think it's entirely possible that he has," Tara replied frankly. "But I also know that you are much too intelligent to be taken in by a fortune hunter."

But the unsolicited vote of confidence didn't make Laura feel better. Suddenly tense and restless, she surrendered to the need for action and rose from the chair. Resisting the urge to pace, she walked over to the bed and picked up the dress she had flung onto it.

"I wonder what he was doing in Rome," she mused aloud, as she slipped the dress on a hanger and carried it to the wardrobe closet. "Do you suppose he went there to see if the *contessa* would loan him the money?"

"Who's to say?" Tara shrugged off the question. "If he did, I doubt that he was successful. The count is notoriously tightfisted, and the *contessa* has very little funds of her own."

Laura had no reason to question the certainty in Tara's voice. Tara was rarely wrong about such things. And it was unlikely that Max was, either.

"Are you all right, Laura?"

She spun around. At the last second, she managed to bite back the sharp retort she had been about to make and smiled instead. "I'm fine." The lie came smoothly. "Why shouldn't I be? After all, I hardly know the man. It's unfortunate that he's in such a difficult financial situation, but it doesn't have anything to do with me. And after what you've told me, you can be sure that it won't."

"Of course." A look of fresh ease claimed Tara's countenance, brightening her eyes and relaxing her smile. "I guess I was worried that you might have become a bit fond of him."

"A handsome devil like him, of course I have." Laura made the breezy admission without hesitation. "Who wouldn't?" She pulled open a bureau drawer and took out her nightgown and matching robe.

Tara laughed. "You're absolutely right," she said, clearly reassured that there was no reason for any concern. "Just the same, I feel better now that you know about this."

"True," Laura agreed in a deliberately casual tone of voice. "As the old saying goes, 'to be forewarned is to be forearmed.'"

"That's exactly the way I looked at it," Tara replied and straightened from the chair. "Are you still going riding with him in the morning?"

"Of course. You don't think I'm going to pass up the chance to gallop across the country, do you? It's been much too long since I've been on the back of a horse. That's the one thing about the ranch that I do miss."

"Just make sure you don't get thrown. Your mother would have my head if anything happened to you."

"Not if it happened on a horse. That's something she would understand."

"You're probably right." Tara glanced at the nightclothes in Laura's hands. "I'll say good night and let you get ready for bed."

"See you in the morning." Laura worked to sound casually off-hand.

But the minute the door closed behind Tara, Laura dropped all pretense that nothing was wrong. Giving rein to the turbulence within, she tossed the robe and nightgown on a chair and crossed to a window. She stared into the night-darkened landscape, indifferent to the scattering of stars and the leafy silhouettes of the trees.

Hurt, that was what she felt. Laura tried to remember the last time she had been genuinely hurt by someone, but couldn't.

She was stunned to discover that she felt like crying. Pride wouldn't let her give in to tears. Instead she went straight to the private bath and stood beneath the shower spray until the feeling went away.

PART TWO

There was a promise of love
And a question of trust,
But a Calder will always
Do what she must.

Chapter Seven

⸺

"Excuse me, miss." The strange voice seemed to come from someplace far away. Yet there was something insistent about it that penetrated Laura's consciousness.

She rolled over in bed and struggled to throw off the heaviness of sleep. Her eyes focused with difficulty on the elderly woman in a maid's uniform walking past her bed, carrying a tray laden with a coffee service.

"His Lordship asked me to bring you coffee." She set the tray on a table in the sitting area. "There's a basket of pastries on the tray as well. If you're going horseback riding this morning, you'll be needing some food in your stomach." She turned back toward the bed. "If you want something more hearty, breakfast will be served in the morning room."

"No, thanks," Laura mumbled, rousing herself with an effort.

"As you wish, miss," the maid acknowledged and bustled from the room.

Laura remained in bed as the events of the previous night came flooding back to her. The memories left her with a heavy feeling. At the same time they hardened something inside her. She threw off the covers, climbed out of bed, grabbed the robe off the foot of the bed, and went directly to the breakfast tray to pour herself that first, bracing cup of coffee. If she felt any lingering sadness, she had pushed it deep inside.

Dressed in riding breeches, boots, and a long-sleeved blouse, Laura descended the stairs an hour later. A black bow held her hair securely against the nape of her neck, and she had a sweater tied around her waist in the event the morning air was crisp.

The butler stepped into the entrance hall and nodded a polite "good morning" to her. "A hot breakfast is being served in the morning room, miss."

"Will I find Sebastian there?"

"No. I believe he's at the stables, miss."

"How do I get there?"

Grizwold hesitated. "The route is a bit confusing," he began with a trace of uncertainty. "I have other duties that require my immediate attention, or I would be happy to show you the way. Perhaps it would be best if you waited out front. His Lordship will be bringing the horses there directly."

"I'll do that. Thanks." Laura continued to the front door and stepped into the sharp spring morning. It was the first time she had ventured outside since their arrival. She ran a glance over the ocher-colored walls of the massive country manor.

It hadn't been that many years ago when her own house, The Homestead, had undergone a major restoration and renovation that had encompassed everything from replacing weakened support timbers and old electrical wiring to a new plumbing and heating system, as well as the addition of two new wings. At the time, her mother had remarked, "I swear it costs more to fix an old house than it does to build a new one. We would have been dollars ahead if we'd torn it down and started from scratch."

By nature, her family was conservative. It was a trait that had rubbed off on Laura, enabling her to understand Sebastian's situation, both current and future. But understanding changed nothing.

The rhythmic cadence of trotting hooves on brick pavement

echoed through the morning air. Laura turned toward the sound as Sebastian rounded the corner, astride a big, bald-faced bay and leading an iron gray hunter. He flashed her that familiar lazy smile, and her reaction to him was the same as it had always been—a quickening of her pulse and a thrilling of her nerve ends.

He slowed both horses to a walk and halted near her. "This is unexpected. I thought I might have to pry you away from your morning coffee."

"You thought wrong," Laura informed him with a saucy look and stepped to the head of the gray horse. "This is a beautiful boy." The horse buried its velvety nose in her hand and nuzzled her open palm. "Is he for me?"

"He is," Sebastian confirmed. "Since you are from the West, I took you at your word that you're a skilled horsewoman."

"I am. If you can put a saddle on it, I can ride it," Laura stated without an ounce of brag. "What's his name?"

"Hannibal." He passed the gray's reins to Laura and started to swing out of his saddle. "I'll give you a leg up."

"I can manage." For reasons of her own, Laura wanted to avoid any physical contact with him just now. With the reins looped over the gray's neck, she grabbed hold of the flat English saddle and stretched a toe into the iron stirrup and pulled herself onto the saddle.

"I had to guess at the stirrup length," Sebastian warned.

"It's almost right," she said and went to work shortening the stirrups by one more notch. "That's the advantage of an English saddle over a western one—it's easy to change from the saddle."

"All set?" he asked when she had finished.

"Ready and eager, I'd say," Laura replied as the gelding shifted restlessly under her and pushed at the bit.

Sebastian pointed his horse down the lane and set off. With re-luctance, Laura's mount settled into a collected trot alongside him. A short distance from the house, Sebastian swung his horse between two trees. A pasture stretched before them, an open invi-tation for a gallop. Neither horse required urging.

There was a sense of rightness to the steady drum of hooves, the whip of the wind in her face, and the feel of a horse beneath her that soothed and invigorated both at the same time. Used to the limitless expanse of the Calder range, Laura looked with regret at the low stone wall that marked the pasture boundary. She followed suit when Sebastian checked his mount to a canter.

"Want to jump the wall?" His eyes sparkled with an unspoken dare.

"Do birds fly?" She shot a laughing smile his direction and sent her horse toward the wall.

Its gray ears pricked forward, signaling its awareness of the obstacle before them. Laura readied the gelding for the jump, felt the gathering of its haunches and the adrenaline rush that came when they took to the air, sailing over the low wall. They landed well clear and galloped on.

Within seconds, she heard the pounding hooves of Sebastian's horse behind her. When he drew level with her, he signaled for Laura to follow him. They galloped across another pasture, jumped a brook and a wide gate, and arrived at a narrow country road, empty of traffic. Both reined their horses down to a walk.

"I needed that," Laura declared and released a contented sigh.

"I thought you might." His glance made an assessing study of her, noting the flush of excitement that gave a glow to her face. "You looked a bit distracted earlier, as if you'd hit a spot of heavy weather."

"I'm never at my best first thing in the morning," Laura said, deliberately making light of his observation.

"I'll keep that in mind." The hint of intimacy in his twinkling eyes had its usual disturbing effect on her. But along with the sensual rush she experienced, there was also a pang that was anything but normal for her.

Other than allowing a small smile to play across her lips, Laura made no reply to his comment and focused instead on the cottage that fronted the road just ahead of him. A milk cow emerged from a shedlike structure next to it, followed by an older gentleman in boots and work clothes.

"Good morning, Mr. Frohme," Sebastian greeted him. "Beautiful day, isn't it?"

"Indeed it is, sir," the man boomed, his glance sliding curiously to Laura. "Certainly a fine one to be taking your lady for a ride."

Sebastian chuckled. "I wish she were my lady."

It was on the tip of her tongue to retort, "It's my money you want, not me." But this wasn't the time or the place for that, so Laura smiled instead and said nothing.

"Give my regards to your wife," Sebastian said to the man. "And I should warn you that Helen mentioned she needs a fresh supply of honey, so I expect she'll be paying you a visit this weekend."

"Home for the weekend, is she? The missus and I will look forward to seeing her."

"They raise honey, do they?" Laura remarked idly after they had ridden past the cottage.

"The best in the Cotswolds," Sebastian confirmed, then smiled wryly. "Or, as Helen would say, the finest from Frohme's. She has a fondness for alliterative phrases." After only the smallest break, he continued, "There's a lovely stretch of river ahead of us. Shall we ride along it?"

"Sounds wonderful." Both horses moved into a trot.

Tara sailed into the sunny breakfast room and cast a cheerful smile at the trio gathered around the table. She was dressed simply in a silk blouse and tan slacks, but it was the tasteful addition of jewelry that gave her the look of country elegance.

"Good morning, all." she said in greeting.

Max had his face buried in the financial section of the *London Times*. He lowered it long enough to grunt a disinterested response, then snapped it back into place. Boone simply nodded.

Helen was the only one to offer an actual response. "Good morning. You slept well, I hope."

"I did indeed." Tara confirmed and sat down in the chair that the butler had readied for her. Immediately he shook out the folded napkin and placed it across her lap. "Don't tell me I'm the last one up."

"Not quite." Finished with his breakfast, Boone picked up his coffee cup. "Laura isn't down yet."

"She isn't?" Tara repeated in surprise. "How odd. I heard her stirring about long before I ever got out of bed."

"I wonder where she is," Boone mused, his forehead creasing with a slight frown.

"Didn't you know?" Helen gave him a wide-eyed look of innocence. "She and Sebastian went riding this morning."

"No, I didn't know," he replied, his mouth tightening with displeasure.

Max lowered the newspaper to glare at Tara. "Didn't you have a talk with her last night?"

"Yes, I—"

Boone never gave her an opportunity to complete her sentence as he turned his hard gaze on Helen. "How long have they been gone?"

"Perhaps a half to three-quarters of an hour. Wouldn't you say, Grizwold?" She looked to the butler for confirmation.

"About that, yes ma'am."

"Where would they have gone?" Boone pressed for more information.

"I expect Sebastian would have probably taken her riding over the countryside." Helen buttered a slice of toast and lifted a curious glance to him. "Why? Were you thinking of joining them?" She instantly followed that question with another. "Do you ride? Of course you do," she said, shaking her head in self-reproach. "For a minute I had forgotten you have a ranch in Texas. I'm surprised Sebastian didn't ask you to join them."

"I'm not," Boone countered in a flat, hard voice.

"That oversight is easily rectified," Helen assured him, a pleasant smile curving her lips. "If you like, I can take you riding."

"Do you think we could find Laura and your brother?" he challenged.

Helen paused a moment to consider the matter. "Springtime rather limits the routes he can take. Farmers take a dim view of riders galloping across the crop fields," she explained. "I should say it's likely we would come across them somewhere."

"Good." Boone removed the napkin from his lap and laid it on the table and pushed his chair back. "Let's go, then."

Helen glanced at the butler. "Grizwold, will you phone the stables and have two horses saddled for us while I go up and change into my riding clothes?"

"Right away, ma'am." He directed a half-bow in her direction and left the room.

"It shouldn't take me more than a few minutes to change. By then the horses should be saddled," she told Boone. "Shall we meet in the front hall?"

"Fine," he agreed, his impatience showing at even this slight delay.

The angle of the sun's rays created a diamond sparkle on the river's surface. Something rustled the underbrush on the opposite bank. Laura's gray hunter snorted and stepped lightly, eyeing the area with suspicion. But the twittering of a bird in the branches of a nearby tree seemed to offer assurance that there was no danger lurking in the deep shadows.

Just ahead of them the riverbank dipped down to the water's edge, forming a natural ford. Sebastian glanced back at Laura. "We'll stop here and give the horses a drink."

"All right."

When they reached the flattened area, Sebastian was first out of the saddle. He held the gray's bridle while Laura dismounted. Side by side, they led the horses to the water and stood to one side while the animals lowered their noses to the water.

"This is a restful spot, isn't it?" Sebastian let his gaze wander over the area before sliding it to her.

"It is," Laura agreed. "Beautiful and serene."

"It's always been a favorite place of mine. I used to come here often when I was a boy, just to get away and be by myself, especially when Charlie and Helen teamed up to razz me."

"Who's Charlie?" Laura asked, although she was fairly certain she knew the answer.

"My older brother," Sebastian replied. "He was killed in a plane crash this past winter, along with his wife Sarah and their three sons."

Their thirst satisfied, the horses lifted their heads, droplets of water falling from their muzzles. Sebastian led his gelding to some grass. Immediately its head went down and it started to graze.

Laura joined them with her mount. "Three sons, that's what you meant when you said something about not expecting to inherit the title, isn't it?"

"Yes." Sadness tinged the smiling crook of his mouth. "Charlie had one more than the requisite heir and spare. It's still hard to walk into the house and not find it full of their voices."

"I imagine it is," Laura agreed, not without sympathy.

"And in England," Sebastian continued, "the tradition of primogeniture is still observed. Both the estate and the title passed to me."

"What did you do before you became the earl of Crawford?" she asked, suddenly curious.

"In theory, I was a solicitor."

"In theory?" Laura repeated, amused by his choice of words.

"I never had any great passion for the profession of law. Therefore, I only dabbled in it when I had nothing better to do," he admitted without apology.

The frankness of his answer surprised a laugh from her. "It sounds as though you were a dilettante."

"I expect I was. The modest income I received from a trust fund my parents set up for me meant that I wasn't obliged to work."

"That's the second time you've used the past tense," Laura observed.

"Yes, well, responsibility has a way of forcing one to grow up, doesn't it?" Sebastian countered, smiling dryly. "And you, what will you do when your tour of Europe is over?"

"I haven't decided yet."

His smile widened into something lazy and sexy. "I have the feeling we are two of a kind."

So did she, which made it that much more difficult to condemn him. Laura started to turn away, but his hand checked her movement. He tucked a finger under her chin and turned her face toward him.

"Is something wrong?" His eyes made a thorough study of hers. "At times it can be difficult to tell what you are thinking."

Laura was deliberately uncommunicative in her answer. "Tara would tell you it's a wise woman who keeps a man guessing."

He smiled. "I expect she is an expert at it, too."

"You're probably right." She almost laughed again. It made her wonder. "Have you always had this knack for making people laugh?"

"I don't know. I've only tried it with you."

"With me? Why?" Laura asked, puzzled by his answer.

He moved fractionally closer, one hand slipping to her waist and the other tucking a wayward strand of hair behind her ear. "Mostly because much of the time you seem too serious, too self-contained. I think I like to reassure myself that you are human and not some beautiful goddess walking among us mere mortals."

The light touch of his hand, like his nearness, only made her want more, as if it might somehow ease the hurt she felt. "I'm no goddess."

"Enchantress, then. Or siren."

"How about vamp?" Laura suggested with an upward tilt of her head.

Sebastian responded with a small shake of his head, his eyes narrowing in disagreement. "Too crass. That is something no one could ever accuse you of being."

"Thanks for the compliment."

"Don't you know the truth doesn't count as a compliment?" he murmured, lowering his head to rub his mouth over her cheek in a nuzzling fashion that had her heart skipping beats.

She closed her eyes, conscious of both the pleasure and the pain she felt. As much as she wanted to surrender to his embrace, Laura had a greater need to confront him with what she knew.

Without any preliminary, she said, "Tara thinks you may have designs on my money."

Sebastian never hesitated. "At the moment I have designs on your virtue," he said and proceeded to nibble on her neck, igniting little shivers of excitement through her body.

A part of her wanted to pretend she hadn't caught his failure to deny her accusation, but Laura couldn't do that. "You also want my money, don't you?"

After a slight pause, Sebatian lifted his head and met her gaze. "The truth?" he asked.

"That would be a change," Laura replied, her throat aching.

"I was attracted to you the moment we met. Believe me, it had nothing to do with your bank balance, considering I was completely unaware that you had one."

She believed him, as far as he went. "But you did find out."

"I did," Sebastian admitted. "And it seemed a bit like gilding the lily, as they say."

Laura was suddenly and inexplicably furious. She shoved his hands away and made a spinning turn. "Don't touch me." Her low voice vibrated with the heat of her anger.

But Sebastian paid no attention to the warning in either her voice or her words as he caught hold of her and pulled her back around. Laura lashed out immediately, swinging the flat of her palm at his face. Sebastian captured her wrist before it could reach its target.

"You said you wanted the truth," he reminded her, something like anger glittering his own eyes.

"I didn't expect you to be so disgustingly cavalier about it." Laura made one twisting attempt to free her wrist, then ceased any struggle, pride keeping her rigid in nonviolent resistance.

"What did you expect?" Sebastian challenged, the hard light in his eyes changing to something softer, more delving in its study of her. "Did you think I would pretend that none of what you said was true? That I would insist I had no interest at all in your money? You're much too intelligent to have believed that. Still you set this trap."

"I set no trap for you," she denied with firmness.

"I don't know what else you would call it," Sebastian countered, his expression smoothing with a new certainty. "And I suspect you did it hoping to catch me in a lie. It would have made it easier to despise me, wouldn't it?"

"I got what I wanted," Laura insisted, icy-hot in her regard of him. "An admission from you that you were after my money."

"That isn't all I'm after. It never was all." He lowered her wrist and bent it behind her, forcing her against his body. Laura remained stiff and unyielding, shutting her mind to the warm heat radiating from him. "Don't you know you are the answer to any man's prayer? And when I found out you were wealthy, too, I thought you were the answer to my prayer. That after the pain and grief of these last months, the fates were finally going to smile on me."

"Next, I suppose, you'll be claiming you're in love with me." Her expression was full of scorn, but there was a big, empty ache in her chest.

"I don't know what love is. Do you?" The look in his eyes was serious enough that it gave her a moment's doubt. "I only know that I can't seem to be around you without wanting to touch you and hold you, and feel the heat of your body against mine."

"That's lust." Laura refused to attach any importance to it.

"Maybe, but it's something I would feel whether you had money or not." When he released her wrist, his hands moved up her arms in a rubbing caress that kept her close to him without force. "You feel it, too."

"A skilled lover knows how to evoke a response in a woman."

"Is that how you reason away what you're feeling?" Sebastian countered.

Laura had a glimpse of something tender and slightly mocking in his look before his mouth came down and claimed her lips in a kiss that was warmly persuasive. If only she weren't hurting so much, if only she could hold on to that righteous anger, she might have been able to hold on to her shield of indifference. But Sebastian had deflected too much of her anger, planted too many seeds of doubt, and she hurt too much. At the moment, more than anything else, Laura wanted to forget—and his arms promised that.

The moment she moved against him in response, the flames leaped and need took hold. It pushed, turning Laura into the aggressor, craving the salty taste of his skin and aching to feel his muscled flesh beneath her hands.

Clothes became an irritating barrier that were quickly discarded. When he sank to the ground beside her, her hands reached to pull his hard, male body to her. Sebastian was slow to react to their pull.

Laura saw he was about to say something and ordered tightly, "Don't talk. Not now."

It was action she wanted, not words. And he gave it to her, his hands and lips seemingly intent on memorizing every inch of her, pushing her to the fever-pitch of need. Then came that exquisite moment when he entered her and two bodies moved as one, hips thrusting, pressure building. Release came in a series of straining shudders that left them both trembling and limp.

For a wordless second they lay on the ground, still partially tangled together. Laura felt the slight chill of the morning air against her bare skin. With its touch came the coldness of reason. She rolled away from Sebastian and reached for her clothes.

"Where do you get the strength to move?" he wondered huskily. "You've stolen all of mine."

"Don't talk," Laura said again, and went about putting on her clothes.

"What do you mean?" He sat upright, his gaze boring into her.

"Exactly what I said." She tucked her shirt inside the waistband of her breeches and zipped them up.

"We have to talk now."

She didn't have to look to know he was frowning. "No, we don't." Laura pulled on one boot and reached for the other. "Everything's been said."

"Laura . . ."

She felt the brush of his hand on her arm and quickly stood up, made a half-turn to look down on him. "I can't trust your words any more than I can trust my feelings." She had never allowed emotions to rule her, and she wasn't about to start now.

"You aren't making any sense—" Sebastian began.

"Then let me say it more clearly." Laura was relieved to find her voice was steady and calm. "That was good-bye."

She saw the disbelief that clouded his face. At the same instant, her finely tuned senses caught the drum of muffled hoofbeats. She turned.

"Dammit, Laura, you—"

"I think you'd better get dressed," she cut in. "It looks like Helen and Boone are riding this way."

While Sebastian muttered a few choice words under his breath and grabbed for his clothes, Laura set about fixing her mussed hair, removing the confining band and bow, finger-combing it into smoothness, and wrapping it once more at her nape with the band.

As Laura refastened her bow in place, Sebastian was struggling with his last boot. He managed to stamp his foot into it mere seconds before Helen and Boone rode up. Greeting them with a cheery wave, Laura walked forward to meet them.

"Marvelous morning for a ride, isn't it?" Her breezy tone had Sebastian clamping his mouth shut in irritation, convinced that nothing ever rattled that woman. She either had nerves of steel or no feelings at all. He didn't believe the latter, so he chose the former.

"We've been looking for you," Boone stated, and Sebastian felt the rake of the man's gaze as he moved to Laura's side.

Helen was quick to explain, "Mr. Frohme told us that he thought you'd ridden this way."

Laura reacted to neither comment as she set her hands on her hips and surveyed Boone with amusement. "That English saddle just isn't your style at all, Boone. I've never seen anyone look more out of place on it than you do. You really should stick with western tack."

"If they had any, I wouldn't be riding this flat thing." He kicked free of the iron stirrups and jumped to the ground, his attention still divided between the two. "Where have you been?"

"Galloping madly across fields, jumping walls and hedgerows," she replied, seemingly oblivious to his probing question. "It's lucky you found us when you did. We were just getting ready to mount up and ride on after stopping to give the horses a drink. Now we can all ride together. Come on. You can give me a leg up."

Sebastian had a clear view of the blatantly provocative look she tossed at Boone before turning away. It cut through him like a knife. If he hadn't just held her in his arms, he would have called her a heartless bitch. He suspected the truth was simply that she was a damned good actress who had total control of her emotions. And judging from the combative light in Boone's eyes when he rode up, Sebastian suspected that if Laura had adopted any other air than one of carefree unconcern, he and Boone would be trading punches about now. Instead, Boone walked right past him, following Laura to the horses.

When he started to turn to retrieve his own horse, Helen caught his eye and signaled him to check his cheek. Reaching up, he rubbed his fingers over the area. They came away with a telltale smudge of coral-red lipstick on them. He fired a wary glance at Boone, wondering how the smear had escaped his notice.

Laura collected the gray's reins, conscious of Boone directly behind her. She turned the horse around, confident that Boone would catch hold of the hunter's bridle. When he did, she automatically checked to make sure the cinch hadn't loosened.

"I didn't expect you to go riding alone with him." Boone's voice was low and heavy with disapproval.

"Why ever not?" Laura countered in a perfectly reasonable tone, then cast a knowing glance his way. "And if you're wondering whether Tara passed on your daddy's message, she did."

"Then why does he have lipstick on his cheek?" Boone challenged.

"I had to tell him good-bye, didn't I?" She gave him a twinkling look of mock innocence. "After all, I couldn't blame him for trying. That would be childish. Don't you agree?"

"I don't have your tolerance for fortune hunters." And Boone didn't pretend otherwise.

"I wouldn't worry about it if I were you. I'm not." She stepped into his cupped hand and he boosted her into the saddle.

Privately Laura couldn't have been happier that Boone had shown up when he did. It had spared her further needless conversation with Sebastian. Her mind was made up. Nothing he might have said would have changed it.

On the ride back to Crawford Hall, Laura deliberately paired up with Boone. With her usual skill she kept the conversation focused on unimportant topics. That wasn't difficult, considering none of the others seemed inclined to talk. By the time the manor house loomed before them, she was beginning to feel the strain of maintaining the facade that she was untouched by all that had happened. Laura welcomed the chance to escape to the privacy of her room even for a few minutes.

But it wasn't to be.

She had barely set foot inside the front door when Tara's voice summoned her from a nearby room. "Laura, is that you? Your brother's on the phone. He wants to talk to you."

"Coming," Laura answered, and threw a questioning glance at Sebastian.

"I think they're in the front parlor." He pointed her toward it.

When she entered the formal parlor, Tara rose from a velvet-covered sofa, a cell phone to her ear. "Here she is now, Trey," she said into the mouthpiece, then passed the phone to Laura.

She lifted it to her ear and said, "Hi. What's up?"

"Don't you ever carry your cell phone with you?"

Laura smiled at the comforting sound of her twin brother's voice, conscious of her tension unraveling.

"Only when I choose to," she admitted.

"That's what I thought," Trey replied with an undertone of censure.

"So what's new at the ranch?" Laura asked and followed it up with a quick, "How's Quint getting along?"

"That's why I'm calling," Trey replied. "Aunt Cat is flying him home on Tuesday. We're going to have a big welcome-home bash for him on Wednesday. 'Course it won't be quite complete without you here."

"Wednesday, you say." Strange as it sounded, even to herself, Laura suddenly had no great desire to continue this European tour. "Hold on a second." She lightly cupped a hand over the mouthpiece and looked at Tara. "Quint's coming home. They're throwing a big party for him on Wednesday. You wouldn't mind if we cut our trip short and flew back for it, would you?"

The request took Tara by surprise. "If that's what you want—" she began.

Laura deliberately didn't wait to hear more. "We'll fly home on Monday," she told Trey.

There was an instant of silence. "Are you serious?"

"Of course."

"Is something wrong, Sis?" Trey asked, and Laura knew that sixth sense they shared was at work again.

She managed a convincing laugh. "Don't be silly. I wouldn't miss this party for the world. It'll be the highlight of the year at the Triple C."

When she finally rang off, Tara stared at her in disbelief. "You don't really intend to fly home on Monday, do you?"

"Why not?" Laura countered.

"We left half our clothes at the hotel in London. Do you realize how much packing we'll have to do before we leave?"

"Then we'd better get at it, hadn't we?" Laura said as Max wheeled his chair into the room.

"Get at what?" he demanded, splitting his attention between the two of them.

"Tara will explain," Laura told him. "I'm going up and start packing."

Chapter Eight

⌒

The plane's shadow raced across the limitless expanse of grass that marked the plains of eastern Montana. From the cabin's porthole window, Laura looked down on the landscape below, devoid of any signs of human habitation. The plane's altitude increased the land's appearance of flatness. But Laura knew the way it rolled and dipped, sometimes smoothly like a calm grass sea and at other times roughly like an angry one.

She hadn't needed a visible boundary to know the minute the private jet had entered the skies above the Calder range. She had known it instinctively, without the need for an obvious landmark. Laura decided it was something that came from being born a Calder.

It was that same instinct that caused her to scan the stretch of land to the southwest. Her search was rewarded with the sighting of a large collection of buildings that seemed to spring out of nowhere. A stranger would have mistaken it for a town, but Laura knew she was looking at the headquarters of the Triple C Ranch

In many respects the headquarters resembled a small town, complete with housing for the hired help and their families; a commissary stocked with food staples, hardware, work clothes, video rentals, and other sundry items; a central mail pick-up and drop-off; a gas station; a fire station; and a fully equipped first-aid station. There was even a cookshack that could be loosely considered a restaurant.

The Triple C was more than forty miles from the nearest town and nearly two hundred miles from anything that resembled a city. Which made it essential for the ranch to be as self-sufficient as possible. It had become such a part of her life that Laura took it for granted, even as she identified each individual building.

But her gaze fastened on the massive, two-story house that towered over all the others, the white of its exterior walls making it stand out against the spring green of the grass. It had long ago been dubbed The Homestead, a name that conjured up images of something rustic and old. The Homestead might be old, but there was nothing rustic about it. It stood tall and proud, a gleaming white jewel atop the knoll.

The door to the cockpit opened, pulling Laura's attention away from the window. The copilot stepped into the opening, flicked a glance at the dozing, jet-legged Tara and directed his gaze at Laura.

"Let Mrs. Calder know that we'll be landing shortly."

"Of course," Laura replied.

When he disappeared back inside the cockpit, Laura reached across the aisle of the private jet and nudged Tara's arm. She stirred, then sent a slightly groggy look at Laura. "Are we there?"

"Almost."

Tara sat up and gently pressed her fingers to her eyes as if to force the sleep from them. But she didn't do anything so indelicate as to rub them and risk smearing her makeup. Lowering her hands, she lifted her head and automatically gave her seat belt a tightening tug.

"What a shame we didn't spend a few days in New York to break up this long flight," Tara declared on a sigh.

"If we had, I wouldn't have made it back in time for Quint's party," Laura reminded her as she listened with half an ear to the grinding whirr of the landing gear being lowered.

"Quint's party *is* the reason you cut our trip short, isn't it?" Tara's questioning look held concern and uncertainty.

"Of course." There was the thud of the landing gear locking into position.

"I wondered," Tara admitted. "I thought your sudden decision might have had something to do with the information Max found out about Sebastian."

Looking amused, Laura eyed her askance. "You aren't really suggesting that I ran from the scene with a broken heart, are you? Honestly, Tara, can you imagine me doing that?"

"Not really, but you did seem quite fond of him."

"I was. He was easily the sexiest guy I've ever met, and, truthfully, I was looking forward to seeing more of him. But finding out he is a fortune hunter was more a blow to my ego than to my heart," Laura insisted

"Naturally," Tara agreed. "And you're much better off with Boone. The man has it all—money, power, position, and good looks."

"True." Through the cabin window, Laura watched the land rushing up to meet them, each blade of grass becoming discernible. "I imagine Boone's in Texas by now."

"If Max has anything to say about it—and he will—you'll hear from Boone again. And fairly soon, I suspect."

The jolting thud of the wheels making contact with the runway stopped further conversation. Which was just as well. Laura's thoughts were on Sebastian, not Boone.

She couldn't help wondering if the day might come when she would run into him again. The possibility was enough to resurrect that familiar flutter of excitement. Instead of being upset that the mere thought of him could arouse her, Laura accepted it.

Distance was what she had needed to acquire the proper perspective on the situation. Just as she accepted that nothing permanent could ever come of the attraction she felt for the man, that didn't mean she couldn't indulge that attraction, in the event of some future chance encounter. It was an attitude that seemed both worldly and wise, and one Laura felt comfortable wearing. In a way it was like an armor to protect her from further hurt.

The plane taxied to a halt on the hangar apron. As Laura unbuckled her seat belt, Tara relapsed an attention-getting sigh. "Laura, darling, if you don't mind, I'll say my good-byes now. There's really no reason for me to get off here, since we'll be flying on to my private airstrip at Wolf Meadow as soon as your luggage is unloaded. Give my regards to your mother and Chase, will you?"

"Of course." Laura crossed the aisle to Tara's seat and bent down to air-kiss her cheek. "Thank you for an absolutely glorious trip." She straightened. "Talk to you soon."

When Laura stepped from the plane into the bright afternoon sunlight, there waiting on the tarmac was her boy-slim mother, Jessy Calder, dressed as usual in boots, Levis, and a cowboy hat. The crisp white blouse she wore was the only thing that set her apart from a working ranch hand. Chase Calder, Laura's grandfather and the family patriarch, stood next to Jessy, gray-haired and stooped, without the rock-hard muscles that once covered his big frame—as evidenced by how heavily he leaned on his cane.

Jessy welcomed Laura with open arms and deep-shining look of love. Even though they had little else in common, the love of a mother for her child and a child for her mother linked them together.

After an exchange of hugs, Jessy stepped back to take a good look at this grown daughter of hers. "We've missed you." In a purely motherly gesture, she brushed the loose blond hair from Laura's face. "You've been gone a long time."

"No longer than when I was off at college." Laura chided affectionately and turned to give her grandfather a big hug.

"It's about time you came back." His wide smile negated the gruff reproach in his voice. "Maybe now I can stop worrying about you."

"You know you don't have to worry about me, Gramps." She planted a kiss on his cheek, leaving a smear of lipstick behind. "I'm a Calder."

"Don't you forget it, either," Chase Calder admonished, his eyes atwinkle with pride.

A movement in her side vision caught Laura's attention. Laredo Smith was standing next to the Suburban's rear fender, his boyish features belying his fifty-odd years. For almost as long as Laura could remember, the long, lanky cowboy had been a fixture at the Triple C. There was a story that Laredo had saved her grandfather's life when Laura was a small child, but that was something people rarely talked about, making it another part of the Calder legend.

But Laredo had always been something of a mystery. Nobody seemed to know for sure where he was from, whether he had family somewhere, or even if Laredo Smith was his real name. Laura had asked often enough but never received adequate answers, certainly not from Laredo. Yet there was never any doubt about the absolute and unqualified trust placed in him by both her mother and grandfather.

"I should have known you would be somewhere close by, Laredo," Laura said, his presence reminding her that even though he lived in an old line shack in the far western corner of the ranch, he was always at the Triple C headquarters, in the vicinity of either her mother or grandfather. She had long suspected, ever since her early teens, that her mother and Laredo were secretly lovers, mostly from the tender way they sometimes looked at each other. But if they were, they were unfailingly discreet.

"I see the world traveler has finally come home," Laredo remarked, leisurely moving to join the threesome.

"I don't think Europe exactly qualifies as the world," Laura chided.

"Maybe not," Laredo conceded.

"Where's Trey?" Laura made a quick scan of the hangar area, but saw no one other than the two men who manned the private airstrip, serving as mechanics, ground crew, and, at the moment, baggage handlers as they unloaded her luggage from the plane's hold. "I thought he'd be here."

"He would have," Jessy assured her. "But some truck driver fell asleep at the wheel and plowed up a large stretch of the boundary fence along the highway early this morning. You know how cattle are. The minute they discovered the downed fence, they had to find out what the grass tasted like on the other side. When Logan called to alert us we had cattle out, he said it looked like there might be close to fifty head scattered up and down the highway. I sent Trey and a bunch of the boys to round 'em up and get the fence back up. They haven't returned yet, so they must be still at it."

If Laura had needed a reminder that the Triple C, for all its immense size, was essentially a working ranch, with cattle representing its livelihood, she had just gotten it. On a priority list, her return hardly held the importance of nearly fifty head of cattle straying off the range.

She put aside her disappointment at Trey's absence and asked instead, "Was the driver all right?"

"He was pretty shook up but otherwise okay," Laredo answered. "The same can't be said for his truck. The tractor got banged up good."

Scowling, Chase peered at something beyond her. "Is all that your luggage, or is some of it Tara's?"

Laura threw a glance over her shoulder. "It's mine."

Laredo looked at her sideways, amusement lurking in his eyes. "Am I mistaken, or are you coming home with more bags than you took?"

"One or two. After all, I had to buy presents for everyone." Laura didn't bother to mention the new wardrobe that filled two of the suitcases. Her mother, who had no interest in clothes, high-fashion or otherwise, never would have understood why Laura thought she needed so many. And Laura had long ago given up trying to explain.

"It might take two trips to get all of that down to The Homestead," Laredo murmured, more to himself than to them.

"By the way, Tara asked me to give you her regards." The minute she mentioned Tara's name, Laura could almost feel the temperature dip. It was a reaction that confirmed what she already knew—that her family had no liking for the woman. Her presence in their lives was something they tolerated, mostly for Laura's sake.

"Is she staying here in Montana or flying home to Fort Worth?" Chase asked, with no great interest in the answer.

"She'll be staying here at Dunshill." Dunshill was the name Tara had long ago given to her summer home, but Laura found she couldn't say it without thinking of Sebastian.

The arrival of the men with her luggage briefly sidetracked the conversation. With Laredo's help, the two men were busy trying to figure out how to fit it all in the back of the Suburban while the others looked on.

After a moment, Jessy glanced at Laura and asked, almost as an afterthought. "So how was your trip? Did you have a good time?"

"I had a marvelous time," Laura stated without reservation. "I could bore you endlessly with stories about the places we went and the things we did. But right now I want to hear all about the welcome-home party you're throwing for Quint."

Fluffy white seed-tufts from the cottonwoods growing along the river's edge drifted in the air like so much confetti as Mother Nature added her own touch to the festive atmosphere. Pennants streamed from the freshly painted gazebo, along with a banner celebrating Quint's return home.

It was a party attended by all the ranch hands and their families as well as a few neighbors. The large turnout showed the high regard they had for this Calder-born son whom they had dubbed "Little Man" as a boy.

As always, there was more food than could be eaten, though an effort had been made to do just that. A few people were still grazing at the dessert table. But for the most part, the eating was done and the socializing had begun, filling the air with the sound of talk and laughter, the strumming of instruments from those musically inclined, and the shrieks of children at play or splashing in the shallow water at river's edge.

Chase was comfortably settled in a lawn chair, letting the sun warm his bones, his cane hooked over the armrest and a cup of cold beer from one of the kegs in his hand. At the moment his attention was on his daughter Cathleen, better known as Cat. With her petite frame, green eyes, and black hair that had yet to show any streaks of gray, Cat was the spitting image of his first and much loved wife, Maggie. Chase had never been able to look at Cat without seeing the resemblance. But today it wasn't the remnants of past grief that brought shadows to his eyes.

When he noticed his son-in-law, Logan Echohawk, wandering by, Chase called him over and motioned for him to pull up an empty chair. Logan dragged the chair closer and sat down, giving his hat a push to the back of his head and showing Chase a profile marked by high, hard cheekbones and a strong, straight nose that spoke of his Sioux ancestry.

"Heck of a party," Logan remarked and hooked one leg across the knee of the other, idly giving the hem of his jeans, which he wore in place of his sheriff's uniform, a tug.

Chase chose not to comment and demanded instead, "Cat's lost weight, hasn't she?"

Logan's gray eyes flicked a glance in his wife's direction, a shadow of worry briefly darkening them. "She's taken this hard. It doesn't seem to matter that Quint's wound was never life-threatening."

Chase nodded in understanding. "Cat's always had a tremendous capacity for emotion, the kind that runs to the extreme, seldom settling for anything in between."

"I always knew she was against Quint going into law enforcement, but I thought it was mostly because she didn't want him to live somewhere far away."

"There was more to it than that."

"Yeah." Logan didn't need it spelled out, either. "I've decided not to seek reelection when my term as sheriff is up. There's enough work on the ranch to keep me busy."

"That's probably a good idea. At least she won't have to worry about something happening to you."

"That's what I thought." With Cat being the subject of discussion, it was automatic that Logan would watch her. He saw the idle glance she sent in the direction of the gazebo, and the second look she took before she began to scan the crowd in a slightly frantic way.

In seconds she was hurrying over to him. "Have you seen Quint around?" She attempted to inject a curious interest in her question without completely succeeding. "I don't see him anywhere."

"I just saw him a couple minutes ago with Trey," Chase answered. "They were headed toward the barn—I imagine to use the facilities."

"He didn't walk all that way on his crutches, did he?" Cat protested, throwing a look in the direction of the century-old, big-timbered barn, as if Quint might still be in sight. "He should have said something to me. I could have driven him up there."

"The walk won't hurt him," Logan assured her.

Temper snapped in her green eyes. "I don't think you realize how weak he is. He's only been out of the hospital two days."

"Actually, it's been three," Logan corrected.

"Two, three, it doesn't matter," Cat declared impatiently. "He's still weak. You can sit there if you want, but I'm going to see if he needs any help."

She had that angry, determined look that Chase recognized well. "No, you're not," he barked, startling her to a stop. "Quint's a grown man—too old for you to be barging into the men's room to wipe whatever needs wiping."

"Just the same," Cat began in protest.

Logan spoke up, "I'll go check on him, just to be on the safe side."

As Logan got up to leave, Chase locked his gaze on his daughter. "You can stay here with me." Cat glared at him for a rebellious moment, then sat down on the very edge of the lawn chair, her body straining forward in its desire to go with Logan. "You do know, Cat, that there is a difference between mother love and smother love," Chase said in warning.

She flashed him an impatient look. "I can't help it, Dad—"

"You'd better." His voice had the ring of command and the experience of his eighty-odd years.

As Logan drew level with an end corner of the barn, he noticed a dark green Suburban coming toward him. He was quick to recognize the vehicle as the one Jessy usually drove. The sun glare on the windshield made it impossible for him to see the driver until the vehicle made a right turn toward the front of the barn. That's when he saw it was Laura behind the wheel.

Logan didn't think much about it other than to absently recall the sundress and flimsy sandals he'd noticed her wearing earlier— reason enough for her to drive back and forth to the picnic area rather than walking.

When he rounded the front corner of the barn, he saw the Suburban parked in front of it, both doors on the driver's side standing open. Even though Trey had his back to him, Logan had no difficulty recognizing the husky-shouldered, narrow-hipped frame of Jessy's tall son. Laura stood just beyond him, partially obscured by Trey, who was busy stowing something in the backseat.

That was when Logan caught a glimpse of a bulky white cast. It didn't require any great deductive powers to realize that it was his son the two were helping into the backseat. The thought of Cat's reaction to this had Logan frowning when he walked up. "What's going on here?"

Laura gave him a laughing look. "Really, Logan," she said in mock reproach, "You're a lawman. I should think it would be obvious to you that Trey and I are kidnapping the guest of honor."

From his crosswise position in the backseat, Quint looked at him, his eyes the same shade of gray as Logan's. "I just want a break from all the commotion and hoo-ha, Dad. We're gonna go somewhere quiet, grab a beer, and talk. Make it right with Mom, will you?"

As a boy, Quint had never sought to be the center of attention, and manhood hadn't changed that about him. Logan smiled in understanding and nodded. "It won't be easy, but I will."

"Tell Aunt Cat that we'll take good care of him," Laura said as she climbed into the driver's seat.

"You'd better, or she'll have your hide," Logan countered.

Laura just laughed and turned the ignition key. As the engine rumbled to life, Trey laid Quint's crutches on the floor of the backseat and closed the door.

"We'll have him home before dark," Trey promised, his voice had the same deep, commanding tone as his grandfather's. One look at those rugged, rawboned features and it was impossible to mistake him for anyone other than a Calder. Those features were like a tribal stamp.

Logan watched the three of them drive off, just as he had done so often during their growing-up years. There was a rightness to it.

Chapter Nine

A wind tunneled through the Suburban's open windows and tangled its fingers in Laura's long blond hair. As usual, she welcomed the feel of it—and the memories it brought back of riding through the streets in Rome in the Porsche with Sebastian. This time, though, the wind filled the vehicle with the earthy smells of the land instead of the intriguing scents of the Eternal City.

Beside her, Trey sat sideways in the front seat and leaned over the back of it to face Quint. "How long before you get rid of that thing?" He flicked a finger at the cast that completely immobilized Quint's leg from the upper thigh down.

"If everything is healing all right, they should put me in a walking cast in a couple weeks. I'll probably have to wear that for at least a month."

"By the time you get out of it, you'll have a closet full of one-legged pants to throw away," Laura teased and slowed as she approached the east gate. Its highway access had long ago made it the main entrance to the Triple C.

"I hope not," Quint replied and twisted his head toward the front, catching sight of the massive stone pillars that curved out into wings and supported the wrought-iron sign that hung between them, spelling out in block letters the name: TRIPLE C RANCH.

"I miss the old sign," Quint said.

For years the original entrance gate had been an unimposing structure consisting of two tall poles and a sun-bleached sign with faded letters that said THE CALDER CATTLE COMPANY, with the Triple C brand burned into the wood on either side.

"Now you sound like Gramps," Laura chided, as she pulled onto the highway and headed north toward the town of Blue Moon. "It's called advertising. You have to let people know where you are, especially the ones with fat checkbooks coming to one of our private livestock auctions."

"I know. It was a business decision to change it," Quint conceded. "But I still like the plainness of the old one better."

Old or new, Trey didn't really care, and it showed in the idle shrug of his shoulders. "It's that old catchword called progress, I guess."

"You'll never convince me progress has come to the Triple C until there's a swimming pool in the backyard," Laura declared.

"That'll be the day," Trey scoffed. "Besides, a swimming pool isn't progress; it's a luxury."

"Surely one luxury is permitted," she replied. "Remember the time you two went skinny-dipping in the river and I stole your clothes. Watching you two trying to sneak to the barn, picking your way across the gravel—I nearly laughed out loud."

"You were watching us." Trey looked at her in disbelief.

"You didn't think I'd steal your clothes and not stick around to see the fun, do you?"

"Quint got you back, though." Trey's smile was loaded with devilish glee. "Remember the minnows in your ice cubes?"

"How could I forget?" Laura shuddered at the memory of the minnow head poking out of the ice cube in her iced-tea glass. "But that wasn't Quint who did it. That was you."

"Trey's right. I did it," Quint spoke up from the backseat, amusement gleaming in his eyes.

"You?"

Trey took considerable satisfaction from the look of astonishment on her face. "And you were always blaming me for everything."

"With cause," Laura reminded him. "Ninety percent of the time you were the culprit."

The good-natured squabbling continued all the way into town. Only three vehicles were parked in the graveled lot outside Blue Moon's lone eating establishment. The neon letters that proclaimed the place as Harry's Hideaway were dark, but the red Bar & Grill sign in the window was lit, confirming the place was open.

Laura parked the Suburban close to the front entrance and climbed out. She briefly surveyed the building's grimy windows and its cracked and peeling paint, then scanned all the weed-choked yards and empty houses just beyond it.

It was her first trip to Blue Moon since she'd returned, and she couldn't help being struck by the changes. "When you said Blue Moon was turning into a ghost town, you weren't kidding," she said to Trey when he jumped out to give Quint a hand. "All it needs is some tumbleweed rolling down the empty streets."

"It's pretty sad, isn't it?" Trey agreed as he collected Quint's crutches and readied them for the moment when he would need them. "Gramps says it's back to the way it was in the old days when the town had to depend on the trade of the local ranchers and the occasional motorist."

"Times have changed since then," Laura said thoughtfully, not altogether sure if the town could still survive on only that.

"I suppose." Trey held the crutches steady while Quint planted his good foot on the running board and gripped the crutches, preparing to swing to the ground. "Still, it reminds me of the story Gramps used to tell about old Fat Frank Fitzsimmons, the first to throw up a ramshackle building here when his wagon broke down. There he was in the middle of nothing on the road to nowhere. A cowboy even warned him that people came this way only once in a 'blue moon.' You've gotta admit, Laura, that hasn't changed, but the town is still here."

"The Triple C can send some of its business Blue Moon's way and help it along." Quint hopped on one foot to get his balance.

Laura smiled at him with a mixture of amusement and affection. "You've always had a soft spot for the weak and helpless." Without waiting for a reply, she made a jaunty turn toward the entrance. "Come on. Let's go get something cold to drink. Heaven knows we won't have to worry about not having a reservation."

The tinkling of the bell above the door announced their arrival when the trio walked in. Not a single table on the restaurant side was occupied, but from the bar came the sharp crack of one billiard ball hitting another, followed by the sound of balls rolling across the table.

A short, balding man pushed through the swinging doors to the kitchen and paused at the sight of them, a half-scowl on his face. "The kitchen won't be open for another hour yet."

"That's okay," Trey told him. "We just want something to drink."

The man gestured toward the bar area. "Have a seat anywhere ya' like. I'll be right with you."

Laura led the way to a four-top in the center of the bar area while Quint thumped along behind, bringing up the rear. After Quint had lowered himself into one of the chairs, Trey scooted another one around to face him.

"Prop your leg up on this," he said and left it to Quint to manage it unaided.

Laura resisted the impulse to help, sensing that Quint was tired of everyone fussing over him. But, then, he'd always had an independent streak that manifested itself in a quiet determination to manage on his own.

Laura suspected that a stranger seeing them together would never guess that the three of them were related. There was a dissimilarity that went beyond the differences in hair and eye coloring. Everything about her said city, from her clothes to her hairstyle and makeup, while Trey had cowboy written all over him, from his hat to his boots and that far-seeing look in his eyes, and it was all wrapped in a kind of restless energy that never let him be still for long. Quint was more difficult to label. Those steady gray eyes and his air of quiet strength seemed to set him apart somehow, as if he could be whoever and whatever he chose. Laura smiled to herself, thinking that he certainly didn't look like a Treasury agent.

The scuffle of footsteps signaled the approach of the balding man. He stopped at their table. "What'll ya' have?"

Trey shot Laura a warning look and muttered low, "For God's sake, don't ask for a glass of wine."

Since she had no intention of doing so, Laura didn't bother to respond and flashed her most winning smile at the man. "Since I seem to be the designated driver, I'll have a glass of iced tea."

"A beer for me," Trey said. "Whatever you have on tap is fine."

"The same," Quint echoed

After the man left to fetch their drink order, Trey swung his attention to Quint. "How soon do you have to report back to work?"

"Never, if Mom has anything to say about it." Quint attempted to make a joke of it, but the underlying truth in his words injected a kind of troubled heaviness. "But I'll be reporting back as soon as the doctor gives me a release, which will probably be in two weeks or so."

"Mothers worry. It's part of the job description," Laura told him.

"Mom's gone above and beyond the call of duty, then," Quint replied and paused when the man returned to the table with their drinks. Trey dug some bills out of his pocket to pay their tab. After the man moved away from the table, Quint resumed their conversation. "I honestly thought Mom would feel better knowing that I'd be stuck behind a desk for the next six months to a year, but I forgot about the Oklahoma City bombings. She's convinced any federal law office is a potential target. Unfortunately, she's right. Dad thinks she just needs some time to get used to the idea of me going back in the field."

"But you don't agree, do you?" Laura guessed.

Quint shook his head. "No. Only one thing would make her happy, and that would be for me to resign and go to work for the Triple C."

"I think that's a helluva good idea," Trey declared.

Quint turned his steady gray gaze on him. "No, it isn't. That ranch is going to pass into your hands one day."

Trey flashed a cynically amused glance at Laura. "He says that like it might be news to me, instead of something I've been told ever since I can remember. And I don't see what difference that makes, anyway." He directed the challenge to Quint. "It would be good to know I have somebody I could trust at my side running things. And in case you haven't looked at that old map on the wall lately, the Triple C's as big as some eastern states—certainly big enough for two."

"You're wrong," Quint stated calmly. "There can't be two people at the top of the Triple C, or you'll end up with divided loyalties. You can see it today in the way some of the old hands wait for Granddad to nod when your mother tells them to do something." He shook his head again. "As much as I might like to, I won't be going to work at the ranch."

Laura caught the note of regret in his voice and wondered if Trey had, too. But Quint's remarks seemed to have a sobering effect on Trey that had him still contemplating them.

"How in the world did this conversation get so serious?" she said in mock reproach. "I thought we were here for a cousins' celebration—although I can't say this is the most festive place I've ever been in." Laura flicked an amused glance at the dingy surroundings that reeked with the stale, sour odors of tobacco smoke and liquor.

"After Europe this place must be quite a comedown for you," Quint observed matter-of-factly.

"I suppose." One bare shoulder lifted in a diffident shrug. "But I think you'll agree Harry's definitely provides a lesson in appreciation for the better-class establishments."

Quint chuckled at her response. "I guess when you're the only watering hole in nearly a hundred miles, quality isn't something you have to worry about."

"How true." Laura raised her iced-tea glass in a toasting acknowledgement of his statement.

Trey made a single sideways twist of his head in disagreement. "If your idea of quality is silk boxer shorts, I'll take Harry's any time."

"Silk boxer shorts?" Quint repeated.

"Yeah. That's what she brought me back from Europe. Can you believe it?" The high arch of his eyebrows left little doubt of Trey's opinion of the gift.

"He refuses to even try them on," Laura complained.

"I have just one question." There was a devilish glint in Trey's dark eyes. "Does Crockett wear them?"

"Who's Crockett?" Quint split his glance between the two of them.

"Laura's new beau." Trey answered, still watching Laura.

"Really." Quint's gray eyes took on the same teasing light that glittered in Trey's. "Someone you met in Europe, is he?"

"In Rome, actually. And his name isn't Crockett, it's Boone. I happened to be gone when Boone called yesterday, and Gramps answered the phone. By the time Gramps got around to giving me the message, he'd gotten mixed up about the name and remembered only that it was the same as a famous frontiersman."

"Of course." Quint nodded, making the connection. "Daniel Boone and Davy Crockett."

"Trey's been calling him Crockett ever since." Laura eyed her brother with mild annoyance.

"Does this beau of yours have a full name?" Quint asked.

"Boone Rutledge. His father is Max Rutledge."

"*The* Max Rutledge? The cattle and oil tycoon from Texas?" Quint questioned with freshening interest.

"The same."

"You've roped yourself a big one."

"I know," Laura replied, conscious of the heady satisfaction she felt at Quint's reaction to the news.

"Is it serious?" Quint wondered.

"It's a little soon to say." Yet she was confident that if she wanted Boone, all she had to do was go after him. It was an idea that had a definite appeal, especially when Laura considered the additional power and prestige that would accompany a marriage to Boone.

"We get to meet him next week," Trey inserted that tidbit of information. "He's coming to the horse sale."

"Actually, Boone and his father are flying in two days early so they can preview the sale lots," Laura explained.

"The sale lots or one filly in particular?" Trey teased.

Quint was more practical. "Will they be staying at The Homestead?"

Laura shook her head. "They'll be at Tara's. She's known Max for years."

"I guess we know where you'll be spending those two days." Trey sent her a knowing smile.

"Boone isn't a man you can catch by chasing him," Laura informed him.

But it was the certainty in her voice that prompted Trey to challenge. "How do you know that?"

"The same way you know which way a cow is going to jump when you try to separate her from the herd. You read the body language. Sometimes all it takes is a twitch of a muscle," Laura replied. Observing his slightly dumbfounded reaction, she laughed. "You didn't think it was some great mystery, did you?"

"I never thought about it at all," Trey replied with easy candor and eyed her with disapproval. "But you've gotta admit the way you talk about catching a man sounds a bit calculating."

"And I suppose you have never calculated what the best way to approach a girl might be," Laura scoffed. "Why is it wrong for a woman to apply similar tactics?"

When Trey started to answer, Quint held up a silencing hand. "Don't get into that argument. I guarantee you'll lose it."

The bell above the door tinkled. Automatically Laura glanced toward the entrance as a scruffy-looking boy of about seven slipped inside. She noticed the way his glance scoured the restaurant area as if looking for someone. An instant later the clatter of billiard balls had his head jerking in the direction of the bar. After a slight pause, he headed toward the pool table. But there was something hesitant, almost fearful, about his movements that captured her attention.

"Someone you know?" Trey asked in jest, observing her interest in the boy.

"No," Laura replied easily. "But if someone washed his face, he might be cute."

"A little young, though," Quint observed.

"I like them young." Laura smiled, all the while keeping a curious eye on the boy as he approached the two men playing pool.

One man, the younger of the two, seemed to be the object of the boy's attention. Dark-haired and burly, he was bent over the pool table, arm muscles rippling as he took aim on the cue ball. The cue stick in his hand shot forward in a lightning-swift strike. Laura heard the rapid roll of the ball and the *click* of it hitting another. On the flat top of the bumper, a chalk cube weighted down two paper bills.

As the ball tumbled into a pocket, the man straightened, a dark scowl of concentration creasing his expression as he studied the lie of the remaining balls on the table. He seemed unaware of the boy watching him until he moved to that side of the table and his glance landed on him.

"What are you doing here?" The man snapped in obvious irritation.

The boy seemed to shrink back. "Mom said I was to tell you supper's almost ready," he said in a small voice.

"You've told me. Now git." Instant obedience was something the man clearly expected. When the boy failed to immediately move, he raged at him. "Can't you see I'm in the middle of a game? Now get the hell out of here."

The young boy threw up an arm as if to shield himself from a blow. The man grabbed it and shoved him toward the exit with a force that sent the boy sprawling against an empty chair.

In a cold fury, Laura sprang to her feet and ran to the boy's side. The minute she touched him, the boy scooted away from her hand.

"The kid's not hurt." The man's voice was almost on top of her.

Laura threw him an angry glare. "No thanks to you."

Just for an instant the man faltered, then recovered. "The kid's got no business bein' in a bar, and he knows it," he declared as if that somehow justified his actions.

By then the boy had scrambled to his feet, moving with an alacrity that told Laura he had probably suffered nothing more serious than a bruise. She stood up and swung around to confront the man.

"That's no excuse to be so rough with him." Her voice vibrated with the heat of her temper.

"Are you blamin' me for him runnin' into that chair?" The man drew his head back in a great show of innocence.

"He didn't run into that chair. You pushed him," Laura stated.

"Like hell I did."

"You can deny it all you want," she said with contempt. "But I know what I saw, and you pushed him."

He took a threatening step closer, gripping the cue stick in front of him like a potential weapon, his arm muscles bulging. "Listen, you smart-mouthed little bitch. Somebody needs to teach you to quit stickin' your nose into other people's affairs."

Suddenly Trey was there, placing an arm in front of her and pushing her behind him. "Lay a hand on her and it's the last thing you'll ever do." His voice was as steely with warning as his look. "Any problem you've got with her, you'll settle with me."

The man wisely backed up. "I don't have any problems as long as you damned Calders mind your own business and stay out of mine," he said with some of his former bluster, then swung back toward the pool table.

Too angry to let him have the last word, Laura took a step after him. Trey grabbed her by the arm and forcibly turned her toward their table.

"Just shut up," he muttered.

Reluctantly Laura acknowledged the wisdom of his advice and let him steer her to where Quint still sat with his casted leg propped on a chair seat.

"Who is that guy, anyway?" she demanded, her temper still simmering

"I think his name's Mitchell. He used to work at the coal mine until he got laid off when it closed down. He had a job for a while stringing fence at the old Connors Ranch. I don't know what he's doing now. Hustling pool, I guess."

"The man should be horsewhipped," she said with conviction.

"Laura," Trey began in a placating tone.

She whirled on him. "Don't you 'Laura' me! I saw the way that little boy tried to protect himself. He's been knocked around before by that bastard who claims to be his father." Just as abruptly, Laura pivoted away from her brother and headed for the table. "What I should do," she muttered to herself, "is turn him in for child abuse."

With the thought still rolling around in her mind, Laura sat down in her chair and glared in the direction of the pool table. Trey followed her, swung a leg over his chair and lowered himself onto it, then reached for his beer.

"For a minute, I thought I was going to have to hobble over there," Quint remarked. "What happened?"

"Nothing really," Trey replied.

"Bullies like that one only pick on women and children." Laura made no attempt to conceal her loathing for such men.

A small smile crooked Quint's mouth. "It might interest you two to know that while you were trading words with your would-be pool shark, the kid was stuffing his pockets with mints from that basket by the cash register. What he couldn't get into his pockets, he shoved in his mouth, paper and all."

"You're kidding," Laura said, shocked.

" 'Fraid not," Quint replied.

Trey chuckled. "Why that damned little thief."

"With a father like that, who can blame him?" Laura retorted.

Trey made no reply to that and took a swig of his beer, made a face, and set the mug on the table. "It's warm," he said in distaste. "What d'you say we get outta here and head back to the ranch before Aunt Cat sends out a search party for Quint?"

"That's a good idea." Quint leaned to the side and scooped his crutches off the floor. "Besides," he said, throwing a teasing look at Laura, "Crockett might call tonight, and we wouldn't want Laura to miss that, now would we?"

Laura just shook her head in mild disgust. "Aren't you two ever going to grow up?"

"Not where you're concerned," Trey replied with a grin.

Chapter Ten

With the horse sale only two days away, there was a steady bustle of activity at the Triple C headquarters. Adding to the seemingly constant flow of horses coming and going from the barns to the work pens, a half dozen buyer's reps had already shown up to get an advance look at the horses being offered for sale. A couple were inspecting the horses in the stalls, but the rest were scattered around the pens, observing the horses being exercised and put through their paces.

As Laredo left the big-timbered barn, he spotted one of the reps standing at the rails of the large cattle pen, watching a cutting horse at work. The minute he got a good look at the claybank stallion through the gaps in the fence rails, Laredo guessed there would be questions and veered toward the rep. He was right.

"Would you happen to know the catalog number for that stud?" the man asked as soon as Laredo reached the fence.

"That's Cougar's Pride," Laredo told him. "You won't find him in the catalog. He's not for sale, but it's his get you'll be bidding on."

Disappointment flickered in the man's expression. He gave the middle rail a slap and made a pushing turn away from the fence.

"Tell Calder if he should change his mind about selling that stallion, I've got a buyer. And with that stud, he can name his price."

"I'll pass it on, but I wouldn't hold my breath," Laredo replied.

The man walked away, and Laredo climbed onto the top rail to watch the champion stallion at work. He had barely settled on his perch when he caught the flash of blond hair and bare skin. And he privately marveled that the rep had noticed the stallion at all with Laura in the saddle.

The flashy dun stallion crouched low, pouncing first one way then the other to frustrate the cow's attempts to rejoin the herd, exhibiting all the agility and cat-quickness of a mountain lion. Laura sat deep and balanced in the saddle, giving the horse no cues, aware that he needed none.

A beauty Laura had always been, easily worth two or three looks. But today it was her attire that was drawing male stares. Brown leather chaps covered a pair of skin-tight jeans, and a matching leather vest stopped just below her breasts, about the same place as the crop top she wore, baring her midriff.

Leave it to Laura to come up with an eye-catching getup like that, Laredo thought and shook his head in amusement.

After working the cow almost to a stop, Laura reined the claybank stallion away from it, letting it rejoin the penned herd. She waved at one of the riders, loosely holding the cattle, and called, "That should do it."

A horse and rider moved into Laredo's side vision. He glanced to the right as Trey halted a three-year-old colt parallel with the fence. Laura spotted him at almost the same moment and rode over.

"You're every bit the horsewoman that your mother is," Laredo told her when she halted the stallion near the fence.

"All I did is sit in the saddle. This guy did all the work by himself." She tunneled a hand under the stallion's black mane and gave him a congratulatory pat. "I swear, no one works cattle with the ease of The King," she said, using the nickname the ranch hands had given to the claybank stud when he was a yearling.

The stallion was the last thing on Trey's mind. "What the hell are you doing in that outfit, Laura?" he demanded, disapproval vibrating in his low voice. "You look like something out of *Playboy* magazine."

Laura never blinked an eye. "Don't be naive, Trey," she chided. "If I were posing for *Playboy*, I'd have to ditch the jeans and the top, and you know it."

As she uttered the last, a Land Rover pulled up to the pens. Her attention immediately swung to it. When a tall dark-haired man climbed out of the driver's side, Laura stood up in the stirrups and waved to draw the man's attention.

"Hey, Boone," she called. "Meet me at the gate."

The minute she said the name, understanding dawned in Trey's expression. "I forgot Crockett was supposed to show up this afternoon. That's why you're dressed so sexy, isn't it?"

Laura didn't deny it as she swung the stallion away from the railing and fired a warning look at her brother. "So help me, Trey, if you call him Crockett while he's here, I'll steal all your shorts and leave you with only the silk ones to wear."

Without giving him a chance to reply, she cantered the stallion the last few yards to the gate. While Trey watched, Boone Rutledge swung the gate open and Laura rode through, then pulled up to wait for him to shut it. She made no attempt to dismount until Boone had moved to the stallion's head. Trey couldn't hear what they were saying to each other, but he could see the way the man's eyes raked over Laura.

"I'm surprised his tongue isn't hanging out," he muttered to Laredo.

"You can say that about nearly every man who sees her," Laredo reminded him.

With Trey looking on, Laura dismounted and managed to

stumble against Boone yet make it look like an accident. But Trey saw through the act.

"You know," He glanced at Laredo, a grimness entering his expression, "having Laura for a sister makes it hard for me to trust anything a woman says or does."

Laredo chuckled, but Trey was dead serious.

Laura stayed against Boone, tipping her head back to look up at him, conscious of his hands clasped around her bare middle, knowing that he was equally aware of it. She laid her hands on his upper arms as if to push away, then left them there to feel the rock-hardness of his biceps.

"I had forgotten how strong you are," she murmured.

"Funny. I hadn't forgotten how beautiful you are." There was a primitive quality to the look of desire in his dark eyes.

Just for an instant, she pressed herself more fully against him to make certain the feel of her body against his would be imprinted in his mind before she drew back. "I was beginning to wonder," Laura said with a touch of coyness, "considering how long it took you to get here."

"Then you did want me to come," Boone stated, a cocky kind of male confidence flaring in his expression. "On the phone you didn't seem all that excited about seeing me again."

"A woman shouldn't sound eager," she told him. "It wouldn't be proper."

"You don't look all that proper." His glance dropped to the bareness of her middle and the navel that was exposed by her low-riding jeans.

She laughed. "That's because I seldom feel proper around you. Besides, being proper can become boring, and I hate being bored." Turning her back to him, Laura unlooped the reins from around the stallion's neck and stepped to his head, then glanced back at Boone. "Want to walk along while I take The King back to his stall and unsaddle him?"

Boone looked at her with surprised frown. "Can't someone else put him up?"

"On the Triple C, a rider takes care of his or her own horse. Only guests can get away with passing them off to someone else. It's an ironclad rule that can be broken only in the event of a dire emergency." Laura paused to slant him a provocative glance. "Did you think I had led a pampered life?"

"A woman like you deserves to be pampered."

"Careful," Laura warned lightly. "Some women might mistake a remark like that for a proposal."

"What makes you so certain it isn't?" Boone countered, matching strides with her when she struck out for the stallion barn.

She gave him a considering look. "It might be," Laura conceded. "You do seem to be the impulsive type."

"And you aren't?"

"Oh, I'm definitely impulsive, but never rash."

"There's a difference?"

"Definitely." But Laura didn't bother to explain the distinction, choosing to change the subject instead. "So what do you think of the Triple C?"

"It's quite a spread." It wasn't so much his words as his expression that told Laura he was impressed by what little he had seen.

"I'll take you on a tour of it after I get The King settled in his stall," she said. "And I'll show you the horses that will be up for auction. That is, after all, the reason you're here." Her sideways glance invited him to deny that the horse sale was the main attraction for him.

Boone didn't disappoint her. "It's hardly the only reason."

"That's good to know. By the way," Laura said, making another lightning-fast change of subject, "did Tara pass along the invitation for you and Max to join us for dinner tomorrow evening?"

"She did."

*   *   *

From her bedroom window Laura saw the Land Rover pull up in front of The Homestead. Even before Boone stepped out of the vehicle, she felt that little hum of excitement that came with being confronted with a challenge. She had spent much of the last two days constantly in his company, at his side, but never alone with him. It was part of her plan—to be within reach, yet out of reach.

Briefly Laura toyed with the idea of making an entrance, then rejected it as too dramatic. She paused in front of the mirror and absently ran a smoothing hand over the waistline of her teal-colored dress, then gave her blond hair a push to increase its fullness and exited the room to run lightly down the oak staircase.

As she reached its broad landing, her grandfather's voice reached out to her. "There you are. I was just about to holler upstairs and let you know your guests had arrived." He stood outside the double doors to the den, his aging body tilted to one side as he leaned on the support of his cane. "I thought you might want to be on hand to welcome this Crockett fellow in person."

Laura opened her mouth to correct him, then saw the twinkle in his brown eyes. "Honestly, Gramps, you are as bad as Trey," she admonished with affection and crossed the living room to his side.

"You mean that isn't his name?"

"It's Boone, and you know it. Now hold still. Your tie is crooked." She reached up to center it. "And please try to be on your best behavior tonight. I think he might want to marry me."

Unimpressed, Chase Calder responded with a harrumph. "He certainly isn't the first."

"I know." Laura smoothed the lay of his collar. "But he's the first I might consider accepting."

"Really?" He showed his surprise.

"Yes, really. So, be good."

"I thought you just met him when you were in Europe."

Laura didn't bother to recount the number of times she had seen Boone, first in Rome, then in England and on the Triple C. "Now, Gramps," she reasoned instead, "when have you ever known me to be slow at making up my mind about anything? And just imagine the kind of splash a marriage between the Rutledges of Texas and the Calders of Montana would make."

His gaze narrowed, anger flaring in the wells of his eyes. "I knew it was a mistake to let you spend all that time in Europe with Tara. That's the kind of talk you hear from her."

"But if I hadn't gone, I might never have met Boone," Laura responded.

"Do you love him?" The question bordered on a challenge.

Considering how close she had come to falling in love with Sebastian, Laura didn't consider love to be the most trustworthy of emotions. But she had long ago learned that where women were concerned, her grandfather tended to be idealistic rather than pragmatic.

"Any woman could love Boone, including me." She believed that. More importantly, Laura was confident of her ability to manage him. "Wait until you meet him, Gramps." She hooked an arm around his and directed him toward the entry. "He's one of those big, tall Texans with a potent animal magnetism that can make any girl's heart beat faster."

But her reply failed to provide Chase with much peace of mind. In his way of thinking, Laura put way too much stock in the things that Tara considered important. And that tended to color his attitude toward this Boone Rutledge.

Chase vaguely recalled having met Max Rutledge before, but most of what he knew about the family was by reputation. Rutledge was a name that carried weight in a lot of circles. And from what Chase had heard, the old man wasn't shy about throwing it around. He was known for being a ruthless businessman and a demanding boss. As for the son, other than some idle talk about him being a disappointment to the old man, Chase knew nothing.

He looked Boone over good when Laura introduced him. The man was tall, as tall as Trey, with a more muscled chest and shoulders. He had his father's hard features and a look of coarse masculinity that Chase supposed Laura had chosen to call "animal magnetism." Try as he might, Chase couldn't fault the courtesy and respect Boone showed him, but he took an instant dislike to the possessive way he looked at Laura. Something about it made his hackles rise in anger, but he couldn't put his finger on just what it was.

All through the social hour that preceded dinner and the meal itself, Chase puzzled over it, contributing little to the conversation. A dozen times his attention strayed to the couple, observing the glances Laura slanted at Boone, subtly suggestive and flirtatious, the same kind that Tara had once practiced on his son Ty. And with each of Laura's attentions, the possessive gleam in Boone's eyes grew brighter.

By meal's end Chase was no closer to identifying the thing that troubled him about Boone. Chase knew he was getting too damned old, and his discernment wasn't nearly as sharp as it once had been.

There was only one man, other than Laredo, whose judgment he trusted. Chase started to get up, then sat back down in his chair and did something he would never have done under any other circumstances.

"Logan, will you give me a hand here?" he said, careful to inject the right note of impatience for his supposed infirmity.

Seated closer, Trey immediately pushed back his own chair. "I'll help you, Gramps."

"No." Chase waved him off. "You take the rest of them into the den. We'll be there directly. It's just going to take me a bit longer than you young folks."

Even with Logan's assistance, Chase made certain they were the last ones to move away from the table. It didn't take Logan long to catch on to his delaying tactics.

"What's the problem?" Logan pitched his voice low to keep it from carrying.

"Laura's new beau," Chase muttered, his gaze tracking the

man exiting the dining room with his granddaughter. "The way he looks at her."

"You mean, like she's a prize to be won?"

"That's it." The fog cleared in his mind. There was heat in the man's look, but no warmth or tenderness, Chase realized.

"I wouldn't worry," Logan told him. "If Laura hasn't noticed it already, she will."

"But will she care?"

It was a question without an answer, and Logan didn't bother to attempt one.

"Tara's to blame for this," Chase grumbled, mostly to himself as they trailed after the others. "The first time she set foot in this house, I should have shown her the door. It would have saved this family a lot of grief—then and now."

With Logan at his side, Chase thumped into the den with his cane. As he headed for his customary seat behind the big desk, he slid a glance around the room and immediately noticed both Laura and Boone were absent.

"Where's Laura?" he asked no one in particular.

It was Tara who answered. "She and Boone went outside to enjoy the sunset." She set a cup of coffee on the table next to Max Rutledge's wheelchair. "Would you like some coffee, Chase? Or something stronger?"

"Coffee's fine," he said and continued on his way around the desk.

"Here you go, Dad." Cat took the cup of coffee that Jessy had just poured and carried it to the desk.

"Is that the famous map of the Triple C Ranch that I've heard so much about?" Max gestured to the framed map hanging on the wall behind the desk. Age had yellowed the background of the hand-drawn map that identified the water courses, outlying camps, and various landmarks as well as the boundaries of the ranch.

Chase stopped to look at it. "My grandfather drew that more

than a hundred years ago. The boundaries haven't changed more than a few inches since that time."

"Not many family ranches can make that boast these days," Max declared.

"It's no boast. It's a fact." Chase maneuvered himself in front of the oversized swivel chair, gripped the armrest, and lowered himself onto the cushioned seat.

"Naturally." Max nodded briefly in a kind of respectful apology. "I didn't mean to imply otherwise."

"Don't pay any attention to him, Mr. Rutledge." Cat smiled affectionately at her father. "Dad's gotten a bit testy lately."

"She's trying to make you believe I've turned into a crotchety old goat," Chase declared.

"I am not," Cat protested, then saw the teasing light in his eyes. "You are impossible, Dad."

"So you've told me before." His attention strayed to the window and the couple moving down the steps and striking out in the direction of the ranch buildings.

"I must say," Max began, drawing Chase's glance back to him, "I never expected to see a set of Texas longhorns this far north. That's quite a pair you have hanging above the mantel. What are they, six feet across?"

"Closer to seven," Chase replied. "They came off the old brindle steer that led every Calder herd north from Texas. Old Captain was always something of a legend back in those early days of the Triple C. It's good to keep a reminder like that around."

"I don't imagine a lot of people know you Calders came here from Texas," Max said with seeming idleness. "In fact, that ranch you own near the Slash R, it originally belonged to your family, didn't it?"

Chase nodded. "My granddaddy Seth Calder settled the place."

"The next time you go down there, you need to look me up,"

Max told him. "Give me a chance to return some of your hospitality, one neighbor to another."

"I appreciate the invitation," Chase acknowledged, "but I'm getting too old to make a long trip like that."

"I know what you mean." Max rubbed a hand over one of his bony, lifeless legs. "Traveling has gotten to be more of an ordeal with each passing year."

"That's why I stick close to home." Chase sensed this conversation was leading to something; he just didn't know what.

"It can't be convenient being an absentee landlord, especially when there's so much distance between the two ranches," Max observed, providing Chase with his first solid clue. "If you ever decide you want to sell the C Bar, let me know. I'm interested in buying it."

"Calder land is never for sale." Chase was cool with his answer.

Max smiled in understanding. "I feel the same way about Rutledge land. I only mentioned buying it because I think it would make an appropriate wedding present." He gave Chase a long, considering look. "Almost from the moment I met your granddaughter, I've never made it a secret that I'd like my son to marry her."

For a moment Chase looked down at the blotter on his desk, smiled wryly, and exhaled an amused breath, then lifted his head to meet Max's puzzled glaze. "It seems I owe you an apology."

"What for?" Max frowned in genuine bewilderment.

"When you offered to buy the C Bar, I assumed it was the abundant water resources on it that you wanted. I didn't realize your motive was something more personal. For that, I apologize, Mr. Rutledge."

"Call me Max," Rutledge insisted. "After all, it's likely we will be related one day soon."

It was a thought that didn't please Chase one bit.

* * *

Brushstrokes of crimson and orange streaked the western horizon and tinted the undersides of the scattered clouds. A soft breeze drifted off the river, the coolness of its breath wafting across Laura's face as she strolled arm in arm with Boone toward the white-painted gazebo near the riverbank.

His glance wandered over the collection of picnic tables. "What's this? Your own private park?"

"Something like that," she admitted. "Situated the way we are, miles from anything that even remotely resembles civilization, there is little in the way of entertainment available. And what there is tends to be rustic." Releasing his arm, she caught hold of an upright post and stepped onto the gazebo. "This is about the only place on the Triple C that is even slightly romantic."

"And private." Boone caught her wrist and bent her arm behind her back to draw her against him. "Do you realize this is the first time I've been alone with you since I arrived?"

Smiling, Laura gazed at him through the tops of her lashes. "Don't count on it lasting," she warned. "Any second kids can show up—to play hide-and-seek or hunt frogs."

"They have to go to bed sometime, though." He bent his head and nibbled on her neck.

The heavy scent of his cologne swirled around her, strong and citrusy. Unbidden came the memory of how quickly Sebastian had identified it on her skin. And Laura knew it wasn't wise to have thoughts of Sebastian in her mind when she was in Boone's arms. There was no choice; Boone would have to change colognes. Laura smiled, knowing it wouldn't be all that difficult to accomplish. She would simply enlist Tara's aid to arrange for his current bottle to be accidentally broken and a different one offered in its place.

"Personally," She moved sinuously against him and let one hand glide up to his shoulder, then slipped the other one free from his loose grip, and curled it around his neck, "I think we should make good use of the little bit of privacy we have now. By tomorrow afternoon the ranch will be packed with people. Between the party tomorrow night and the auction the day after, it isn't likely we'll have a moment to ourselves."

He raised his head, his dark eyes like a black fire as he pushed his hands into her hair and framed her face with them. "We'll make time," he told her with a kind of savage insistency in his voice.

But Laura knew it wouldn't happen; she would see to that. "Let's make use of this time instead." She applied pressure to the back of his head, urging his mouth down to hers.

The rough hunger in his kiss was exhilarating. Laura gave herself up to it without inhibition, letting her body come awake to the arousing caress of his hands on her hips and back, molding her ever more firmly against him. She felt the rigid outline of him pressed against her stomach, the hardness of it leaving her in little doubt of his desire. But it had to be more than just sexual desire, something any woman could satisfy. It had to be more personal than that.

Instinctively she knew that marriage to Boone would never work if it came about solely through Max's force of will. Such an event would result in Boone's eventual resentment of her, possibly even hatred. She had to be the trophy he brought home, not the woman he'd married merely to satisfy his father.

As much as she might want to let him take her where he wanted to go, Laura knew she had to hold back, for a while longer anyway. His big hand molded itself over her breast, and she trembled with the longing she felt. It was almost with relief that she heard boyish tittering coming from somewhere close by.

With a reluctance that wasn't feigned, she pulled away from his kiss and said huskily, "We have company."

Boone threw an irritated glance at the two boys, dressed in straw cowboy hats and boots and clutching fishing poles and a worm can in their hands.

The distraction allowed her the opportunity to create a little more space between them. "We might as well walk back to the house," she told him. "As long as we stay here, they'll be stealing peeks." When he looked at her with a kind of angry impatience, she reminded him, "I did warn you."

In response, his fingers dug into her elbow. "Let's go," he muttered and propelled her out of the gazebo.

Chapter Eleven

⌁

Private aircraft, everything from turboprops to executive jets, were parked wingtip to wingtip, taking up every available inch of apron area next to the Calder airstrip. In addition, much of the ranch yard had been turned into a parking lot to accommodate the host of Mercedes, BMWs, Jaguars, and other vehicles, proof, if any was needed, that the June sale had drawn a record attendance.

The well-heeled crowd drifted between the sale-ring area inside the massive old barn and the shimmering white refreshment tent located just outside it, equipped with closed-circuit television to keep prospective buyers abreast of the latest horse coming up for bid. Max Rutledge had his wheelchair parked in front of the big screen, ash building up on the smoldering cigar between his fingers as he stared intently at the rider of the horse currently on the block.

It was a tradition that any horse deemed to be exceptional was shown by a member of the Calder family. It was Laura who rode the horse in the ring. They made an eye-catching pair, the horse's coat a gleaming black and Laura dressed from head to toe in an off-white outfit studded with silver and turquoise.

Max was struck again by the class and elegance she exuded even in those rodeo queen clothes. He couldn't look at her without thinking of the grandsons she could give him. Boone shifted in place beside him and tossed back a swallow of watered-down bourbon.

Max threw him a half-irritated look, started to speak, then hastily checked to make sure there was no one within close earshot.

"Are you making any progress with her?" he grumbled out of one side of his mouth.

"When have I had the chance?" Boone muttered back at him. "I haven't had more than five minutes alone with her since we got here."

"Mmm." Max grudgingly had to acknowledge the truth of that. "We'll have to do something about that." The gavel fell, stopping the bidding on the black horse, and a scattering of applause from the barn reached them. Max stuck the cigar between his teeth and checked the sales catalog on his lap. "You'd better get in there. That filly we want is coming up right after this next yearling colt."

When Laura rode the horse out of the ring, one of the ranch hands, Ken Garvey, waited outside the gate for her. "Good job," he said, catching hold of the bridle's headstall. "He went for a good ten thousand over our top estimate."

"Blackie sold himself." She dismounted and passed him the reins.

"After you showed what he could do." He looked at her with an approving smile.

Praise was never idly handed out on the Triple C; it had to be earned. Laura accepted it with a simple, "Thanks," and headed for one of the barn's side exits.

Once outside, she paused to push the brim of her hat lower and shield her eyes from the sun's bright glare, then started toward the tent. She hadn't taken more than a dozen steps when she ran into Tara.

"This is shaping up to be one of the most successful sales the Triple C has had to date," Tara announced, her expression aglow.

"It is, isn't it?" Laura agreed.

Tara's tone turned a touch wistful. "I wish your father were here. He and I put together the very first auction the Triple C held." She turned a loving look on the towering structure before them. "You should have seen this old barn before we started renovating it. There was a century of grime covering everything. It's amazing how varnish can reveal the true beauty of those old hand-hewn timbers."

"How true." It was a story Laura had heard countless times in the past, but she never bothered to remind Tara of that. The auctions had always been a nostalgic time for Tara, and Laura knew that she was the only member of the family with whom Tara shared her recollections of those long ago days.

"Your father and I worked so well together. We were truly partners," Tara recalled somewhat absently. "It was one of my happiest, most fulfilling times. I told Ty these auctions would turn into one of those not-to-be-missed events. And I was right." Breaking free from her memories, she turned to Laura, her dark eyes bright and shining with triumph. "Did you notice? This time we even have some Hollywood celebrities in attendance?"

"They are hard to miss."

"Their presence will only bring more people to the next one," Tara stated with certainty. "You might suggest to your mother that prior to the next auction she contact some of the publicity agents for the major stars and see if she can't encourage more to attend."

"That's a good idea. I'll do it."

"By the way," Tara said as she tipped her head toward Laura in a confiding manner, "the Texas crowd has been abuzz ever since you arrived at the party last night on Boone's arm. And you can be sure they noticed the way Max practically dotes on you. You two are definitely the couple of the moment. It's hardly surprising, though. With Boone so dark and you so fair, you make a striking couple."

"I suppose we are," Laura agreed, fully aware of the stir they created, and the way heads continued to turn every time she was with Boone.

"Believe me," Tara declared, "you are going to start receiving a horde of invitations from Texas. But don't accept a single one until you've spoken to me. It's important that you be highly selective about which ones you accept, if any. It will only enhance the whole Calder mystique that's out there."

Laura frowned. "I don't think I understand your reasoning."

"Darling, if you should decide to marry Boone, people need to realize it's a marriage of equals. And when the day comes that you and Boone throw a party of your own, they'll come in droves."

It was a tantalizing picture that Tara painted in her mind. With no effort at all, Laura could see herself in it. The practical side of her surfaced to remind Laura that standing here talking about it wouldn't make any of it come true.

"Speaking of Boone," she began, "is he still at the tent with Max?"

"As a matter of fact, I just passed him going into the barn." Tara replied. "If you want, I'll let Max know that's where you are."

"Thanks," Laura said and moved away to retrace her steps to the barn.

The sudden loud blast of a horn stopped her, its harshness out of place amid the auction's steady hum of voices. She threw a look around to identify the source. Her searching glance landed on an old blue pickup with scratched paint and dented fender parked off to the side, away from the expensive vehicles. She probably wouldn't have thought much about it except that she saw a child's head bob up in the cab, then turn and look out the rear window.

One glimpse was all Laura had before he disappeared from sight, scooting down in the seat, but she immediately recognized the little boy from the bar.

"Hey, Sis." Trey walked up, leading a red roan filly. "What are you staring at?" he asked, turning to look.

"Do you see that truck? There's a little boy in it. I swear he's the same child that Mitchell guy was shoving around at Harry's. What would Mitchell be doing here?"

"I think we should find out. It's for sure he isn't here to buy horses." Eyes narrowed, Trey scoured the immediate vicinity, then shifted his attention to the rows of parked cars.

Laura spotted him an instant before Trey did. "There he is." She nodded at the man, trotting into view from behind the caterer's truck parked next to a second smaller tent used as a food prep station. His attire alone, faded jeans and a wrinkled plaid shirt, set him apart from the others in attendance.

"I see him," Trey stated. "Looks like he's headed back to his truck."

"I wonder what he was doing over there." Laura sent a curious glance in the direction of the caterer's tent.

"We'll know soon enough," Trey replied.

Positioned as they were, Mitchell had to pass them to get to his pickup. Intent on the truck with the boy inside, the man didn't notice Trey and Laura until he was a few yards from them. Immediately he slowed to a walk, something hot and wary leaping into his expression.

"What are you doing here, Mitchell?" Trey said in peremptory challenge.

The man sneered, "If it's any of your business—"

Trey cut in, his voice cold and hard, "It is our business. You're on the Triple C."

Mitchell clamped his mouth shut for a long second, then jerked a thumb in the direction of the tents. "My wife's workin' out here today. I just stopped to find out what time she'd be gettin' off.

Now that I've found out, I'm leaving. Are you satisfied?" The sneer returned.

"As long as you're leaving, we won't stand in your way." Trey continued to regard him with cool distrust.

Mitchell glared at him for a silent second, flicked a look at Laura, and stalked off. As he headed for his truck, Laura caught another glimpse of the boy stealing a peek out the rear window before he ducked out of sight again.

"Poor kid," she murmured to Trey. "I can't imagine anything worse than a child being left in the care of a brute like that."

"Hey, Trey!" Someone called from the barn area. "The filly's up next."

Trey lifted a hand in reply, gathered up the reins, and grabbed hold of the saddle horn. "Keep an eye on him and make sure he really does leave," he told Laura and swung into the saddle.

"Will do," she promised.

When Trey reined the roan filly toward the barn, Mitchell jerked open the truck's driver side door and threw a look at Laura. Rather than make it obvious that she intended to watch him, Laura headed toward the barn, taking an angle that kept the pickup in her side vision.

The pickup sputtered to life, belching dark smoke from its tailpipe with each rev of the engine. She was nearly to the barn before it reversed out of its parking spot and backed into a right turn that pointed it in the direction of The Homestead.

Keeping one ear tuned to the pickup's idling engine, Laura entered the barn through a side door and worked her way through the scattering of prospective buyers standing along the wall until she reached the barn's opened double doors. She stood to one side and looked out as the pickup rolled slowly forward on a path that took it unusually close to the row of parked vehicles. It was obvious to Laura that Mitchell was in no hurry to leave, and she wondered why.

"Ladies and gentlemen, you are going to like this next filly we have for you," the auctioneer's baritone voice came over the sophisticated sound system that had been set up in the barn. "She's a three-year-old by Cougar's Pride out of a fine San Peppy mare."

Laura glanced toward the sale ring as Trey rode in on the horse, stopped in the center, and reined the athletic filly into a fast spin that had nearly everyone in the place sitting up a little straighter. Laura smiled, feeling a surge of pride, both in the filly's talent and her twin's skill in the saddle. Then she shifted her attention back outside to check on Mitchell.

The pickup had stopped. At the same instant that fact registered, Laura noticed a thin slip of a woman hurrying toward it from between the cars. She was dressed in the white top and black skirt of the catering staff and carried a sack in her hands. There was something furtive in the glance the woman threw over her shoulder.

The minute she reached the pickup, she hurriedly stuffed the sack through the opened window, pressed her fingertips to her lips, and transferred the kiss to the little boy in the passenger seat, darted another worried look over her shoulder, and hurried back to the catering truck. Simultaneously the pickup roared away from the site.

It was only a guess, but Laura thought it was a fairly accurate one that the sack had been full of food, no doubt the same as that being served in the refreshment tent. Her mouth moved in a wry smile as Laura realized the Mitchells would have plenty to eat tonight, courtesy of the Calders.

With the mystery of Mitchell's presence solved, she shifted her attention to the sale ring, where the bidding was under way. The auctioneer's rapid and rhythmic chant filled the barn. She scanned the crowd and located Boone standing near the rear.

The initial bidding was fast and spirited as Laura picked her way through the mix of spectators and buyers. One of the spotters pointed to Boone. At a nod from him, the price jumped two thousand dollars.

"You know your horseflesh," Laura murmured when she reached Boone's side. "I think she's the best of the lot."

"My father agrees with you." He automatically curved an arm around her waist, more in a statement of ownership than affection, and nodded again, raising the last bid by another two thousand.

Aware of the knowing looks they received, Laura leaned lightly against him and spread the flat of her palm over the front of his shirt and the iron-hard muscles beneath it. She made no further comment, choosing to feign an interest in the bidding. When the hammer fell, the top bid was Boone's.

His success brought a round of congratulations and good-natured back-slapping from those close by them. It faded with the entry of the next horse into the sale ring.

Tilting her head back, Laura smiled up at Boone. "I hope you read the fine print in the sales agreement."

"Why?" Wariness leaped into his eyes.

"Somewhere in there, it states that the buyer must appear in person to pick up any stock purchased," she teased. "Which means, if you want that filly, you'll have to come get her yourself."

The minute he realized she wasn't serious, Boone responded to her smile. "I might be able to arrange such a visit," he said and flicked a glance at the crowd, nearly elbow to elbow. "Maybe there won't be so many people around then."

"I can almost guarantee it," Laura replied.

Another private jet soared into twilight's purpling sky, its navigational lights winking as it banked south. Laura glanced idly in its direction, then surveyed the ranch yard, now nearly empty of vehicles. The few that remained were clustered mainly around the tents. Now that the sale was over the cleanup would begin.

"The Rutledges are gone, are they?"

Laura turned as her mother walked up to join her. "About

twenty or thirty minutes ago," she confirmed. "Boone will likely be back at the end of the week to pick up the horses they bought."

Jessy studied her daughter with a quietly inspecting look. "Chase tells me you're thinking about marrying him."

"It's possible."

"Is that your idea or Tara's?"

"Mine, of course, although I'm not surprised that you might think otherwise." Laura was too used to the dislike that existed between Tara and her mother to take offense at the comment.

"I suppose I'm really wondering if you're in love with Boone or in love with what you think he can give you." As one, both set out in the direction of The Homestead.

"Isn't it possible that it's both?" Laura countered.

"It's possible," Jessy agreed. "But when you're with him, you don't act like someone in love. You're too coolheaded."

"Maybe I'm like you," Laura suggested. "You don't act like a woman in love, either. But I've seen the way you look at Laredo sometimes. And the way he lightly rubs your back when he thinks no one is watching. Just out of curiosity, Mother, why haven't you married him?"

"Don't change the subject, Laura."

"Don't dodge my question. Is it because he's nothing more than an ordinary cowboy—and not a particularly good one at that?"

"That has nothing to do with it." The denial was quick and decisive.

"Then why?"

"The decision was Laredo's." She turned a look of cool challenge on Laura. "Maybe you should ask him."

"Maybe the next time I see him, I will," she replied.

But she didn't. She was too busy plotting out how she wanted Boone's next visit to go.

* * *

A cane thumped across the hardwood floor and halted in front of the doors to the den. Chase looked in and saw Laredo leaning against the desk, one leg hooked over a corner while Jessy sat behind it, her blond head bent over the stack of checks she was signing. Planting the cane in front of him, Chase rested both hands atop it and leaned his considerable weight on it.

"When's dinner gonna be ready?" he demanded gruffly.

Laredo pushed off the desk and came erect. "As far as I know, we're just waiting for Trey and Laura to come down."

"They should be here shortly," Jessy added and laid the pen aside.

"One of you needs to holler up there and tell them to shake a leg." Chase swung away and propelled himself toward the dining room with his cane. "A man could starve to death around here."

Laredo came sauntering after him. "As little as you eat anymore, I'm surprised you even know when it's mealtime."

"I may not eat much," Chase told him. "But that doesn't mean I don't get hungry."

As they rounded the archway into the dining room, the clatter of booted feet running down the stairs echoed through the big house. Trey swept into the dining room about the time Chase reached his chair at the head of the table.

Chase glanced at the doorway, but Jessy was the only one who came through it after Trey. "Where's Laura?" He frowned.

"Better not wait dinner on her." Trey pulled out his customary chair and lowered himself onto it. "She's on the phone with Crockett. She's likely to be cooing in his ear for another hour yet."

"Now, Trey," Jessy murmured in light reproval.

"It's true." He pulled his napkin off the table and laid it carelessly on his lap. "What do you want to bet we'll have the dubious pleasure of his company again this weekend? What's he been here—three or four times since the sale? For the life of me, I don't understand what Laura sees in him."

"You mean other than the fact he's rich and good-looking," said Laredo.

"And full of Texas swagger," Trey added, his disgust for the man showing. "Or haven't you noticed the way he walks around like he's the he-bull of the prairie."

"If he seems a bit standoffish, maybe it's because you haven't acted all that friendly to him," Jessy suggested.

"I've met his kind before." Trey's tone was dry with cynicism. "I have a hunch he figures he's too important to need friends. And I'm not the only one who thinks that. Quint feels the same way about him."

Trey's assessment of the man was one that Chase shared. What he disliked about Boone was more an aura than any overt action. It pleased him that Trey had picked up on it. It certainly didn't surprise him that Quint had.

"Speaking of Quint," Jessy began, making a tactful change of subject, "have you talked to Cat lately? I was curious how Quint's getting along since he reported back for work."

"Fine, I guess," Chase replied. "Although Cat did say that he tires quickly."

Trey smiled. "I talked to him last night. He said he was getting stronger every day. Now that they put the walking cast on him, he's gotten rid of the crutches and started using a cane. Sort of like you, Gramps."

"With one difference: he's a few years younger."

They were halfway through the meal before Laura joined them. "Sorry I'm late," she offered in breezy apology as she slid into her chair.

"Trey explained that you were on the phone with Boone," Jessy said in a show of understanding.

"I was. Then I had to call Tara and talk to her."

"About what?" It was Chase who made the challenge.

"Boone wanted to fly up this weekend, but he's going to be tied up at the ranch. He wants me to fly down there instead." She took the platter of roast beef that Laredo passed to her. "So I had to call Tara and see whether she would be free to go with me. After all, it wouldn't look right for me to stay at the ranch with Boone without someone to serve as a chaperone, and I knew it would be impossible for you to get away, Mother."

"It is," Jessy confirmed, yet it stung that she hadn't been asked first. "So, are you going?" she asked.

Laura nodded and forked a slice of beef onto her plate. "We'll leave Friday morning, probably around ten o'clock, and fly back Sunday afternoon sometime."

The wheelchair made almost no noise as it rolled across the stone floor of the living room in the sprawling ranch house. Ignoring the soft whirr of its motor, Boone crossed to the bar, took a glass off the shelf, and reached for the bottle of bourbon.

"I heard the phone ring." Max Rutledge's voice reached across the room to demand his attention. "Is she coming or not?"

"She's coming." Boone poured a full jigger of liquor into the glass, added some ice cubes and a splash of water. "So is Tara."

"Smart girl," Max said with approval. "There are some who'd look sideways at a woman who'd spend the weekend here alone."

"That's what she said," Boone acknowledged.

"Tomorrow you go into town and buy her a ring. Get her something big and flashy that she can show off, but nothing as ordinary as a diamond—unless you can find a yellow one. A yellow diamond," Max repeated, warming to the possibility. "That's exactly what you need to get."

"Isn't that rushing things a bit?" Boone countered. "I've only known her a little more than a month."

"If you haven't gotten her to fall in love with you in a month, you never will." His dark eyes narrowed on Boone in sharp suspicion. "Or is that the problem? You figure she's going to turn you down."

"I don't think that at all." But at the same time, he wasn't certain she'd accept him, either. It was the pressure of that uncertainty that had Boone downing a hefty swallow of bourbon.

Chapter Twelve

The clip-clop of shod hooves on brick pavers echoed through the stillness of the English afternoon. As a groom walked the chestnut gelding up the ramp and into the horse van, Sebastian exchanged the bill of sale in his hand for a check from the buyer. A glance confirmed it was made out for the correct amount, and Sebastian slipped it into his inside jacket pocket.

"I'm confident the horses will make suitable mounts for young riders, Mr. Melrose," Sebastian stated. "I know they served my nephews well."

"They're fine, sound animals. My daughters will be thrilled to have them." The heavyset man threw a look over his shoulder as the groom emerged from inside the van to load the second horse. "Myself, I've never understood the connection between horses and young girls, but mine are completely daft about them." When the second gelding walked up the ramp, the man touched his hat to Sebastian. "It was a pleasure doing business with you, Your Lordship."

Nodding, Sebastian murmured an appropriate response, his attention distracted by the approach of a vehicle. Quick to recognize the driver behind the wheel as his sister, he turned to meet her while the man went to help the groom secure the horse van for travel.

Helen stepped out of the car, greeting him with a wide smile. "Since I was in the vicinity, I thought I would join you for tea."

"I'm glad you did."

She threw a curious glance at the horse van. "Is that Jaspar and Big Mike in there?"

"It is." Sebastian opened the front door for her.

Helen stepped inside then waited for him, her expression puzzled and slightly uncertain. "Did you sell them?"

"To Mr. Melrose," he confirmed and led the way toward the twin library. "It seems his twin daughters have outgrown their ponies."

"I had no idea you were thinking of selling them."

"Under the circumstances, a six-horse stable is a luxury I can't afford." Upon entering the library, he crossed to the desk and rang the kitchen. "Inform Grizwold there will be two for tea. We're in the library."

"I hope you received a good price for them." Helen sat down in one of the overstuffed chairs and curled her legs underneath, making herself at home.

"The sum is more than enough to finance a trip across the pond," Sebastian replied.

It took a moment for the significance of his statement to register. "Are you going over there to see her?" Helen asked as if none too sure of his reason.

"If I don't, I will always wonder what might have happened if I had made one more attempt to win her."

His expression was much too serious for Helen to doubt the truth in his words. Neither had to say Laura's name; they both knew to whom he was referring. The mere reference to Laura prompted Helen to glance at the wall where the portrait hung. But the space was blank.

Her gaze flew to Sebastian. "What did you do with the portrait of Lady Crawford?"

"As soon as Melrose agreed to buy the horses, I had Grizwold take it down and crate it for shipment."

"You're taking it to America with you."

"I thought it might make a useful peace offering." His mouth quirked in an attempt at a smile.

Helen saw through it. "You really care about her, don't you?"

"I must. It's been impossible to get her out of my mind." The portrait was merely one reminder of Laura. Sebastian knew there were few rooms in Crawford Hall that he could enter without seeing Laura in them.

Logan drove into the ranch yard and headed straight for The Homestead. A car was parked in front of it. There was nothing unusual about that, but the compact sedan wasn't one that he recognized as being from the area. As he pulled up beside it, Logan automatically glanced at the license plate and saw it was a rental.

It was a habit to be interested in any stranger, and his attention quickly shifted to the man standing near the top of the veranda steps. Tall, and well-dressed in a sports jacket and slacks, he looked to be somewhere in his early thirties. Most distinctively, no hat covered his head, and he wore shoes, not cowboy boots. Lean of face and fair-complected, he had a touch of red in his light brown hair.

Logan climbed out of the Jeep Cherokee and approached the steps. "Afternoon."

"Good afternoon," the man replied with a British accent, then glanced in the direction of the front door. "No one seems to be in. I knocked, but there was no answer."

"No one knocks at the Triple C." Logan gestured toward the door in invitation. "They just walk in." He continued past him to the door.

"Unannounced?" the man questioned.

"That's right." Logan opened it and smiled, waiting for the man to join him. "Only strangers knock."

A wry amusement curved the man's mouth as he crossed to the door. "Then it must be obvious to you that I am a stranger here."

"It is," Logan confirmed easily and followed him into the house. "By the way, my name's Logan Echohawk."

"You're the sheriff, aren't you?" The man looked at him with new interest. "Laura mentioned you."

"You're a friend of Laura's?"

"We met in Rome."

Hearing the familiar thump of a cane, Logan turned as Chase hove into view. "Oh, it's you, Logan. I thought I heard voices," he said in lieu of a greeting. He started to turn away, then paused to peer intently at the stranger. "Who's that with you?"

"A friend of Laura's," Logan replied. "Is Jessy here?"

"In the den." Chase bobbed his head in its direction. "Why? What's up?"

"It looks like we have some rustlers working the area. Miller has about ten head of cattle missing from his west pasture, and a black pickup with a gooseneck trailer and Wyoming plates was seen in the area," Logan explained, aware that even though Jessy was technically in charge of the operation, Chase liked to know all that went on. "I thought I'd better pass the word so you and your people could keep an eye out."

Chase nodded and made a wordless sound of approval then fired a look at the stranger. "If you're here to see Laura, you're out of luck. She left yesterday."

"I see." The answer was clearly one the man had not anticipated. After a momentary pause, he asked, "When do you anticipate she will return?"

Chase treated him to a hard stare, then turned, leaning heavily on his cane, and yelled, "Jessy! Come here a minute." The minute she walked out of the den, he waved a hand at the stranger. "There's a young man here who wants to know when Laura'll be back. I can't remember what she told us."

"She said she'd be flying back tomorrow afternoon." Jessy directed her answer to the man and stepped forward, stretching out her hand in greeting. "I don't believe we've met. I'm Laura's mother, Jessy Calder."

"Sebastian Dunshill. It's a pleasure to meet you, Mrs. Calder." He grasped her hand and bent slightly at the waist.

"Dunshill," Jessy repeated with recognition. "You must be the current earl of Crawford. Laura told us about her visit to your home in England. I'm afraid she never mentioned that you might be coming."

"She didn't know. I wanted it to be a surprise." He smiled with a touch of self-deprecating humor. "But it turns out that I am the one who is surprised. I should have known Laura would find it difficult to remain in any one place for long."

Chase studied him with sharpened attention. "You seem to know my granddaughter rather well."

"Well enough to know she likes places that are loud and crowded. I mean no offense, but from what little I have seen of Montana, it is neither."

"None taken." A smile deepened the corners of Chase's mouth.

"It's clear you have important matters to discuss," Sebastian said with a glance at Logan. "So I will take no more of your time. If you could perhaps direct me to a place nearby where I might find suitable lodging, I'll be on my way."

Chase didn't think twice. "The most suitable place is right here on the Triple C."

There was a small hesitation during which Sebastian appeared to consider something more than the invitation. "As much as I would like to accept your offer of hospitality, there are some things you should know, and I would rather you heard them from me."

Chase studied him with a steady and close regard. "Sounds like this might involve some heavy talking. Why don't we go into the den and sit down?" He started to lead the way, then paused. "Your business isn't so urgent that it can't wait, is it, Logan?"

"No. I've already said most of what I came to tell you anyway."

"Good. Let's go." Pushing off with his cane, Chase headed for the den.

Heat lightning flashed in the east while the Texas sky overhead glittered with stars. The night air had a sultry feel to it that added to the languor Laura felt as she stood within the loose circle of Boone's arms and gazed into the land's thickening shadows.

The low-built ranch house sprawled behind them, its thick walls and wide overhangs designed to ward off the scorching summer heat. Light spilled from some of its windows onto the broad patio, but none reached the corner she occupied with Boone.

"I love lazy summer nights like this," Laura murmured candidly, tightening the wrap of his arms around her waist. Her glance drifted to the shimmering surface of the swimming pool. "If I wasn't so full from dinner, I'd go change into my suit and take a dip in the pool."

Boone buried a kiss in her hair. "I have a better idea." His hands shifted to the sides of her waist and turned her to face him.

Laura let her hands slide to the top of his shoulders and tilted her head to one side in an alluring pose. "And what might that be?"

She hadn't missed the touch of his right hand until it was there in front of her. But it wasn't his hand that captured her attention; it was the small velvet-covered box it held. She stared at it, conscious of the exultant leap of her heart.

"What's this?" Laura feigned ignorance even as her head told her the jewelry box had to contain a ring.

"Open it," Boone instructed.

Careful not to allow more space to come between them than necessary, she took the box and snapped it open. There was nothing faked about her sharply indrawn breath of surprise as Laura caught her first glimpse of the ring. It was a marquise-cut diamond, the same pure yellow as the Texas sun, and just about as big and brilliant, set in a platinum mounting.

"Marry me, Laura." His words had more the ring of demand than a proposal.

More than anything she wanted to slip the ring on and see how it would look on her hand. But Laura knew this was no time to appear too eager. Instead she looked up at him with questioning eyes. "Are you sure, Boone?"

"I've never been more sure of anything in my life." The heat of need was in his voice and in the possessive rake of his eyes.

"In that case, my answer is 'yes.'" She took the ring and slipped it on her finger. The fit was perfect, and the look of it was stunning, just as she had known it would be.

"Laura Rutledge," she said, as if trying the name on for size, then declared with feeling, "I definitely like the sound of that."

Boone didn't bother with words to make his feelings known as his mouth claimed hers. Laura welcomed the crush of his arms and returned the heat of his kiss, for now holding nothing back.

The afternoon sunlight flashed on the ring as Laura ran lightly up The Homestead's front steps, still riding on a triumphant feeling. She spared a backward glance at Tara, who followed more slowly.

"There's so much to do, my head's spinning just thinking about it all," Laura said on a wondering note.

"You have to start first with 'where' and 'when,'" Tara replied, ever the practical one.

"But that's just the tip of the iceberg." Laura crossed to the front door.

"You really need to bring a wedding consultant on board," Tara told her.

"The sooner the better," Laura agreed and opened the door. "Would you get the names of some for me?"

"Of course."

Once inside the entryway, Laura set her small carry-on on the floor and called out, "Hello! Where is everybody?"

The answer came from her mother. "We're in the living room."

Eager to share her news, Laura sailed down the wide hall to the living room. Her bright-eyed glance made a sweep of her mother, grandfather, and Laredo, all seated in the room. She came to a stop when she saw that the man standing by the fireplace wasn't her brother.

"Sebastian," she said his name on a breath, soft and warm.

But it was the shining look in her eyes, completely uncalculated, that caught and held Jessy's attention, though that moment of surprise and complete spontaneous reaction didn't last.

"Hello, Laura. Surprised to see me?"

The minute Sebastian spoke, a practiced smile of beguiling charm curved Laura's lips. "Surprised and pleased," Laura declared, moving toward him. "And your timing couldn't have been better. Now you can join in the celebration. Congratulations are in order." She lifted her left hand and wagged her ring finger at him, letting the yellow diamond catch fire in the living room's light.

Jessy's estimation of the young Englishman went up a notch when he glanced at the ring and never turned a hair. "I think I am supposed to ask who the lucky fellow is?"

"Boone, of course." Laura swung toward Jessy, but Jessy found it impossible to tell whether the excitement in her daughter's expression was genuine. "He asked me last night. If it hadn't been so late, I would have called you. Then this morning I decided I would much rather deliver the news in person. Have you ever seen such a rock?" She crossed to Jessy's chair to give her a close-up look at the ring.

Chase leaned over to see it. "It's yellow," he observed dryly. "Is that for caution?"

"Well said," Sebastian replied. But Laura ignored him as she gave her grandfather an admonishing look.

"Gramps," Laura said in a tone of indulgent reproach. "It's yellow for happiness."

"And when's the wedding to be?" Sebastian inquired.

"We haven't set the date yet," Laura replied easily.

"But it will be soon," Tara inserted with ringing certainty. "Boone made it clear that he was not in favor of a long engagement."

Sebastian merely smiled. "It's a viewpoint shared by most men, I dare say."

"Where's Trey?" Laura asked, then held up a hand to stave off any answers. "I forgot. He told me he was jackpot roping somewhere this weekend. I suppose it'll be after sundown before he gets home." The opening of the front door was accompanied by a hard thud. Laura glanced in its direction. "That must be Vince. He said he'd bring my luggage from the plane." Her glance ran to Sebastian in light challenge. "Instead of standing there looking decorative, you can be useful and carry them upstairs for me. I'll show you the way. Come on."

Jessy couldn't help noticing that Tara looked anything but happy when the two retraced Laura's steps to the entryway together. She wasn't surprised that Tara disapproved of Laura associating with a man who had little money. Personally, Jessy had her own reservations about Sebastian Dunshill, but his lack of wealth wasn't one of them.

"A wedding here at the Triple C, won't it be wonderful?" Tara declared. "Of course, Laura hasn't said that she wants it here, although I'm certain she will. Naturally it would have to be an outdoor affair to accommodate all the people who will come. Wouldn't it be lovely to have the ceremony on the veranda?"

"Very lovely," Jessy agreed. "Although it might be a bit difficult seating people on the slope."

"I hadn't considered that." Tara appeared to give the matter some thought, but Jessy noticed the way her attention covertly strayed to Laura and Sebastian when they started up the oak staircase. "Perhaps something on the lawn. It would be simple enough to bring in beautiful white arbors, or even some pillars to echo the front of the house." The moment the pair reached the top of the stairs, Tara leaned forward and lowered her voice to a secretive level. "There is something about Sebastian that you really need to know—"

Jessy didn't give her a chance to say more. "If you are referring to his current financial problems, we already know. He told us."

"How very clever of him." But there was contempt in Tara's voice. She smoothed the lay of her skirt. "I'm surprised you allowed him to stay. It's obvious his chief interest is in Laura's bank account. You should have ordered him off the ranch the minute he arrived. He's nothing but a fortune hunter."

Chase made a small snorting sound. "If we had done that with everyone whose motives or sincerity we doubted, your foot wouldn't have crossed our doorway in years."

Tara tilted her chin at a combative angle. "My concern is strictly for Laura, and I don't particularly care whether you believe that or not."

"I'm sure you believe that," Jessy said. "But it doesn't really matter. Sebastian came here to see Laura. If she wants him to leave, she can tell him so."

Upon entering the bedroom, Laura gestured to the walnut dresser's curved front with a sweep of her head. "You can put them down over there," she told Sebastian.

Her luggage consisted of no more than a garment bag and a slim, weekender-sized suitcase. He set the suitcase on the floor and draped the bag over it, then turned to her expectantly.

His gaze was alive to her, compelling in its warmth. The spacious and slightly grand bedroom suddenly seemed small with him in it. But Laura knew it was purely her own reaction to him, the livening of all her senses and that faint thrum of excitement that ran through every nerve.

"What? No tip?" He smiled with his eyes.

"Since when does a gentleman expect a tip for helping a lady," she countered, matching the lightness of his tone even as her gaze wandered over his lean, smooth features. Laura remembered every detail of his face, including the scattering of pale tan freckles. She turned slightly serious. "I was surprised to see you when I walked in today. At the same time, though, I think I always knew you would show up sooner or later."

"What made you so certain of that?" His look seemed to delve for the deeper meaning behind her words.

"Under the circumstances, you couldn't afford not to, now could you?" Laura taunted without an ounce of malice, then made a little pout of mock regret. "What a pity that you arrived too late."

"What makes you think it's too late? Surely you don't believe that gaudy rock on your finger changes anything, do you?" Sebastian replied with amusement. "You know as well as I do that that ring can come off as easily as it went on."

She laughed in her throat. "It can, but it won't."

"You don't truly expect me to believe you're in love with him, do you?" Skepticism riddled his voice.

"I'm marrying Boone, aren't I?" Laura reasoned, then snapped her fingers in an exaggerated show of dawning realization. "That's right. I forgot. You don't regard love as an essential part of marriage, do you?"

"Was that supposed to be a wounding blow—or merely a knife flick?" Sebastian smiled as if to show that she had drawn no blood with it.

"It's nothing more than the truth," Laura replied easily. "You're wasting your time, Sebastian, and you have precious little of it to waste."

He leaned a hip against the dresser and folded his arms in front of him. "I don't see it that way."

"Suit yourself." She lifted her shoulders in a shrug of indifference.

"Ah, now therein lies the problem." He lightly shook one finger at her as he pushed away from the dresser. With a negligent ease, he eliminated much of the space between them. "No one suits me as well as you do." His fingertips lightly touched the underside of her jaw as if to tilt her face toward him.

"I believe you," Laura said, conscious of all the raw stirrings within. "But it doesn't change anything. I'm still going to marry Boone."

"So you said before." His hand drifted down to her throat, touching it without quite touching it, even as his mouth moved inexorably closer to hers.

As Laura debated whether to allow Sebastian to kiss her, the decision was removed from her hands by Tara's summoning voice. "Laura!"

"Nice try," she said to Sebastian and stepped away, laughter dancing in her eyes as she moved to the door. Exiting the bedroom, she crossed to the top of the stairs. "Did you call me, Tara?"

"I'd like a quick word with you before I leave." She stood by the bottom newel post, looking up. "Would you mind walking me to the door?"

"Not at all," Laura replied, conscious of Sebastian coming out of the bedroom behind her. Then, "Thanks for carrying my luggage up," she said to Sebastian, tossing the words over her shoulder, and ran lightly down the stairs to join Tara.

The instant her foot left the last step, she struck out for the foyer, ignoring the sharp probe of Tara's gaze. Laura knew exactly what Tara wanted to discuss, and it wasn't the wedding.

Tara didn't waste any time getting to the point. "You need to send that man on his way, Laura. The sooner the better." Her voice was hard with demand, and there was an angry snap in her dark eyes.

"Why? He's no threat." Laura smiled with confidence. "I know his game."

"Perhaps you do," Tara conceded coolly. "But I warn you, Boone is the jealous type. He'll be furious if he finds out he's here."

Laura bristled inwardly. "Then he'll have to get over it, won't he?"

"That is not a wise attitude to take."

"Maybe not," Laura agreed, albeit reluctantly. "At the same time, I don't see why you're making such a big fuss about Sebastian being here. He won't be staying long—not now that he knows he is completely out of the running." She flashed the engagement ring as a reminder to Tara. "What choice does he have, other than to charm his way into some other woman's bank account?"

"True. But he is a charmer," Tara added almost as a warning.

"Don't worry," Laura assured her. "I may make a fool of him, but he will never make a fool of me." As far as she was concerned, that closed the subject. "Don't forget to call me as soon as you have the names of some wedding coordinators."

"I'll get on that as soon as I get home," Tara promised.

Chapter Thirteen

The yellow sun sat high in the summer sky, throwing its brightness over the big land. Coffee cup in hand, Laura wandered onto the front veranda, careful to stay within the shade of its roof and avoid the full glare of the sun. Her gaze traveled over the ranch yard, seeking out each and every area of activity, but at this late hour of the morning, there was little to be found.

Almost belatedly she became aware of a figure in her side vision. Laura turned and smiled when she saw her grandfather sitting in one of the wooden rockers, eyes closed and chin buried in his chest.

She walked over to the rocker and pressed a light kiss on top of his gray head. "Good morning, Gramps."

He came awake with a start, blinked, and hurriedly rubbed a hand across his mouth as if to rid it of any inadvertent drools. He threw a quick identifying look at her. "It's you," he said, then glanced at the coffee cup in her hand. "You just getting up?"

"More or less," Laura admitted and again let her attention wander to the ranch yard. "Where is everybody?"

"Your mother's at the ranch office, and Laredo said he was going to South Camp this morning. Trey went to doctor a couple of steers in the home pasture." There was a trace of sly humor in the sideways glance he sent her. "Or was it the Englishman you were wondering about?"

"As if you didn't know."

"He rode along with Trey. I don't imagine he would have if you had gotten up at a decent hour."

"You know I've never been a morning person, Gramps." Laura raised the cup to her mouth and breathed in the coffee's fragrant aroma before taking a sip of it. At the same time, she kept a covert watch in the direction of the home pasture, so named for its nearness to The Homestead. "How long have they been gone?"

"A couple hours, maybe more. You can bet Trey will be back in time for lunch."

"In that case, I'll miss them," Laura said with a touch of regret.

Her remark drew a frown from Chase. "Why?"

"Allie wants me to run into town. According to the trusty range telegraph, Fedderson's received a batch of fresh strawberries this morning, and Allie wants some for dessert tonight," Laura explained, referring to the woman who ran the kitchen at The Homestead, and had for the last ten years. "I offered to go after lunch, but she's worried that they'll be sold out by then. I was going to ask Sebastian if he wanted to ride along with me, and we could grab a bite to eat at Harry's"

"If he was here, I'd give you odds that he would jump at the chance," Chase observed dryly.

"Probably." She took another idle sip of her coffee. "You do know that Sebastian is very anxious to get his hands on my money."

"I know." Chase nodded and slanted a twinkly look at her. "Judging from the way he looks at you, I think he'd enjoy getting his hands on you as well."

Laura clicked her tongue in mock dismay. "You aren't supposed to notice such things, Gramps."

"I may be old, but I'm not dead," he retorted.

She laughed. "I should hope not."

But Chase didn't choose to get sidetracked by her comment. "I get the impression you might have some feelings for this Englishman. Otherwise, knowing what you do about him, you would have already shown him the door."

Laura pitched her shoulders forward in an uncaring shrug. "If Sebastian chooses to stay, knowing that I am going to marry Boone, it's his time he's wasting."

"That reminds me," Chase said. "Crockett called earlier this morning. He said he'd try to reach you tonight sometime."

"You might as well give up, Gramps. You are not going to rile me anymore by calling him Crockett." A trio of riders approached the home-pasture gate. Laura crossed to the edge of the veranda, put two fingers to her mouth, and whistled shrilly. Trey answered with an acknowledging wave and swung the gate open from horseback, held it open for the other two, then maneuvered it shut.

One rider split away to head for the corrals while Trey and the second man branched off toward The Homestead. Laura watched them approach at a steady trot, her attention centering on Sebastian. A straw Resistol sat atop his head, its brim shading his face. He wore a pair of faded Levis and a plain blue shirt. From a distance, he could have passed for one of the ranch hands, but the riding boots gave him away.

When the pair reined up near the front steps, Laura declared, "You almost look like a cowboy in that saddle, Sebastian."

"If I do, the credit belongs to your brother," he replied. "He informed me that if he caught me posting at the trot—his words—he would knock me out of the saddle straight to kingdom come."

"Trey!" Laura was too stunned by his rudeness to a guest to do more than stare at her brother.

"Good God, Laura, it's one thing for you to do it, but if he started bouncing up and down, you know all the other guys would look at him sideways the whole time he's here," Trey said with force.

Sebastian made light of it. "When in the West, do as the westerners do. Of course, I also didn't know how far it might be to kingdom come, and I felt certain I didn't want to find out."

As always, the dryness of his humor made Laura laugh. "I'm glad you're back all in one piece. I have to go into town. Want to ride along and see what one of our western villages looks like?"

"It's almost lunchtime," Trey said in protest.

"We can grab a bite at Harry's. The food won't be as good as what Allie will put on the table, but it'll do," Laura replied and looked at Sebastian. "What d'you say? Are you coming or not?"

"After tangling with that steer, I'll need to wash up a bit."

"No problem," she said. "I still have to get my purse and the keys to the pickup."

"I'll take care of your horse," Trey offered. "You go on inside and clean up. Knowing Laura, she's just as apt to leave without you."

"Only if he dawdles," Laura teased as Sebastian swung out of the saddle and handed the horse's reins to Trey.

"I have been accused of many things, but never dawdling," Sebastian countered as he came up the steps.

"There's always a first for everything," Laura retorted and headed for the door.

After it closed behind them, Chase fired a glance at Trey. "Did he really tangle with a steer?"

"I guess you could say that. After we got the steer down, he sat on his neck to hold him while Baker and I doctored the gash on his hip. At least he pitched in to help, which is more than I can say about Crockett." Clicking to the horses, Trey reined away from the house and set out for the barns.

The shadow raced alongside the pickup as it sped over the highway. On either side of it the land rolled away, stretching from blue horizon to blue horizon.

Laura took her eyes off the road long enough to run a glance over Sebastian's profile. "You're unusually quiet."

"I suspect this land is to blame," he said with an absent smile. "It gives one a new appreciation for that trite phrase 'wide open spaces.' "

"I suppose." She looked around, trying to see it through his eyes. "I can remember my gramps once saying, 'This land makes a small man smaller and a big man king.' "

"I suspect your grandfather looked every inch the cattle king in his day." There was an underlying note of admiration and respect in his voice. The sound of it warmed something deep inside Laura and brought a faint swell of pride.

"From the stories I've heard, he wasn't a man to tangle with," she said.

"I dare say he still isn't."

In the distance the rooflines of Blue Moon jutted into view. "Town's just ahead of us—such as it is," Laura said. "When I was growing up it was a lively place. But that was back when the mine was in full operation."

"A mine? What kind?"

"Coal. There's tons of it underground. I can take you to a half dozen places on the Triple C where seams of it are exposed. Back in the old days it was just about the only fuel they had to heat their homes, other than cow chips, of course."

"And what might cow chips be?"

Laura smiled at Sebastian's puzzled look. "Manure."

His eyebrows shot up in instant reaction. "Indeed, burning coal is infinitely preferable to burning manure for heat." As they approached the outskirts of town, Laura reduced the truck's speed, and Sebastian directed his attention to the buildings before him. "When did the mine close?"

"About a year ago, I think. The entrance to it is ahead on the right." Laura pointed to the tall gate, chained and padlocked to prevent access. "After it closed, there was a mass exodus from town, with almost everybody moving away to find other jobs. The population of Blue Moon probably numbers only around thirty or forty people now."

She flipped on the left turn signal and waited for a southbound semi to roar past, then made the swing into Fedderson's lot. "Strawberries, here we come."

"You intend to purchase strawberries at a petrol station?"

"There's a grocery store inside, as well as post office and a small snack area. They even have a miscellaneous section where they sell everything from automotive supplies and hardware items to trinkets and magazines. Fedderson's is really what used to be called a general store. Clothing is about the only thing they don't sell." Laura pulled up in front of the building and switched off the engine. After slipping the ignition key into her purse, she climbed out of the pickup while Sebastian exited the passenger side. "The Feddersons don't actually own it anymore. Old Mrs. Fedderson sold it about eight years ago to Ross and Marsha Kelly," she explained as she started toward the store entrance. "He drives a truck, so he isn't here very often."

"Surely his wife doesn't run it all by herself, does she?" Sebastian reached ahead of her to open the door.

"Her brother works here, too, mostly at night. He's a Vietnam vet who lost his leg in the war. Between the two of them and some part-time help, they do fine." Laura preceded him into the store.

Marsha Kelly was behind the counter, a slightly built brunette with apple cheeks and the first few strands of gray showing in her hair. Her smile was quick and warm when she recognized Laura.

"Hi, Laura. Let me guess: you're here for the strawberries," she said.

Laura responded with a confirming nod. "Allie's orders. I'm supposed to buy a whole flat."

The woman grinned. "I swear I've had more customers this morning than I had all last weekend." She pointed to her right. "All the strawberries I have left are on that table over by the fresh produce."

Laura made her way to the produce aisle, trailed by Sebastian. After that, she simply had to follow her nose to the source of the sweet strawberry smell. Half the table was already bare of fruit, but one look at the berries' red, ripe perfection and Laura understood why.

"Don't they look luscious," she marveled as she scooped up a flat of them.

"Indeed they do," Sebastian agreed and reached for the flat. "Let me carry that for you."

"Thanks." Laura surrendered it to him without hesitation and retraced her path to the counter. "You still have six quarts left," she told Marsha.

"They'll be gone before the afternoon's over, I imagine. Is there anything else you need?"

"Not this trip." Laura removed the wallet from her purse as Sebastian set the flat of strawberries on the countertop.

"By the way," Marsha said as she rang up the sale, "let Allie know that Ross is making a run to the Gulf Coast this week. He'll be bringing back shrimp and some honest-to-goodness home-grown tomatoes, if he can find any."

"I'll tell her," Laura promised and pushed a twenty-dollar bill onto the counter.

"I need some more ones. Just a second." The woman reached under the counter and pulled out a thick bank-deposit bag, un-zipped it to reveal a bulging stack of bills, then exchanged a ten-dollar bill from the cash drawer for ten ones.

At the sight of such a large quantity of cash, Sebastian frowned in concern. "I should think having so much money on hand would be an invitation for robbery. Aren't you worried about such a pos-sibility, being a woman, here by yourself?"

"Not really," Marsha Kelly replied with marked indifference. "Everybody knows I keep a loaded .38 under the counter as well. And they also know my brother Bob made sure I know how to use it. When you live in the middle of nowhere, with anything re-motely resembling the law a good fifty miles away, people have to be willing to protect their own property."

"I see," Sebastian murmured.

Smiling to herself, Marsha glanced at Laura and tipped her head in Sebastian's direction. "Is this your fiancé?"

"The ever-reliable range telegraph has been at work, has it?" Laura wasn't at all surprised that the news of her recent engagement had already made it to Blue Moon. "Actually, Sebastian is just a friend," she explained, then made the introductions. "Marsha, I'd like you to meet His Lordship, the earl of Crawford, Sebastian Dunshill, from England. Marsha Kelly, the proprietress of Fedderson's."

Flustered by the title, the woman searched for an appropriate response. "Welcome to Montana, Your High—" She darted a frantic look at Laura, unsure of the proper way to address him.

"Sebastian will do," he said graciously.

"Sebastian," Marsha repeated, and awkwardly bobbed her head.

"It's a pleasure to meet you, Mrs. Kelly."

"The same," she mumbled, suddenly at a loss for words, and belatedly remembered to give Laura her change. "I think that's the right amount."

"It is," Laura confirmed. "We're on our way over to Harry's to grab some lunch. Could I leave the strawberries here and pick them up when we're done?"

"That will be fine," Marsha assured her.

"Thanks." Laura started to move away from the counter, then paused when she saw Sebastian selecting a handful of strawberries. "What are you doing?"

"A little something to whet our appetites." His mouth slanted in a lazy smile. "Allie won't miss these few."

When he finally turned away, he held a half dozen berries in the cup of his hand. Laura sketched a farewell wave to the woman and pushed her way out the door.

Somehow Sebastian managed to reach the pickup ahead of her and opened the driver's side door. "Thanks," Laura said, but he stopped her before she could slide behind the wheel.

"Have a strawberry." He offered one to her, holding it by its green cap.

Rather than allow him to feed it to her, Laura took the plump berry from his fingers and bit into it. She hadn't expected it to be so juicy. She hurriedly reached up to catch the drips before they fell onto her clothes.

"Mmmm, delicious," she murmured and popped the rest of the succulent berry into her mouth except for its leafy cap. "They're so sweet they don't even need sugar."

"Really?" he said in a doubting voice when she reached up to delicately wipe any bit of juice from her lips with her fingertips.

As his head bent toward her, she was slow to recognize his intention. When she did, Laura was aware only of the quick thrill that raced through her, knowing his lips would soon be covering hers. The pressure of them was persuasively light yet delving—and all too brief.

Sebastian drew back only inches. "Nothing enhances the flavor of a strawberry like a kiss."

"That was sneaky," Laura said in mock reprimand.

"You knew sooner or later I'd steal a kiss." His gaze drifted once more to her lips.

"But I didn't expect it to be in a public place in broad daylight," Laura chided, not the least bit offended. In truth she would have been disappointed if he hadn't made a play. "I expected you to be more discreet than that."

"What could be more discreet than this?" Sebastian countered, his crooked smile barely wavering. "The cab of the truck blocks any view of us from inside the store, and I'm shielding you from the sight of anyone who might be watching across the street.

"It was still a sneaky thing to do." Laura plucked a berry from his hand and climbed into the truck.

"I noticed how much it upset you," Sebastian replied, eyes agleam as he pushed the door shut and walked around to the passenger side. Laura started the truck and waited for him to slide onto the seat next to her. "We're off to Harry's, are we?"

"We are." She reversed the pickup away from the store and pointed to the bar and grill across the highway.

"Is there a Harry?"

"Not any more. He died a few years ago. His son Jack runs it now. According to Trey, he has the place listed for sale."

He studied the building with its chipped and peeling paint. "I should think my chances of selling Crawford Hall far exceed his."

"Is that what you're going to do?" Feeling a sharp twinge of regret, Laura threw him a quick look.

"My options are limited," Sebastian reminded her dryly.

"And I'm one of them," she said with a slight taunt.

"Easily the most beautiful one." Sebastian replied.

"Too bad," Laura declared with a saucy lift of her head and drove across the highway and into Harry's graveled parking lot.

Sebastian climbed out of the pickup and looked around with interest. "Is this the extent of Blue Moon's business district?" he asked and took a bite of berry.

"It is now," Laura confirmed.

"Are you particularly hungry at the moment?"

"Not really. Why?" She halted halfway to the door, a little surprised by his question, and a lot curious.

"I'd rather like to go for a walk and look around. After all, this may be my first and only visit to a true western town."

"Ghost town, you mean," Laura inserted dryly, but she had only to remember her own visit to the lush English countryside to realize how starkly different this was to him. "But you're right. It's nothing like England. We'll start the tour over there." She motioned to the side street.

They set off at a leisurely pace, walking along the edge of the street for a block before they reached a sidewalk. Sebastian studied the first grouping of buildings.

"Most of these look new," he observed.

"Relatively speaking, they are. Most of them were built between twenty and thirty years ago by Dy-Corp when the mine first opened. That one over there is a medical clinic. It's staffed by a physician's assistant two days a week now. There's talk of it shutting down. The one on the left used to be a branch of the sheriff's office, but everybody works out of the county seat now. About the only police presence in Blue Moon is Logan. Since he lives west of here, he usually makes a patrol through town on his way to the sheriff's office in the morning and again when he comes home at night.

"Did I mention I met your uncle the day I arrived at the ranch?"

"No, you didn't."

"He gave me the impression he was a man who knew his business," Sebastian said and held out his hand. "Have a strawberry."

"As long as it's just a strawberry I get," Laura said in playful warning and took one from him. When they reached the end of the block, she made a left turn. "Now we're entering Blue Moon's residential area. The homes along here are mostly old and mostly empty."

The grass grew tall in the yards, tall and already seared by the relentless sun. The few occupied homes were easy to spot, thanks to their mowed lawns and the flowering plants sitting in pots on their porches or front steps. But those few splashes of color only seemed to emphasize the rundown and neglected state of the rest. Laura found it a bit depressing until she spotted the corner house on the next block. There was an immediate lifting of her spirits at the sight of it.

Without thinking, she reached over to lay a hand on his arm, seeking Sebastian's full attention and using physical contact to obtain it. "I was wrong. There is a touch of England here in Blue Moon."

"I beg your pardon?"

Laura ignored his doubting look and grabbed hold of his hand. "Come on. We need to cross the street." With traffic in Blue Moon all but nonexistent, she didn't bother to look to see if there were any cars coming; she simply led him across the street at a running trot. "See that place ahead of us?" She pointed to the white house on the corner lot, its front lawn alive with varying shades of reds, pinks, and whites, punctuated by touches of yellow and peach. "It's the Fedderson house."

"Those are roses, aren't they?" Sebastian realized.

"Tons of them. I couldn't have been much more than four or five years old the first time I saw them," Laura recalled with a nostalgic smile. "I had never seen so many flowers in one place before. Mom says that after that, every time we came to town I'd hound her until we drove by here. I've had a soft spot for flowers ever since, especially roses."

Sebastian's glance shifted from the house and its rose garden to the treeless expanse of plains that surrounded the town. "I can see why it would make such an impression."

Laura nodded absently and slowed her steps to prolong the view of the garden. Climbing roses rambled over the picket fence, up trellises, and over arbors while mountainous shrub roses hugged the sides of the house and its porch, leaving room in the lawn's center for beds of hybrid roses.

"I was told old Mr. Fedderson planted these as a tribute to his wife," Laura recalled idly.

"I assume her name is Rose,"

Laura flashed him a grin. "Obvious, isn't it," she said as they neared the corner. "The last I heard she was still alive." She grew thoughtful. "Do you know it's been years since I've been by the house—probably not since I started high school."

"Your tastes likely changed to something more sophisticated."

"Ouch. That was a dig." She fired him a look of pretended offense.

"Not really." Sebastian smiled. "Most teenagers like to act smug and worldly—and much too mature to savor something so simple as the joy of flowers."

Suitably mollified by his explanation, she agreed, "You're probably right." She stepped off the curb and started across the street, her attention still focused on the riotous abundance of blooms. Not until she was nearly to the other side did Laura notice the slight white-haired woman in a faded housedress sitting in a lawn chair near one of the rose beds. Laura leaned sideways and whispered to Sebastian. "Look. There's Mrs. Fedderson. We'll go say hello." Without waiting for his reply, she quickened her steps and cut across the lawn toward the elderly woman. "Good morning, Mrs. Fedderson. It's Laura Calder."

The woman lifted a frail hand to shield her eyes from the sun's high glare. "Laura," she said in recognition. "My, haven't you grown up to be a pretty girl," she declared, then peered past Laura, eyes squinting at the sight of Sebastian. "Is that young Trey with you?"

"No, Trey's at the ranch. This is a friend from England. His name is Sebastian Dunshill." This time Laura didn't bother with his title.

"From England, you say?" The woman repeated with a slightly worried look. "My hearing's not too good."

"From England, yes," Sebastian confirmed, slightly raising the volume of his voice. "It is a pleasure to meet you, Mrs. Fedderson. Laura was insistent that I see your rose garden. You do have a most spectacular display."

After listening intently, the woman nodded. "The roses. Yes, Laura always did like them. My Emmett planted all of this for me."

"So she told me," Sebastian replied.

Laura caught a movement in her side vision and turned, smiling at the sight of a young toddler, still in her pajamas, her dark, uncombed hair hanging in straggles about her smudged face. Clutched in her stubby fingers were a bunch of rose petals as she made a beeline straight for Mrs. Fedderson.

Bending down, Laura touched the woman's arm and pointed to the little girl. "I think you have a dirty-faced angel coming to pay you a visit."

"What?" The woman frowned, then saw the child.

The little girl toddled right up to the chair and held out the crushed petals. "Coo-kie," she said, giving Laura the impression she wanted to trade the flower for a cookie. To her shock, the old woman scowled at the girl, demanding, "Where's that brother of yours?"

"Coo-kie," the girl repeated and dropped the petals in the woman's lap.

"He sent you, didn't he?" Rose Fedderson accused and flung a shooing hand at the girl. "Go on. Scat! He's not going to steal from me this time." She struggled to push herself out of the lawn chair.

"What are you talking about, Mrs. Fedderson?" Laura said in protest and reached out to offer a helping hand.

"That brother of hers is a thief, that's what I'm talking about." There was no mistaking the conviction or the anger in the old woman's voice. She made a painful turn toward the porch. "It took me a while to figure out why things were coming up missing." Head down and back hunched with age, she started for the house at a hobbling gait. "The little brat sends that baby over here. Then he slips in the house and takes my things." When she saw the little girl toddling after her, she flapped her hands. "Shoo! Shoo!"

Sebastian came up alongside her and pointed. "You wouldn't be referring to that young man, would you?"

Laura turned in time to see a dark-haired boy making a mad dash across the backyard of the neighboring house. He had something tucked under his arm, but her glimpse of the object was too brief for Laura to identify it.

"Come back here, you little pup!" Rose shouted. "Come back here, I say!"

"I'll catch him for you." Sebastian broke into a long, loping run, giving chase after the boy.

Laura scooped the little girl into her arms and caught a strong whiff of a stinky diaper. "Where do they live? Do you know, Mrs. Fedderson?"

"Down the street, two or three houses. The one with all the trash in the yard," she said with contempt.

"Coo-kie," the little girl demanded and pushed out her lower lip.

"Later," Laura said and set off to take the girl home, careful to keep her head averted to avoid inhaling the smell of the dirty diaper.

Chapter Fourteen

Laura took one look at the weed-choked yard, littered with broken toys, junked auto parts, and an old sofa with ripped cushions and a missing leg, and knew this had to be the right house. When she started up the front walk, Sebastian came trotting around the corner of the house.

"He ducked in the back door and locked it," he said and went up the front steps two at a time.

Laura reached the porch as Sebastian put a shoulder to the door and forced it open. When he swung the door wide, she caught a glimpse of the boy racing toward the rear of the house, but it was enough.

"That's the Mitchell boy," Laura said in surprise.

Sebastian hesitated in the doorway. "Do you know the family?"

"Not really. I had a run-in with his father a week or so ago." Remembering the man's hot temper, Laura stepped cautiously into the house and set the girl on the floor. She immediately toddled over to a bedraggled-looking doll on the living room's floor and picked it up. "Hello!" Laura called. "Anybody home?"

Beyond some rustling movement coming from the rear of the house, there was only silence. Laura ventured a little farther into the room. She muttered to Sebastian, "I wouldn't be surprised if the swine hasn't gone off somewhere and left the children to fend for themselves."

Sensing Laura's wariness, Sebastian made a thorough visual inspection of the areas within their view. "Is there a mother?"

"She's probably working," Laura said and bent down to the little girl. "Where's your daddy, sweetheart?"

The little girl immediately lost all expression and backed away from Laura, turned and dashed off to sit against the wall next to an old armchair.

"He knocks you around, too, does he?" Laura concluded, her dislike of the man deepening to an anger. She straightened. "This time I am going to report him. Do you see a phone?"

"No." More sounds came from the rear. Sebastian listened for a moment, then moved toward them. "I think I'll see what our little thief is doing."

Laura followed him into a narrow hall that led to the back of the house. The doorway to the bathroom stood open. She glanced in, but saw nothing but a pile of dirty towels and discarded clothes.

The next door was shut. Sebastian pushed it open. Looking past him, Laura saw the unmade bed. She was almost sorry Mitchell wasn't in it.

Sebastian swore under his breath and charged into the room. "What's wrong?" The question was barely out of her mouth when Laura saw a pair of slim bare legs, a woman's legs, on the floor near the foot of the bed.

Alarm shot through her as she pushed into the room. By the time Laura reached the fallen woman, Sebastian was already crouched beside her, his fingers pressed against the inside of her wrist, checking for a pulse.

Her stomach lurched sickeningly when Laura saw the woman's

face. There was little about it that resembled the woman she'd seen slipping food into Mitchell's truck the day of the auction. Her features were distorted by dark, purpling bruises that marked nearly every inch of them. One eye was swollen completely shut, and there was dried blood on her chin from a severely cut lip, partially covered by an inexpertly applied Band-Aid with stars scattered over it, the kind meant for a child.

When Sebastian gently lowered the woman's arm to her side, Laura asked, "Is she—"

"No. Her pulse is strong. Her breathing is steady. But she's been severely beaten, mostly about the face, it appears, although there is some bruising on her arms."

"And I know exactly who did it," Laura stated, giving rise to the anger that had been simmering ever since she realized Mitchell lived in this house.

"What did you say their name is?"

"Their last name is Mitchell. That's all I know."

Sebastian bent close to the woman. "Mrs. Mitchell, can you hear me?" He gave her shoulder a gentle nudge. "Mrs. Mitchell?" The undamaged eye fluttered open, then closed with the release of a low moan. Sebastian tried again to rouse her. "Mrs. Mitchell!"

Again she opened the one eye. This time it stayed open as the woman attempted to focus on Sebastian. "Who . . . ?" The movement of a cut lip must have produced an instant jab of pain as her hand moved shakily to her face.

"I'm a friend of the Calders," he answered, knowing his own name would be meaningless to her.

The woman's obvious pain was more than Laura could take. "I'm going to find a phone and call for help."

As she started to turn away, the woman's voice lifted to stop her. "No, don't!"

There was just enough strength in her voice to make Laura pause. "You've been badly hurt."

"No. No, I'm all right," she mumbled and made a weak attempt to rise.

Sebastian checked her attempt, warning, "Careful. You may have some internal injuries."

"No." Her hand trembled over the swollen surfaces of her bruised cheek and eye. "My face . . . that's all." She directed a pleading look at Laura. "Don't call anyone. Please."

The appeal was so poignant that Laura was torn between doing what she knew was right and giving in to the woman's wishes. Sebastian delayed the moment of decision.

"Let's get her off the floor and onto the bed." He nodded in the direction of the unmade bed and the table lamp that lay atop it, its shade dented and askew. "Straighten the covers, will you?"

"Of course." Laura moved quickly to retrieve the lamp and set it on the bedside table, leaving the shade atilt for the time being, while Sebastian cradled the slight woman in his arms.

The bedcovers were a tangled mess. Rather than take the time to straighten them out, Laura merely threw them back to expose the bottom sheet and moved out of Sebastian's way. When he gently lowered the woman onto the mattress, Laura hurriedly plumped a pillow and slipped it under her head, her heart tearing and her anger growing at the little sounds of pain the woman attempted to smother.

Sebastian sat on the edge of the bed next to the woman, his gaze examining her again. "You really should have a professional assess your injuries, Mrs. Mitchell. You could very well be concussed."

A tear trickled from the corner of her eye. "No, please." The words were a sob. Then a look of panic flashed in her face, and again she attempted to rise. "My babies—"

"Your children are fine." It required no great amount of pressure for Sebastian to force her to lie flat.

"Your daughter is in the living room playing with her doll," Laura told her. "And your son"—she turned, not at all sure where the little thief was until she saw him standing in the doorway—"is right here."

The woman relaxed against the mattress in relief, but it was short-lived as she roused herself again. "I need to see to them."

Sebastian wouldn't hear of it. "First we need to get you fixed up. There will be time enough later to tend to the children."

The woman again settled back, but Laura suspected her easy acquiescence was based more on her lack of strength than an acceptance of Sebastian's reasoning. Sebastian straightened from the bed, shook the top sheet loose from the tangled covers, and gently drew it across the woman, then stepped over to Laura's side.

"You aren't really going to listen to her, are you?" Laura demanded in a hissing whisper.

"What do you suggest?" he countered smoothly. "Her injuries are undoubtedly painful, but they are certainly not life-threatening."

Laura desperately wanted to shoot down his logic, but the only argument she could summon was a weak one. "We can't be certain of that."

The look he gave her spoke volumes, but he chose not to offer a direct response. "I'm going to find the kitchen and get some ice for that eye of hers. Why don't you get a wet cloth and clean her up a bit?"

The instant Sebastian moved toward the doorway, the boy bolted for the living room. Laura couldn't help thinking that he was too young to have such a strong instinct for flight.

She followed Sebastian into the hall and turned right, toward the bathroom, while he went in search of the kitchen. She flipped on the bathroom light switch, made a brief survey of the small, cramped space, and located a linen cupboard built into the wall next to the bathtub. Dirty laundry, a mix of clothes and towels, was piled in front of its door. Laura pushed it out of the way with her foot and opened the door. The shelves were bare of all except two towels and three washcloths. She took the top one off the stack and crossed to the sink.

When she turned on the faucet, Laura noticed the medicine cabinet behind the mirror above the sink. She swung the mirrored door open and scanned the contents. There, on the top shelf, was a bottle of disinfectant. She took it down, found some cotton swabs in a basket sitting on the toilet's tank lid, and removed two from the pack.

Armed with a wet washcloth, cotton swabs, and a bottle of disinfectant, Laura returned to the bedroom, placed the bottle and cotton swabs on the nightstand and sat down on the edge of the bed. The woman lay there, not stirring.

Rather than startle her, Laura said, "Mrs. Mitchell, I'm going to clean you up a bit."

As gently as she could, she went to work on the dried blood crusted on the woman's chin. At some point in the process, she sensed she wasn't alone. She glanced at the doorway and saw the little boy peering around the doorjamb. He quickly ducked out of sight.

Seconds after she returned to her task, Laura sensed his eyes watching her again. This time she didn't turn but concentrated instead on the blood trail until she had cleaned up all of it except for that under the star-studded bandage. Carefully, Laura peeled it off.

As she went to lay the used bandage on the nightstand, she glanced at the boy. "Did you put this bandage on your mother's cut?" The boy didn't say a word, just stared back at her. "That was a very good thing to do."

Once all the dried blood was removed, Laura poured disinfectant into the bottle's lid, saturated the cotton swab with it, and warned her patient. "This is going to hurt, Mrs. Mitchell."

The woman winced noticeably but made no sound. A sharply indrawn breath came from the boy by the doorway. After she had treated the deep split in the woman's lip, Laura used a clean corner of the wet washcloth to wipe the rest of the woman's face.

Almost with the first touch of the cloth on her bruised skin, the woman murmured in a sigh, "That feels so good."

Once again, Laura felt the warring between anger and compassion. "Your husband did this to you, didn't he?" she accused.

The woman looked at her, insisting, "He didn't mean to."

"I'll just bet he didn't," Laura muttered with heat.

"You don't understand," the woman protested.

"No, and I never will." She couldn't bring herself to pretend otherwise.

Approaching footsteps sent the boy scurrying to the living room again. Laura stood up when Sebastian entered the room, carrying a sealable plastic bag filled with ice cubes and water. During the brief moment when their eyes met, Laura picked up something, but she couldn't tell if it was frustration or exasperation.

"This should help the swelling, Mrs. Mitchell." He eased the ice bag onto her black eye and used the extra pillow to prop it in place.

"Thank you," the woman murmured and searched out Laura with her other eye. "Thank you both."

"You lie there and rest a bit," Sebastian said and took Laura by the arm, turning her toward the door.

The woman reacted with a flash of panic. "You aren't going to call anybody, are you? Please, I—"

"We won't. I promise," Sebastian assured her. "Lie still. And keep that ice bag on your eye."

The woman subsided against the pillow, but her worried glance followed them when Sebastian escorted Laura from the room. Laura studied the grim set of Sebastian's mouth.

"What's wrong?"

"I suspect I know what the boy stole from Mrs. Fedderson," he stated. "A sack of marshmallows. Would you care to guess why?"

Laura had a bitter feeling that she knew the answer. "He was hungry."

"Precisely," he said, his speech cold and clipped. "The shelves in that kitchen are regrettably bare. No milk, no bread, no tins—in fact, there is little beyond flour, salt, cooking oil, a few spices, and a package of dried beans."

"I think Mitchell's been out of work for some time."

"The cause is irrelevant. Those children need food." Sebastian made it a flat statement of fact. "You stay here while I go to Fedderson's and pick up some groceries for them."

"Here." Laura dug into her purse and pulled out the truck keys. "You might as well drive the truck back. It'll save carrying the groceries all this way." She hesitated. "How are you fixed for cash?"

There was a touch of drollness in his crooked smile. "I'm not in the poorhouse yet."

The left-handed reference to his current financial straits prompted Laura to extract a pair of twenty-dollar bills from her wallet. "I'll contribute to the cause just the same." She pushed the money and the keys into his hand as the little girl waddled past them into the bedroom, leaving the stench of a soiled diaper in her wake. Laura wrinkled her nose at the odor. "Better pick up some disposable diapers, too. There's one on top of the dresser but it's probably the last."

Sebastian hesitated. "On second thought, perhaps you should go instead. If the husband should come home and find you—"

"He wouldn't dare lay a finger on me." Laura pushed her chin forward at a combative angle, her dark eyes snapping with temper.

The corners of his mouth twitched. "I am quite certain you are more than a match for him, but I prefer not to take the risk."

"He would be twice as angry to find a strange man in his house," Laura warned.

His mouth curved in one of those lazy, sexy smiles. "I do believe you are concerned for my well-being. How encouraging."

"I was merely thinking of how difficult it would be for you to attract the interest of some wealthy woman if that handsome face of yours is bashed in." Laura countered.

"You find it handsome, do you?" Teasing laughter danced in his eyes, a match to the amused smugness of his smile.

"Too bad it's all you have to offer," Laura retorted, enjoying the playful banter that had them matching wits.

"It isn't *all*," he stressed suggestively and tucked both the money and the keys into her purse before adding more bills from his pocket. "Go to the store. There will be a better time to jog your memory."

Desire tingled through Laura at the look of promise he gave her. Rather than let him see it, she challenged instead, "Why are you so insistent on staying here? Are you hoping that I'll regard you as brave and heroic?"

"Perhaps it's simply that I suspect you don't have a clue how to change a soiled nappy."

It took her a second to remember that "nappy" was the English term for diaper. "And you do?" She eyed him skeptically.

"I had some experience at it when my nephews were small," he replied.

"Really? I would have thought that was the nanny's job."

"Even a nanny is entitled to a free day. Wouldn't you agree?"

"How incredibly domestic you sound," Laura mocked.

Sebastian sighed in disappointment. "You were supposed to remark on what an excellent husband I would make."

"You would—for somebody else," she added naughtily. "But you have convinced me. You can stay here and deal with the soiled nappy; I'll go to the store." Smiling, she touched his cheek in farewell and headed for the door.

It was a good forty-five minutes later when Laura parked the pickup in front of the house, collected two sacks of groceries from the back of the truck, and started up the front walk. Sebastian was at the front door, holding it open for her to pass through.

"There's more in the back of the truck," she told him as she went by.

One eyebrow arched at the sight of the half dozen sacks that remained. "Did you buy out the store?"

"You were the one who said the shelves were bare," Laura replied over her shoulder. "Where's the kitchen?"

"Straight back."

The little girl came running to meet her, swinging the bedraggled doll by its arm. Gone were the pajamas, the dirty face, and the diaper smell. Even her hair had been combed and pulled back from her face by a pair of pink barrettes that matched the pink dress she wore.

The change in the little girl's appearance wasn't the only thing Laura noticed as she passed through the front of the house. The living room had been tidied, the clutter picked up, books and magazines stacked neatly on the coffee table, and the toys stowed in a basket.

When she reached the kitchen, Laura suspected that Sebastian's hand had been at work there as well. Both the countertops and table were cleared. She shoved one grocery sack onto the counter and set the other one beside it, then left to bring more, passing Sebastian along the way.

It required two trips by each of them to unload the truck. When Laura returned from the second trip, she caught the boy perched on the counter, trying to rip open a bag of potato chips. He jumped to the floor the instant he saw her. Before he could run off with his prize, Laura grabbed the back of his shirt collar.

"Oh no, you don't." Without losing her grip on the boy, she snatched the bag from his hand, hauled one of the kitchen chairs up to the sink counter, and lifted him onto it. "I see Sebastian wasn't able to corral you. Before you eat anything, you're going to wash those dirty hands." She handed him a bar of soap and turned on the faucet. When he threw her a measuring look, she responded with a no-nonsense one of her own. "I mean it."

Deciding that she did, he pushed his hands under the water. While he went about washing his hands, Laura opened the sack of chips, shook a few into a bowl, and set it on the kitchen table.

"That's all you can have for now," she told him. "And be sure to share with your sister."

Sebastian joined her in the kitchen with the last two sacks, his glance sliding to the boy. "I see he came out of hiding."

"I caught him trying to steal the bag of potato chips." She gave the boy a towel to use to dry his hands and turned off the faucet. After two quick wipes on the towel, the boy jumped off the chair and ran to the table.

"According to the little girl, his name is Mike," Sebastian murmured as he began removing the food items from the sacks. "Her name is Amy."

"She looks like an Amy—now." Laura used the pause to lend emphasis to the latter word, then sent him a teasing glance. "Where did you learn to fix a little girl's hair? Certainly not from looking after your nephews."

"Would you believe that was my first attempt?"

"Really?" she said, admitting to a little surprise.

"It was. Although"—Sebastian paused to briefly comb his fingers into her hair—"I have played with a woman's hair on occasion. It can be quite stimulating. Remind me to demonstrate."

She laughed in her throat even as her pulse quickened. "You never give up, do you?"

"Like England's illustrious statesman, Winston Churchill, I can be very tenacious."

"You're wasting your time," Laura warned lightly and flashed her engagement ring as a reminder.

"Perhaps," Sebastian replied, clearly unconvinced.

Laura carried a gallon jug of milk to the refrigerator. "If you come across a package of hot dogs, leave them out. Every child

I've ever known loves them. I thought we could fix some for lunch and heat one of those cans of soup for Mrs. Mitchell."

As soon as the groceries were put away, the two of them set about fixing lunch for the children. Carrot sticks, fresh grapes, and milk rounded out the meal of hot dogs and chips. Sebastian buckled the little girl in her high chair while Laura poured some vegetable beef soup into an oversized mug she found in the cupboard.

"If you can handle things here, I'll take this in to Mrs. Mitchell," she told Sebastian.

"I believe I can manage," he replied and deftly righted the little girl's drink cup before it toppled off the tray and onto the floor.

Confident that he could, Laura exited the kitchen, soup mug in hand. Briefly she tried to visualize Boone in Sebastian's place, but it was simply too ludicrous. If Boone had been with her, he would have handled the situation differently: the authorities would have been called, the injured woman whisked off to the nearest medical facility, and the children turned over to a social service agency. He wouldn't have seen the need to involve himself personally. Laura wasn't entirely sure why she had.

The woman was awake when Laura entered the bedroom. "I brought you some soup," she told her.

"Thanks." The woman pushed herself up into a sitting position, but it was obvious that she was in pain.

Laura set the mug on the table and helped the woman adjust the propping pillows behind her. "Sebastian mentioned he gave you a couple aspirins. Did they help any?"

"A little. I'll be fine, though," she added hastily.

The anger came back for the man who inflicted this abuse on her. "I hope you feel better than you look." Laura didn't try to soften the sharp edge of her voice as she placed the mug in the woman's hands. "Can you manage to feed yourself?"

The woman nodded in answer and dipped the spoon into the soup. Laura watched her take the first few spoonfuls. Then the effort seemed to exhaust the woman. She rescued the soup mug from the woman's loosening grip and set it on the table.

"Tell me when you want some more, Mrs . . ." she began, then stopped. "It doesn't feel right to keep calling you Mrs. Mitchell. What's your first name?"

"Gail."

"Mine's Laura." Rather than tower over her, Laura settled onto the edge of the bed.

The woman named Gail made a weak attempt at a smile, hesitated, then said, "He didn't mean to hurt me, you know. Gary is really a good, kind man."

"Maybe I should bring you a mirror so you can see what he did to you," Laura suggested dryly. "There isn't much good or kind about it."

"He didn't mean to," she insisted again. "He'd been drinking. It never would have happened if he hadn't."

"How often is he sober?" Laura challenged, irritated at the way the woman kept defending this animal who masqueraded as a man.

Avoiding a direct answer, Gail plucked at the top sheet. "None of this started until the mine closed. Before that he was a wonderful, loving husband and father." She let her head rest against the headboard and gazed at the ceiling as if recalling better times. "We were going to leave when everybody else did, but neither one of us wanted to go back to the city, and the county had an opening in the road maintenance department. Gary was sure he was going to get the job. Every month they kept saying next month. In the end they didn't hire anyone. Budget problems, they said. By then we had used up what little savings we had. Then his unemployment insurance ran out."

It wasn't hard to guess what happened next. "And he started drinking."

Instantly defensive, she met Laura's skeptical gaze. "Gary is a proud man. You have no idea how much it hurts not to be able to take care of his family."

Laura wouldn't relent in her opinion of the man. "Is that the reason your cupboards were bare? He was too proud to apply for food stamps?"

The woman turned her face away. "We get food stamps."

The statement confused Laura, but only for a second. "Let me guess: he sold them for cash so he could buy booze?"

"No," she denied, stung by the remark. "He needed gas money for the truck so he could go look for a job."

"Where? At Harry's?" It was tough talk, but Laura was determined to open the woman's eyes.

Tears welled. "He goes there sometimes. You can't expect him to sit at home all the time."

"And when he goes there, he drinks, then comes home and beats on you."

"It isn't like that. Not always." Her voice had a sob in it. "He loves me."

"His kind of love you don't need," Laura stated, then tried another tactic. "Gail, this isn't good—not for you or your children."

"I know, but"—this time she did sniffle back a sob—"if he could just find a job, everything would be all right again. I know it would."

Personally, Laura had her doubts that a job would bring about an abrupt change in his behavior. Maybe with counseling it might in time, but she couldn't see Mitchell ever agreeing to that, certainly not voluntarily. It was something a judge would have to order him to do; even then Laura suspected he wouldn't be all that cooperative.

"I'm afraid you're dreaming, Gail." Exasperated with the woman's loyalty, Laura gave up and reached for the mug. "More soup?"

In silence the woman downed a few more spoonfuls. "Where are the children? I can't hear them."

"In the kitchen having lunch. I went shopping," Laura informed her, "and restocked your cupboards and refrigerator."

"You didn't have to do that." But there was abject gratitude in the look she gave Laura. "We'll pay you back as soon as we can."

"Of course." But Laura wasn't about to hold her breath waiting for that day to come.

The woman started to take another sip of soup, then returned the spoon to the mug, and pushed aside the top sheet. "I think I'll finish the rest of my soup in the kitchen with the children."

"Are you sure?"

"Yes." She swung her legs out of bed. "I'm fine."

Laura couldn't help wondering which one of them she was trying to convince. She waited while Gail changed into a pair of jeans and an oversized tee, then walked with her to the kitchen. The boy, Mike, was on his second hot dog when they arrived.

The little girl was more interested in the grapes on her plate than the hot dog. She was the only one to comment on her mother's appearance, pointing to her face and saying, "Mama, owie."

"Yes, Mama has an owie," Gail confirmed and sat down at the table with them. She darted a self-conscious glance at Sebastian but avoided looking at Laura. "It was very good of you to help us like this. I'm sure there's somewhere you should be, and it really isn't necessary for you to stay. I can manage now, thanks to both of you."

"We'll go—on one condition," Laura said, unmoved by the wary and slightly resentful look Gail Mitchell slid her way. "The next time it even looks like your husband is going to strike you, you call the police."

"Our phone's been disconnected."

"That must make it a bit difficult for a prospective employer to contact your husband about a job," Laura murmured, unable to resist getting in another jab.

"Laura is right," Sebastian said gently. "Don't subject yourself to another beating like this. The next time you could be seriously hurt. Get away from him however you can, and run to a neighbor or the tavern. But don't remain here."

"All right."

But Laura had the feeling the woman was just saying that; she wouldn't run from the house and leave her children behind. In her place, Laura wouldn't, either.

Angered by the hopelessness of the situation, Laura turned to Sebastian. "We'd better go. Allie will be wondering where the strawberries are."

Their leave-taking was brief. Chin high and temper simmering, Laura exited the house and struck out for the pickup parked at the street curb.

"There is only so much help you can give someone, Laura," Sebastian said in that understanding voice of his.

She threw him a glare. "Don't say another word," she warned. "Or I'll haul off and hit you just because you're a man."

Taking her at her word, Sebastian held his silence and climbed into the truck. After a stop at Fedderson's to pick up the flat of strawberries, Laura pointed the pickup toward the Triple C head-quarters, rolled the window down, and let the hot afternoon wind tunnel into the cab. She rested an elbow atop the opened window and combed a hand into her wind-whipped hair to keep its length out of her face while the pickup ate up the miles.

The speed and the big, empty land worked to unravel the high tension in her nerves. A long, slow sigh at last slipped from her.

"Is it safe to assume that your temper has cooled?" Sebastian queried in a dryly amused voice.

Absorbed in her own thoughts, Laura failed to hear his re-mark. "Sorry, did you say something?"

"Doing some heavy thinking, were you?" he guessed.

"Something like that," she admitted with a shrug, then eyed him curiously. "What are you going to do if you should lose Crawford Hall?"

"I don't know." His mouth twitched. "But I give you my solemn oath that I won't take to drinking and beating up women."

It was a frivolous answer to what had been a serious question, and yet so typical of him that Laura had to laugh. At the same time, she knew Sebastian had spoken the truth.

"Do you realize we never ate lunch?" she asked, suddenly conscious of the emptiness in her stomach.

"Have a strawberry." He hand-fed her one. Just like that, the entire incident at the Mitchell house seemed to lose much of its frustration. Once again her smile was carefree.

Chapter Fifteen

The Mitchell woman dominated the dinner conversation at The Homestead that evening. "I'm afraid I couldn't even pretend to be sympathetic," Laura declared. "As far as I'm concerned, Mitchell should be strung up by his balls for what he did to her."

There was an instant of stunned silence, broken by Jessy's low-voiced, "Laura."

Chase spoke up quickly, "Now don't shush her, Jessy. It's the first unladylike thing that's come out of her mouth in years. She just might be a Calder after all."

"Hear, hear." Sebastian toasted her with his wineglass.

"It might not be a bad idea to mention this to Logan the next time you see him," Laredo suggested. "If nothing else, he can swing by there now and then. It might help convince the wife that she can call for help."

"Good idea," Jessy agreed.

"I wouldn't bother calling him tonight," Trey said. "Logan says things always get crazy on nights when there's a full moon, and we have one tonight."

Laura perked up. "We do?"

Trey nodded. "About as big and round as it gets."

She turned an eager glance on Sebastian. "How about we saddle a couple horses and go for a moonlight ride?"

"I would enjoy that." His answering look was lively and warm, and Laura felt that familiar curl of excitement deep in the pit of her stomach.

"Good." Laura pushed her chair back from the table. "If you'll excuse me, I'll go change into my riding clothes."

"But what about dessert?" Jessy looked at her in surprise. "Allie's made a fresh strawberry tart."

Laura exchanged knowing glances with Sebastian. "I'll pass. I've already had my quota of fresh strawberries today." She rose from her chair and headed into the hallway.

An hour later the first blush of sunset tinted the evening sky as Laura left the barns and rode toward The Homestead, a saddled horse in tow. Chase was ensconced in his rocker on the veranda, pushing it back and forth in a slow rhythm.

Laura reined in her horse, halting it near the front steps. "Where's Sebastian? I thought he'd be out here by now."

"He's on the phone with his sister," Chase replied. "I expect he'll be out directly."

"I hope so. The moon will be rising soon." Laura hooked a knee around the saddle horn and resigned herself to waiting, conscious of the day's heat rising from the sun-baked ground and the utter stillness of the air.

"You surprised me today," Chase continued his idle rock.

"How's that?"

"Getting personally involved with that Mitchell woman. That's something I would have expected from Quint—or even Trey. But it isn't like you."

She smiled in a chiding fashion, not in the least offended. "Now, Gramps, you know very well that I wouldn't have walked out and left her lying on the floor all battered and beaten."

"No. You would have called an ambulance."

"Believe me, I wanted to," Laura admitted without apology. "But she wouldn't hear of it. And once she managed to convince

Sebastian her injuries weren't serious, there wasn't much I could do."

"And there was the business with the groceries. You went and got them yourself instead of simply handing her some money."

"She was in no condition to go," Laura reminded him. "And the children were starving. I'm not heartless."

"Sometimes I think you like to pretend that you are."

"Don't be silly." She dismissed his claim.

"No, you're guilty of letting your head make most of your decisions instead of following your instincts."

"If I had followed my instincts today, the police would have been called and an arrest warrant issued for Mitchell," Laura informed him.

"Not if the wife refused to file charges against him, it wouldn't have," Chase countered. "I think that young English fella knew it."

"He should. He's a lawyer, or a solicitor, or whatever they call attorneys over there," Laura replied with a careless shrug and idly tapped the reins against her boot.

"He seems to be a good influence on you."

Once more Chase had her full attention as a suspicion formed. "Don't tell me you're trying your hand at some matchmaking, Gramps."

"Good God, no." He was emphatic in his denial. "I think you've made the right choice. This Crockett will make you a much more satisfactory husband."

"Really?" Laura was surprised and a little pleased by his unexpected endorsement of Boone. But there was a part of her that wasn't sure she believed him.

"In your own way, you're an ambitious woman. . . ." He paused to study her for a moment. "Perhaps in the mold of Lady Elaine. If the stories that have been handed down about her are true, she thrived on business and politics. Considering the way Tara has filled your head with stories about her, I wouldn't be surprised if you toyed with the idea of marrying a titled Englishman, especially after meeting Sebastian. But it would never have worked."

"How could it, when he was after my money?" Her voice had a little edge to it.

"That's your pride talking, not your head." His accusation stung. "The money part of it wouldn't have mattered."

"Really?" Laura challenged coolly.

"Yes, really. From what I've always heard, those English blue-bloods are pretty much a closed society. They might have tolerated you, but I doubt you would have ever been accepted into the ranks. It's for sure they would have made it tough on you. I suppose in time you might have been able to talk Sebastian into trying his hand at politics. He has the looks and charm for it—maybe even the intelligence. It's the sort of challenge that would definitely suit you. But all the odds are against you," he declared, then nodded. "Like I said, you're better off with Crockett. His father has all the money and power you could ever want. And you've got Tara to pave your way into Texas society. You're walking into a ready-made situation that isn't going to require much from you at all."

A knowing smile curved her mouth. "Honestly, Gramps, you are about as subtle as a bullfighter with a cape." She unhooked her leg from around the saddle horn and slipped the toe of her boot back in the stirrup.

"What?" He gave her a suitable innocent look.

"Come on. That whole monologue was an attempt to convince me I should marry Sebastian, and you know it."

"Why would I want my only granddaughter to marry some foreigner and move halfway across the world?" he argued, then snorted. "It's bad enough that you'll be living in Texas."

His exaggerated denial was almost laughable. Yet it filled Laura with an almost overwhelming sadness. This old stoop-shouldered man idling away the hours in a rocker was a far cry from the big, robust grandfather of her youth.

The front door opened, and Sebastian stepped onto the veranda, eliminating the need for Laura to respond to her grandfather's last remark. "It's about time you showed up," Laura declared and gave a tug on the reins of the second horse, pulling it around to the front of her saddle.

"Chase did explain that Helen phoned, I hope." Sebastian crossed to the top of the steps and started down.

"He did," she confirmed.

"By the way, Helen asked me to give you her regards." He took the reins from her outstretched hand and moved to the near side of the saddle.

"That was thoughtful of her." Laura waited until he had mounted, then threw a wave to her grandfather and reined her horse away from the veranda. "No problems at home, I hope." She slid him a questioning look when he swung his horse alongside of hers.

"No new ones," Sebastian replied.

"Just the same old money ones." She tried for lightness, but she knew it fell short.

He arched her a curious look. "Do I detect a trace of bitterness?"

"Probably," she admitted a little grimly. "But it doesn't have anything to do with you. It's Gramps. Age has started affecting his judgment. It just doesn't seem fair. And don't say it," Laura warned. "I already know that life isn't fair."

"I shan't bother to remind you, then." His smile was easy and warm. As always, Laura found it impossible not to respond to its sexy charm.

She lifted her horse into a trot, pointing it south toward the tree-lined river. Sebastian's mount followed suit as dusk settled over the land.

With her back to the house, Laura never saw Trey walk onto the veranda, a cordless phone in his hand. He halted when he caught sight of the two riders already halfway across the ranch yard, and carried the phone to his ear. "Sorry, Tara. I was too late. They've already left."

"They?" Tara stiffened instantly. "What do you mean, they have left?"

"Laura and Sebastian. They've gone riding," Trey replied.

"Where?"

"With Laura, who knows? There's a full moon tonight, and she decided to go riding. Do you want me to leave her a message to call you tomorrow."

"Yes, you do that, Trey," Tara stated and hung up, but she didn't turn away from the phone. The phrase *ride in the moonlight* echoed through her mind. There was nothing about the sound of it that Tara liked.

She was well aware that Laura was attracted to Sebastian even though she had walked away from him. It infuriated her the way the Calders had welcomed him when he had shown up at the ranch. Her mood didn't improve when Tara recalled the lack of enthusiasm the family had shown when they learned of Laura's engagement.

The longer she thought about it, the more convinced Tara became that Jessy was hoping to undermine Laura's engagement to Boone. She suspected that Chase was probably in on it, too. Considering the way he had allowed his own daughter to marry a common lawman, it was obvious he had no understanding of the importance of marrying someone of similar status and wealth.

Ordinarily Tara would have been confident that Laura wouldn't be swayed by Sebastian's charm, regardless of any attraction she might have for him. But if, as she suspected, the family was involved, they could tilt the balance.

"We'll put a stop to that right now," Tara murmured and picked up the phone, rapidly punched an eleven-digit number, and waited through three rings.

"Rutledge residence."

"This is Tara Calder. Let me speak to Max, please."

"One moment."

Only seconds later, his familiar voice came over the line. "Tara, this is a surprise."

"Not a pleasant one, I'm afraid. I thought I should let you know that Sebastian Dunshill is here in Montana. In fact, he's staying at the Triple C."

"What's he doing there?" The sharp demand in his voice matched her own feelings.

"Obviously he's making one more try to win Laura. He's wasting his time, of course. Just the same, I think it might hasten his departure if Boone were here."

"Do you think that's necessary?" Max challenged.

"I wouldn't say it's necessary." Tara was walking a fine line here, and she knew it. Max would be insulted if she told him her suspicion that the Calders were less than thrilled about Laura's engagement to his son. "I just want the man gone, and I know Boone's arrival would accomplish that."

"Didn't you tell Chase about Dunshill's financial troubles?"

"I told both Chase and Jessy, but they have chosen to leave the decision as to whether he stays or goes to Laura. She finds his persistence a bit more amusing than I do." Aware that she had to be careful, Tara managed a slightly theatrical sigh. "It's hardly surprising, though. Any woman's ego would be flattered to have a man follow her halfway around the world. It's natural that Laura wants to savor the feeling, considering that she'll be married soon."

"I suppose. She is young."

Tara jumped on his comment. "Too young to understand the way people can talk. That's why I want to make certain Sebastian's visit is a brief one."

"I agree."

"Wonderful." Tara smiled in triumph.

The moon resembled a giant silver dollar in the eastern sky, its light so strong that any point in the landscape cast a shadow, including the two riders cantering their horses across the grass plains. The rhythmic cadence of pounding hooves, the belly grunts of the horses, and the occasional creak of saddle leather were the only sounds to be heard in the hushed night.

Cresting a rise in the undulating prairie, Laura reined her horse down to a walk. Sebastian checked his own mount and swung in alongside of her. Hatless, Laura wore her hair in a French braid that ended in a queue between her shoulders. The play of moonlight over the planes and angles of her face enhanced the classic perfection of her profile.

With an effort, Sebastian dragged his gaze from her and made a sweep of the unbroken land before them. "It would be remarkably easy to believe we are the only two on earth."

"Very easy," Laura agreed. "I love riding at night."

"Really? And I was convinced you favored places that were loud and crowded."

"Usually. It depends on my mood." She lifted her gaze to the immense sky and its incredible encrusting of stars. "You must admit there's a definite magic to this night. There must be a million stars up there, all of them so far away, yet they seem close enough to touch."

"Indeed." But it was Laura he wanted to touch.

"You get a feeling of peace, don't you?" She studied the glittering canopy above them and let a little sigh slip out. "I guess that appeals to me tonight."

"Yes, it tends to make the troubles at the Mitchells' seem like a bad dream," Sebastian said, following his own train of thought.

With a downward dip of her chin, Laura angled a glance his way, something light and teasing in her eyes. "Did I mention that my grandfather thinks you are a good influence on me?"

"Which is undoubtedly the reason you are convinced age has impaired his judgment."

Her laugh was soft and musical, in perfect harmony with the surrounding hush. "How astute. Are you that quick in court?"

"A solicitor doesn't argue cases in court. That is the role of a barrister."

"I believe you told me that once before. Oh, look. A falling star." She pointed to a white scratch in the sky an instant before it vanished from sight. "Did you make a wish?"

"It went too quickly."

"They always do."

A coyote yipped somewhere off to the east, an eerie sound in the quiet land. Sebastian's horse swiveled an ear in its direction but never changed the pace of its steady walk. Turning in the saddle, Sebastian rested a hand on the cantle and looked behind them. The buildings of the ranch headquarters had long ago disappeared from view. Only a faint glow in the distance remained to suggest its location.

Facing the front again, he remarked, half in jest, "I hope you know where we are."

"I do. See that dark line of trees over there?" She nodded to the southwest. "That's the river we crossed when we left the ranch yard. It makes a big, sweeping curve to the south. All we have to do is follow it and it will lead us home."

"Upstream or downstream?"

"Downstream. Worried about getting lost, are you?" Laura said with a laugh.

"No, but I like to be prepared."

"Don't tell me you were a Boy Scout."

"Sorry, no."

After a short run of silence, Laura remarked. "It's a warm night. Usually it cools off after the sun goes down. It might be cooler by the river. Let's ride that way." She laid the reins against her horse's neck, pointing it toward the dark line of trees, and tossed a challenging look at Sebastian. "Race you there." She dug her heels into her horse's side. It shot forward, reaching a full gallop in two strides.

Sebastian gave chase, bending low in the saddle, urging his horse on. The river was less than a quarter mile distant. Laura's horse was in the lead by a nose when she checked its headlong pace and reined it away from the treed bank. Sebastian broke in the other direction and circled his horse back to join up with her.

"I won." There was laughter in her eyes and in her face, a glowing joy from within that only added to her natural beauty.

"A head start and a lighter weight in the saddle might have had something to do with that," Sebastian suggested with a grin.

"Life isn't fair that way," Laura reminded him, playfully.

"But races are supposed to be."

"In that case"—her horse danced sideways as she scanned the shadowed edges of the tree line—"we'll have another one."

"Where is the starting point?"

"Up there." Energized by the run, her horse bounded into a canter the instant Laura signaled him forward. Sebastian quickly urged his horse alongside her. Together they loped parallel to the river until Laura pointed to a break in the trees growing along the banks.

"That is my own private swimming hole, wonderfully secluded," she told him, a naughty look shining in her dark eyes. "The perfect spot for skinny-dipping. Are you game? Be warned, though, the water is only chest-deep."

In response, Sebastian kneed his horse into a gallop and tugged his shirttail loose from the waistband of his jeans. Reaching up, he undid the top two buttons, conscious of hooves pounding the ground directly behind him. By the time his horse plowed to a stop near the open section of riverbank, he had pulled the shirt over his head and unfastened his jeans.

Wasting no time, he peeled out of the saddle and dropped the shirt on the ground along with the reins. He had already tugged off one boot when Laura swung off her horse. The second boot followed the first. Then it was an easy strip of his jeans, shorts, and socks.

He threw one look at Laura, catching a glimpse of her as she shrugged out of her bra, and he ran for the water. His second step into the river, he planted his foot and pushed off, making a shallow dive into the center.

When he surfaced, Laura was there, stretched out in an effortless sidestroke, the moonlight silvering the paleness of her skin. "Cheater, you had fewer clothes."

Letting one foot touch the bottom, Sebastian wiped the water from his face. "This time the advantage was mine; last time it was yours. That's only fair, don't you agree?"

She slapped the surface with her hand, sending a spray of water at his face, and the water fight was on. It ended the only way it could, with Sebastian pulling her under the water.

They pushed to the top in unison, emerging only inches apart. Laura swiped a hand across her face and gave a brief toss of her head to shake off the excess water, then fastened her gaze on Sebastian, a darkening in her eyes that was full of invitation.

"I'm cold." She crossed her arms behind his neck and dipped her head toward his mouth. "Warm me up."

"That was my plan all along," Sebastian murmured and met her halfway, his mouth moving onto her lips, parting them to deepen the kiss.

The buoyancy of the water made her weightless in his arms, leaving his hands free to explore every tantalizing dip and curve of her body. But he kept coming back to her breasts and the nipples that the chilly water had turned pebble-hard.

With a faint groan of need, he lifted her partway out of the water, but the slickness of her wet skin made it difficult for him to keep his grip. She would have slipped if she hadn't wrapped her legs around his middle, solving the problem for him. Her fingers dug into his hair as he rubbed his mouth over a gleaming white breast, briefly teething its hard point before sucking it into his mouth.

Need grew, stimulated by everything from the rounded cheeks of her buttocks and the hard peaks of her breasts to the writhing push of her body against him and the little animal sounds she made in her throat.

Adjusting his stance to gain a better footing on the muddy river bottom, Sebastian pried a leg from around his middle, lowering her. In the next second her hand was there, guiding him inside her.

Only briefly was he conscious of the water lapping against them as he drove into her again and again. Then he was lost to everything except the hot race of his blood and the screaming ache for release. It came with an explosive, shuddering rush that had both of them straining to hold on to the intense pleasure of it.

His foot slipped, and they both went under, the suddenness of it separating them. Sebastian broke the surface an instant before Laura came up sputtering and coughing. But her sputtering quickly dissolved into laughter.

"I've never made love in the water before. Next time I'll remember to hold my breath," she declared, then shivered. "Brrr. Now it really is cold. This time I think we need to get dressed. Come on." She caught hold of his hand and led him toward the shore. Glancing back, she noticed his enigmatic smile. "What are you looking so pleased about?"

"To be frank, it had crossed my mind that this might be another one of your good-bye scenes. Obviously it isn't, since you don't seem averse to talking."

"But you will be leaving sometime," Laura said lightly, releasing his hand and crossing to her pile of clothes.

"Why? Because of that ring on your finger?" Sebastian mocked. "Rutledge isn't going to make you happy."

"You're wrong," she replied easily and stepped into her jeans, tugging them up her wet legs.

"Am I?" He aimed a taunting smile her way as he scooped his jeans off the ground. "You're obviously not in love with the man, or you wouldn't be cheating on him already."

For a stunned instant, Laura simply stared at him, then slipped on her bra and worked to fasten it. "I'm not really cheating on him."

"Then what am I?" Sebastian challenged lightly. "A last fling before you walk down the aisle?"

The corners of her mouth deepened in a smile. "That's exactly what you are. Disappointed?"

"Not in the least." Jeans on, he sat on the ground and pulled on his boots.

"Good. Because when you leave, I don't want you to go away mad."

"But it wouldn't bother you at all if I left with a broken heart, would it?" Sebastian picked up his shirt and unfastened the rest of the buttons.

A laugh bubbled from her. "And it's very likely you will be brokenhearted, because you'll leave the way you came, with empty pockets."

"No one can fool you, can they?" He smiled.

"Actually, you did, but not for long." After tugging on her last boot, Laura stretched out a hand so he could pull her upright.

Together they walked over to where the horses were grazing and gathered up the trailing reins. "In time you will become very bored with Boone," Sebastian stated as he swung into the saddle.

"And why is that?" Laura asked, her enjoyment for this back-and-forth banter showing in her expression.

"Because you'll find you can't match wits with an unarmed person."

She made a face of mock dismay. "Ooh, that's an old joke, Sebastian."

"But extremely accurate in this case."

"He suits me," Laura declared and pointed her horse toward home.

With their hair wet and clothes damp from the brief swim, neither was inclined to dawdle along the way. They cantered across the moonlit plains on a straight course to the Triple C headquarters and crossed the river just south of the barns.

After seeing to the horses and stowing the tack, they set out for The Homestead. Sebastian's hand brushed the back of her hair as he companionably draped an arm around her shoulders.

"Your hair feels dry," he remarked idly.

"Almost," Laura confirmed and let her glance wander over the white-pillared facade of the big house, noting its many darkened windows. "I wonder what time it is."

"Somewhere around midnight, I imagine. Hardly late by your standards."

"By Boone's it is. Ranchers are always early risers."

"I've noticed that," he murmured.

"Uncivilized, isn't it?" Laura replied, tossing him a smile.

"Very," he agreed. "Were you planning to call Boone—and ease your conscience a little?"

"Not for the reason you think. I just remembered he was supposed to call tonight."

"Poor man," Sebastian murmured in feigned sympathy, letting his arm fall from her shoulders as they started up the veranda steps. "No doubt he expected his loving fiancée to be sitting by the phone waiting for his call. Instead she's off swimming nude in the moonlight with another man."

"I don't think I'll tell him that." Laura said, matching his teasing tone.

"I wouldn't, either, if I were you," he agreed, perfectly straight-faced. "I suspect he wouldn't be very understanding."

"Would you be?" she countered, stepping back as Sebastian opened the front door for her.

"I'm here, aren't I?"

Having no quick answer for that, Laura walked into the house. The utter stillness of it had an immediate impact as she instinctively spoke in a hushed voice, "I think everyone's asleep."

"As you said, it is late," he murmured. "Long past time for naughty little girls to be tucked into bed."

"That sounds remarkably like an offer." She slanted him an upward glance of amusement.

"That doesn't sound like a refusal," Sebastian countered and let her lead the way across the darkened living room to the oak staircase.

"Rein in the horses, Charlie," Laura admonished him. "Right

now I think a hot shower will provide all the warming up I need."

"If you should change your mind, you do know where my room is," he said, following her up the stairs. "And the name is Sebastian."

"My mistake, and I do know where you're sleeping. But it isn't in my bed."

"Perhaps another night," he suggested and accompanied Laura to her bedroom door.

Turning, she put her back to it. "I doubt you'll be staying that long."

"You might be surprised." He leaned a hand on the doorjamb near her head. "I enjoyed our moonlight excursion immensely."

As he dipped his head toward hers, Laura turned the doorknob and backed into her bedroom, eluding his kiss. "Good night." Her eyes laughed at him as she closed the door.

Sebastian remained where he was, and waited. In mere seconds the door was jerked open, and a stunned Laura faced him. "The portrait," she began and threw a quick glance at the painting propped on a chair in her bedroom, as if to confirm it was still there. "How . . . When . . . ?"

It was the first time he'd known her to be at a loss for words. "I didn't spend the entire time after dinner on the phone with Helen."

"But . . . why?" Confusion clouded her expression, along with a certain wariness.

"I should think it's obvious; I wanted you to have it," Sebastian replied easily. "After all, Lady Elaine was never an ancestor of mine, while it seems quite likely that you are related to her."

Turning, Laura moved out of the doorway and walked back to the chair with the painting. "But it's always hung in Crawford Hall."

Sebastian let his hand fall from the doorjamb and wandered

into the room behind her. "It would have ultimately fallen to the gavel, as Crawford Hall will, along with the bulk of its contents. Rather than have that happen, I prefer to give it to you as a memento of your visit to England."

"You said it had little value. Surely you could have kept it." Her gaze studied him, alert to any change in his expression, no matter how small or brief.

"I have no need for a portrait to remind me of you." A wry smile curved his mouth. "Forgive me for sounding maudlin, but you have haunted my mind since the day you left Crawford Hall. It came as a bit of a start to realize that I had fallen in love with you."

Amused, Laura cocked her head. "You don't really expect me to believe that, do you?"

Sebastian chuckled. "Ever the skeptic, aren't you? I would have an easier time of it if your name was Smith or Brown and your bank balance no better than mine. Ironic, isn't it? Initially I pursued you for your wealth, and now I wish you didn't possess it."

"You are a smooth one, Sebastian." There was a trace of admiration in her chiding tone.

"Naturally. That's why you find me so irresistible. In fact, I suspect you're more than a little in love with me right now." Standing less than an arm's length from her, he raised his hand and traced the curve of her cheek with his fingertips. Her skin tingled from the featherlight contact.

"Maybe a little," Laura conceded, honest with herself and him. "You are always so full of surprises. But I am not about to marry you."

"Boone is a much safer matrimonial choice, isn't he? He has money, while I am a . . . poor risk, shall we say?" Sebastian remarked, eyes twinkling.

She laughed. "An extremely poor risk."

"But our life together would never be dull. I doubt the same could be said of a life with Boone."

"Just the same, he suits me."

"Not as well as I do," Sebastian countered, then paused. "I have a proposition for you."

"I can hardly wait to hear this," Laura mocked.

"Return his ring, marry me, and keep your money."

His words brought a little surge of hope, but Laura quickly saw through them. "How very clever."

"Clever?" One eyebrow arched in silent inquiry at her choice of adjectives. "I thought it was very simple and straightforward."

"But if I keep the money, you'll lose Crawford Hall. Then where would we live?" Laura challenged.

"I have a small flat in London."

She shook her head. "That wouldn't do at all. I'd want to live in something big and grand..." The pause was deliberate. "Something like Crawford Hall. And if I'm buying a large estate, why not the family manor? It would be logical to own the place that goes with title. And you're counting on that, aren't you?"

There was a flicker of annoyance in his expression. "Clearly your mind is much more devious than mine." His mouth had a slightly grim set to it that seemed to match the new, cool amusement in his eyes. "Enjoy the portrait, Laura. At least I'll have the consolation of knowing that every time you look at it, you'll think of me and wonder."

He made a leisurely turn and walked out of the room, pulling the door closed behind him. Laura stood there, certain she hadn't been wrong in her assessment. His leaving was merely an attempt to plant some doubt in her mind. And yet...

She looked at the painting and wondered.

Chapter Sixteen

⎯⎯⎯⎯⎯⎯⎯⎯⎯⎯⎯

⌒⌒⌒

The first rays of sunrise poured through the bedroom window. Conscious of the glare of it against his eyelids, Sebastian turned over and punched the pillow under him, bolstering its thickness. The muffled sound of footsteps came from the hallway, signaling he wasn't the only one in this house of early risers who was awake. For a moment he lay there, listening to the quick tattoo of the footsteps descending the stairs.

Giving up any thought that he might go back to sleep, he threw back the covers and rolled out of bed. After a quick trip to the bathroom, he padded over to the closet, briefly surveyed the clothes on hangers, and picked up the suitcase on the closet floor. He placed it on the bed and flipped it open, then walked to the chest of drawers.

More footsteps moved along the hall and stopped at his door. A knuckle rapped twice against it, and the latch clicked as the door swung open.

Trey poked his head into the room. "I thought I heard you moving around in here. We're moving cattle this morning. I thought I'd see if you wanted to—" He broke off in mid-sentence the instant he noticed the suitcase lying open on the bed. "You aren't thinking of leaving just when things are about to heat up, are you?" There was something of a challenge in his question.

Sebastian paused, sending him a curious look. "I beg your pardon."

"We're going to have company tonight," Trey told him. "Crockett's flying in. I have the feeling a little blackbird called Tara might have told him you were here."

"In that case, it might be better for all concerned if I leave."

"It might." Trey stepped into the room and leaned his tall shape against the doorframe, loosely folding his arms in front of him. "Personally, though, I'm hoping he'll screw up. That isn't likely to happen if you're gone."

"Are you hoping we'll get into a physical fight over your sister's hand?" Sebastian mocked lightly.

"Knowing Laura, she'd like that. No, it'll be enough if you just get under his skin." Trey pushed away from the door and walked to the bed. "If he's the bastard I think he is, he'll take care of the rest himself. It's for sure you won't be needing this." He closed the suitcase, checked to make sure it was securely latched, and carried it to the closet. After a scan of the clothes hanging up, he turned. "If you're going with me, you'd better put on those jeans you wore yesterday. If you wear any of those," he jerked a thumb in the direction of the closet, "you're likely to scare the cattle."

"You are making the assumption that I'm staying," Sebastian observed dryly.

Trey paused with one hand on the doorknob. There was something about the calm steadiness of his gaze that reminded Sebastian of the elder Calder. "Aren't you?"

The lazy challenge made Sebastian smile. "It would seem so." He pushed the drawer shut and walked over to retrieve the Levis.

"We'll pull out as soon as you come down," Trey informed him. "I've got a thermos of coffee in the truck, and I'll have Allie throw a breakfast sandwich together for you."

Sebastian spared a glance at the dawn blush outside his window. "Tell me, is it tradition that a cowboy must be in the saddle before the sun is up."

"You could call it that, I suppose," Trey again. "But for something to become a tradition out here, there's always a good reason for it. In this case, when you're moving a herd of cows from one pasture to another, it's easier to make the gather early, before the calves nurse and cows scatter to graze. This way you have a better chance of arriving with your herd intact. See you downstairs." With that he exited the room, leaving Sebastian to dress.

Laura didn't get out of bed until nearly eleven o'clock. It was closer to eleven-thirty when she came downstairs. After a cup of coffee and a slice of toast, she placed a call to Boone, only to be informed by the Mexican housekeeper that neither Senor Max nor Senor Boone was in.

With Sebastian off somewhere with Trey, Laura opted to visit her Aunt Cat Echohawk rather than while away the afternoon at The Homestead by herself. Between catching up on the latest news about Quint and discussing possible wedding plans, it was four o'clock before she set off to make the hour-long drive back to the Triple C.

When she pulled into the ranch yard, Laura spotted Sebastian and Trey walking up the incline to The Homestead. She honked the horn as she drove by them, then parked near the base of the veranda steps and climbed out to wait for them. A smile curved her mouth when she noticed both the telltale red of a sunburn and the stiff way Sebastian was walking.

"You seem to be moving a little gingerly, Sebastian. Have a few sore muscles, do you?" Laura teased.

"More than a few, I suspect," he admitted with an airy honesty. "This is the first time I have spent an entire day astride a horse."

"Poor man. Too bad Grizwold isn't here to draw you a hot bath so you can soak away some of that soreness."

"There is much to recommend the comforts of Crawford Hall," Sebastian declared on an exaggeratedly wistful note.

The front door opened behind Laura, but she was too accustomed to the comings and goings of people at The Homestead to pay any attention to it. "I guess you'll have to settle for a hot shower," she told Sebastian. "But you're going to need some lotion for that sunburn."

As she turned to climb the steps, her gaze lifted. Surprise brought her to a complete stop when she saw Boone standing at the top, a dark impatience glittering in his eyes and a hint of grimness around his mouth.

Recovering from that initial shock, she glided up the steps and into his arms, all smiles. "Boone, darling. When you did you get here?"

"About an hour ago." His hands gripped her upper arms, his look softening when he met her upturned gaze. Then it hardened once more when his glance flicked past her to Sebastian.

"Why didn't you call and let me know you were coming?" The protest was nothing more than a ploy to reclaim his attention. "Not that it matters. I'm just glad you're here."

"It's my fault, Sis," Trey spoke. "Boone called last night to say he was flying in this afternoon. I took off this morning and forgot to leave the message for you."

"There was no harm done. Was there?" When Laura looked to Boone for confirmation of her claim, he was staring at Sebastian.

"I didn't think you'd have the guts to show up here, Dunshill," Boone said tightly, then allowed a cold smile to twist his mouth. "You're a little late, though. Laura's marrying me."

She laughed softly. "How very macho you sound, Boone. After you see what he brought, you're going to be glad he came. Come on." She linked an arm with his. "Let's go inside so I can show you."

She ushered Boone into the house, trailed by Sebastian and Trey, the sound of their footsteps accompanied by the jingle of

Trey's spurs. In the living room she stopped and placed a detaining hand on Boone's broad chest.

"You wait here and I'll bring it down." As she crossed to the staircase, Laura threw a glance at her brother. "Give me a hand, will you, Trey?"

"Sure," he agreed and lengthened his stride to catch up with her.

Sebastian paused in the living room and slipped off the straw Resistol. Reaching up, he combed his fingers through the sides of his hair, flattened by the hatband. All the while he visually tracked Laura's ascent of the stairs, he was conscious of Boone's gaze boring into him, but he chose not to acknowledge it. With each passing second the silence in the room thickened.

The instant Laura disappeared from sight, it was broken. "I don't give a damn what you brought, Dunshill." Boone's low voice vibrated with anger. "You're not wanted here. Unfortunately, Laura is too polite to tell you to hit the road."

Sebastian smiled without humor and sent him a sideways glance. "But you are bound by no such constraints, are you?"

"Your fancy talking doesn't impress me. Neither does your title," Boone retorted. "We both know you're after one thing—to con Laura out of her money. Haven't you figured it out yet that Laura is wise to you?"

"Oh yes." Sebastian nodded. "She's made that abundantly clear."

"Then get yourself on the next plane out of here," Boone growled as footsteps and jangling spurs came from the upper hall.

Sebastian merely smiled. "All in good time, old boy."

Laura's reappearance at the top of the steps, accompanied by Trey carrying the framed painting, forced Boone to bite back any sharp retort he might have been inclined to make. She ran lightly down and across the room to Boone, slipping an arm around his waist and fitting herself to his side.

"Look." With an outstretched hand, she indicated the painting that Trey held up to view. "The portrait of Lady Elaine. Isn't it wonderful?"

"It certainly is." A little tightness remained in the smile Boone gave her. It went with the resentment in the glance he sent Sebastian. "That was very generous of you, Dunshill."

"It was, wasn't it?" Laura agreed and turned a curious look on Sebastian. "Considering how desperate you are for cash, I don't understand why you didn't call Max. As interested as he was in acquiring the portrait, you could have sold it to him for considerably more than its worth. Why didn't you?"

"If I'd wanted him to own it, I would have," Sebastian replied smoothly. "But I preferred that you have it."

"I'm glad you did. I absolutely love it," Laura declared, her attention once again on the portrait that bore such a striking resemblance to her.

"I think we should hang it above the fireplace at the Slash R, don't you?" Boone's remark was far from an idle one. It was a pointed reminder of his pending marriage to Laura.

"That might seem a little vain," Laura suggested. "But we'll find the perfect place for it."

"While you two thrash out where the portrait is to be hung, I think I'll make good use of the shower facilities." Excusing himself, Sebastian crossed to the stairs.

"That goes for me, too," Trey said and lifted a hand to Boone. "See you later at dinner."

Laura covered their departure by giving Boone an embracing squeeze. "I'm so glad you came."

"Why didn't you tell me Dunshill was here?" His sharp gaze searched her face.

"When did I have a chance?" she countered in wide-eyed innocence. "I was out when you called me, and you were gone when I called you back."

"I'm surprised you didn't show him the door, considering what you know about him."

"But, darling," Laura turned into his arms and ran her fingers along the open front of his shirt collar, "I couldn't be that rude, not when he gave me the painting of Lady Elaine."

"Just how long has he been here?"

"A couple of days," Laura answered with a shrug. "Hardly long enough to get over his jet lag. More important," she said, linking her fingers behind his neck and arching against him, "how long will you be staying?"

"I'm not leaving until he does." It was a flat, hard statement.

Laura's smile widened. "In that case, I'll make sure he stays a long time."

"Dammit, Laura." The words came from him in an explosive burst.

She tipped her head back and laughed low in her throat. "Really, darling, you can't possibly be jealous of him. Not now." Rising on her tiptoes, she rubbed her moist lips over the tight line of his mouth until his arms circled her and crushed her in a hard, claim-staking embrace.

Laura couldn't say why she was reluctant to send Sebastian on his way. It would have been an easy thing to do. She suspected it was a natural resistance on her part to having someone else impose his will on her.

She suggested as much to Tara the following day when she and Boone spent the afternoon poolside at Tara's summer home in Wolf Meadow. When someone from the ranch in Texas called Boone on his cell phone, Tara had used the private moment with Laura to remark, "I imagine Boone was upset when he discovered Sebastian was at the ranch."

"He definitely wasn't happy." Laura rubbed a generous amount of sunscreen lotion on her leg.

"I'm surprised he didn't insist that you ask Sebastian to leave."

"He tried," Laura replied. "But he needs to learn that I won't be pressured into doing things."

"Don't be foolish, Laura," Tara stated with unexpected sharpness. "The pressure is coming from Max. You can never butt heads with Max Rutledge and win."

With a little shock, Laura realized that Tara was right, both in her identification of the source and her assessment of the outcome. "I'll figure out a way to handle him." Laura didn't kid herself that it would be easy.

"Laura," Tara said in warning, but she was prevented from saying more by Boone's return, his phone call finished.

"Everything all right at the ranch?" Laura recapped the lotion bottle and set it on the pool deck next to her chair.

"No major problems."

"Good." Her smile was quick and warm. "I have a suggestion to make. Why don't we go out to dinner tonight? Just the two of us."

"That would be a change," he replied dryly.

"That's what I thought."

Tara allowed a little frown to mar her smooth forehead. "But where will you go?"

"Harry's, of course."

"Harry's!" Tara repeated in distaste.

"I know it's a far cry from the Mansion on Turtle Creek, but they do serve a good steak," Laura replied and swung her long legs off the lounge chair. "I'm going to cool off in the pool. Join me?" she said, issuing the invitation to Boone.

"I'm right behind you."

In the purpling twilight of evening, the huge neon sign mounted atop the porch roof glowed a gaudy green, proclaiming in gigantic capital letters that it was the site of Harry's Hideaway. The hiss and sizzle from the neon tubing dominated the stillness when Sebastian stepped from the ranch pickup. His glance strayed to a second vehicle parked in the lot, its doors emblazoned with the distinctive Triple C brand.

"I suspect Laura will not be very pleased to see us," he said to

Trey when he climbed out of the driver's side and gave the door a closing push.

Trey shook his head in mild disagreement. "Crockett will be the one with his nose out of joint. Laura will be amused, wondering if fists will fly." Trey headed for the entrance, mounting the porch steps two at time. "Don't get suckered into one if you can avoid it. That would be playing into Crockett's hands."

"Why do you call him Crockett?" Sebastian wondered.

"It's a family joke." Trey opened the door and held it for Sebastian, letting him enter first, then followed him inside. "Welcome to Harry's." Amusement gleamed in his brown eyes. "I was told it wouldn't be anything like one of your English pubs."

To the left was the dining area, the source of the food smells and the muted clatter of dishes. Most of its tables were empty, but Sebastian's searching glance easily located Laura and Boone seated at a secluded table, separate from the half dozen other diners. Despite the low lights, Sebastian knew the instant she noticed him. It was almost a tangible thing. Any chance that it was wishful thinking on his part was eliminated when Boone's dark head swung around to face the door.

Trey raised an acknowledging hand in Laura's direction and struck out for the bar area on the right. It was dimly lit except for the brightly colored jukebox along the front wall and the hanging lights over the twin pool tables.

"Grab a table," Trey said as he branched off toward the silent jukebox.

None were occupied, giving Sebastian an ample choice. He picked the nearest one and pulled out a chair. Taking a seat, he glanced briefly at the two men hunched over their drinks at the end of the long bar. Behind him, the jukebox came to life, filling the half-dead bar with a lively country music tune.

Seconds later Trey joined him, swinging a leg over the chair back and lowering himself onto the seat. "That oughta wake up everybody."

The swinging doors to the kitchen swept open, and a short,

heavyset man in an apron bustled over to their table, took their order for two beers, and bustled behind the bar to fill them.

With an effort, Sebastian kept his glance from straying to Laura's table. "Is it usually this quiet?" he asked to make conversation.

"It livens up a little on Saturday night," Trey told him. "Back in Gramps' day, this used to be a roadhouse, complete with poker games in the backroom and a pair of soiled doves upstairs."

The man hustled back with two frosty mugs of beer, set them down, and scooped up the money Trey shoved onto the table. "I'll be back in the kitchen for a little bit. If you need anything else, just holler. That's what everybody else does."

"Will do." Trey nodded, took a swig of beer, and wiped the back of his hand across his mouth, blotting away the traces of foam. He slid a questioning look at Sebastian. "Do you dance?"

Sebastian smiled. "Are you asking? If you are, you should know that I prefer to lead."

Trey laughed, strong and hearty. "Wouldn't we look cute?" he declared and shook his head, the laughter still there, under the surface. "Actually, I had something else in mind. There's a slow song coming up next. I thought you could ask Laura to dance. It's a passion of hers."

"I know," Sebastian said.

The remark drew an assessing look from Trey, but no direct comment. "If Crockett knows anything other than the two-step or the box step, I'll be surprised. What about you?"

"Laura is fully aware that I can dance, if that was your thought."

"It was only half of it," Trey replied. "Me, I know a couple variations on the box step and that's about it. It really grates to watch some other guy make it look effortless, especially if he's dancing with my girl."

The hard-driving song on the jukebox ended in a crescendo of drums and guitars. The noiseless void lasted only seconds before the lilting strains of a waltz came over the speakers.

"That's your cue," Trey said and shot a look at his sister's table, then swore under his breath. "Too late. I think they're leaving."

Turning his head, Sebastian saw Laura moving toward them with a model's grace, the pale gold of her hair catching the shine of the interior lights. There was something almost regal about her carriage that came across as a kind of innate elegance, transcending the simplicity of her dress. He felt a pride in her that could have been stronger only if he were the man walking with her instead of Boone Rutledge.

Instead of veering off toward the front door, the couple continued toward them. "Well, what do you know," Trey murmured. "I think he asked her to dance."

Arriving at the small dance floor, Laura made a swinging turn into Boone's hold, her left hand gliding onto his shoulder. It was Sebastian who watched with envy as Boone held her close, shuffling his feet and making no attempt at waltz steps. And Laura didn't seem to care.

Stool legs scraped the floor near the long bar, Sebastian took little notice of it, or of the footsteps moving in the general direction of the pool tables.

One set of footsteps stopped, and a man's voice spoke loudly, "Well, lookee there. If it ain't that smart-mouthed Calder bitch."

A burly, dark-haired man with a half-empty beer mug in his hand stood near the edge of the dance floor, a look of utter loathing in his expression. If either Laura or Boone reacted to the man's remark, Sebastian didn't see it.

Trey nudged his arm. "That's Mitchell," he murmured.

Sebastian made the connection to the abused woman instantly.

As if determined to get a rise out of the couple on the dance floor, Mitchell jeered, "What're ya' doing here? I thought you and your fancy man got your kicks barging into people's houses uninvited."

This time Laura retaliated. "If I find out you've hit your wife again, it's the police who'll be barging in."

"That was an accident. You ask my wife; she'll tell you," Mitchell insisted with an indignant anger.

"Only because you'll beat her again if she doesn't," Laura retorted, giving up any pretense of dancing.

Mitchell took a threatening step forward. "Listen, you stupid little bitch—"

"You don't talk to her like that." Boone moved into his path, a hand shooting out to shove Mitchell back.

In a sudden fury, Mitchell threw the contents of his mug in Boone's face and laughed at the sight of Boone shaking his head and wiping the beer from his eyes. The laughter acted like a goad. Boone lashed out, a fist connecting with the side of Mitchell's face, staggering him.

When Boone moved in, Mitchell swung the heavy mug at his head. The force of the impact knocked him sideways. Laura cried out, and Sebastian and Trey came out of their chairs as one. Dazed, Boone attempted to shake off the effects of the blow and barely managed to dodge a second swing of the beer mug.

Laura was all ready to throw herself at Mitchell when Trey grabbed the arm that wielded the beer mug, and Sebastian caught the other one. "That's enough, Mitchell," Trey warned.

"He started it," Mitchell flared. "I was only defending myself."

There was no chance for a response as Boone came at Mitchell, taking full advantage of the fact his arms were being held. He slammed a fist into his stomach. The instant, Mitchell doubled over, Boone unleashed an uppercut that snapped Mitchell backward.

Laura threw herself in front of Boone, gripping his upper arms in an attempt to hold him off. "What are you thinking?"

"He needs to be taught a lesson he won't forget," Boone growled in answer.

"Not this way," she stated and threw a glance over her shoulder as Sebastian and Trey succeeded in lifting the semiconscious man onto a chair.

The commotion had drawn the owner from the kitchen.

"What's going on here?" he asked, but none too sure he wanted to know.

"Just a little misunderstanding. It's over now," Trey replied. "Get some whiskey."

The owner hustled toward the bar while Mitchell's beer-drinking buddy remained where he had been, halfway between the bar and the pool tables, quietly taking it all in.

"He's all right, isn't he?" Laura asked.

"He will be," Trey said as Mitchell groggily lifted his head and raised a hand to his sore chin.

It took a second for his eyes to focus clearly. When they did, he searched out Boone. "That was assault. I'm gonna sue you Calders for every dime you've got. Don't think I won't"

"You just try it," Boone snarled.

"Come on. I want to go home." Laura made a determined effort to turn Boone toward the door.

"You go on home," Mitchell taunted. "And stay the hell away from mine."

Laura could feel the bunching of Boone's muscles. "Darling, please," she murmured insistently. "I want to get out of here."

With obvious reluctance, Boone dragged his gaze from Mitchell and curved a protective arm around her. He escorted her to the door, tossed some bills on the counter to cover the cost of their meal, and opened the door for her.

PART THREE

Amid the fury and grief
The truth shines so bright.
A Calder gives her promise
To the only man who's right.

Chapter Seventeen

The warmth of the summer night closed around her the minute
Laura stepped outside. But it failed to relax the tension that
screamed through her nerves. She stiffened slightly at the guiding
touch of Boone's hand on her back.

Neither said a word as they walked to the Suburban. Boone
helped her into the passenger seat, closed the door, and circled
around to the driver's side to slide behind the wheel. Seconds after
he started the engine, air blasted from the dashboard vents, the
temperature of it gradually cooling.

All tight with anger, Laura faced the window and stared into
the nothingness, an elbow propped on the door and curled fingers
pressed to her mouth. Utility poles whipped by outside the window as the silence between them grew more oppressive.

Laura finally broke it, her voice taut with the effort to keep her
temper in check. "I can't believe you did that."

"What did you expect me to do?" Boone demanded. "Sit and
say nothing like Dunshill, while some drunk calls you names?
Sorry, I'm not made that way." There was a flexing jump of a
muscle along his jaw, but Laura was too angry to notice.

"That's not what I'm talking about. It's the way you hit

Mitchell when he was completely defenseless. That was vicious and uncalled for."

A breath of disgust exploded from Boone. "Leave it to a woman to think like that. If you'd ever been in a fight, you'd know that when you've got a man down, you keep 'em down any way you can." He slanted her a sharp look. "Who is this guy? What was that business of you being in his home?"

Tersely Laura provided him with a recap of the circumstances surrounding the one and only time she had been inside the Mitchell house. When she finished, this time it was Boone who demanded, "What the hell were you thinking? Nothing but trouble comes from involving yourself in somebody else's domestic problems. That's why we have police and social workers."

It was a view she once would have echoed, but somewhere along the line doubt had crept in. "What kind of world would it be if everybody felt that way?" Laura said, voicing the question that was in her mind.

"That sounds like the kind of crap Dunshill would spout," Boone said with contempt. "People like that are nothing but trash. I don't want you associating with them anymore. I don't care how well-intentioned the reason."

For a tight-lipped moment, Laura said nothing. "You are going to be lucky if Mitchell doesn't sue."

"If he does, he'll find out you don't sue a Rutledge and get away with it."

Sebastian and Trey returned to a darkened house. The silence of it pushed at them the minute they walked inside. Pausing in the entryway, Trey swept off his hat and listened a moment, then glanced at Sebastian.

"I had a feeling everybody might be in bed. My sister doesn't get mad often, but when she does, she tends to stay mad for a while. And she wasn't too happy when she left Harry's."

"It was an unpleasant scene." Sebastian glanced in the direction of the second floor, his expression thoughtful. "No doubt Rutledge is of the opinion Mitchell provoked the attack and therefore justified it. As so often happens in the heat of battle, a man's actions are more often dictated by instinct than good judgment." It was an absent comment, his thoughts centering on Mitchell's drinking and the potential repercussions on his wife.

"That's the first time you actually sounded like a lawyer," Trey said with amusement. "I think I'll go raid the refrigerator and see if I can't rustle up something to eat. Care to join me?"

"Thank you, but no. I think I'll follow the example of the rest of the family and retire for the evening."

"See you in the morning, then." Trey's long strides carried him in the direction of the kitchen.

Sebastian made his way to the staircase at a slower pace. When he reached the top of the steps, his gaze automatically strayed to Laura's bedroom door. A slit of light showed beneath it. He hesitated, then crossed to it.

Indecision held him motionless in front of it for several long seconds. There was only silence from within. He raised his hand and started to knock, then changed his mind and lowered it as footsteps crossed the living room below him.

Obeying the hush of the rest of the house, he moved silently away from her door. By the time he reached the bedroom, Trey was halfway up the steps, the white of a sandwich showing in his hand.

As Sebastian turned the doorknob to his room, Laura's door sprang open. She stood within the doorframe, fully backlit, the silken texture of her night-robe glistening, creating a sensuous outline of her feminine shape.

For an instant she froze at the sight of Trey. "I thought—" Laura began. Then her gaze flew past him, straight to Sebastian. He turned from it and entered his bedroom. "Never mind," she said to Trey and spun away from the door.

Trey cast a considering glance after Sebastian and crossed the few feet to her room. He paused at its threshold. "You okay, Sis?"

"Of course." The curtness of her voice said something else.

He studied the stiff, tight way she held herself. "Are you still going to marry that guy?"

Laura flashed him an angry look, dark eyes snapping. "Shut up, Trey. Just shut up." She grabbed the door and gave it a swing, shutting it in his face.

The morning sun was still low in the sky when Laura came down the steps the next day. The familiar thump of her grandfather's cane came from the hallway that led to his ground-floor room in The Homestead's west wing. The sound of it grew steadily nearer, signaling his approach. Laura had a warm smile ready for him when he hobbled into view.

"Good morning, Gramps."

He paused in surprise. "You're up early."

"I don't always sleep until noon." Laura saw no reason to admit that her sleep had been less than restful. "Have you seen Boone?"

"He had breakfast with everybody about an hour ago, then commandeered the den." He nodded in the direction of the room, its doors firmly shut in an apparent request for privacy. "Said he had some calls to make."

"I see," Laura murmured.

"There's a pot of coffee waiting for me on the veranda," Chase told her. "You're welcome to grab a cup from the dining room and join me."

Her hesitation was momentary. "I'll do that."

When they reached the entryway, they separated, Chase continuing outside while Laura crossed to the dining room. She found the housekeeper, Allie McGuire, busily clearing away the covered warming pans from the side table. She offered to fix Laura a hot breakfast. Laura declined in favor of a slice of toast slathered with jam.

Carrying both the empty coffee cup and the toast, Laura joined her grandfather, taking a seat in the twin to his rocker. "Where's Sebastian this morning?" she asked while he filled her cup with coffee from the insulated carafe. "Did he go off again with Trey?"

"Not today, he didn't. Said he wanted to walk off breakfast." Chase's glance made an idle sweep of the ranch yard. "He's wandering around there somewhere."

Laura nibbled on the jam-covered toast without really tasting it. A sip of coffee only seemed to add to the restlessness that had plagued her all night.

"I suppose you heard about the fight last night." As much as she was loathe to discuss it, she also knew it was a subject that had to be confronted.

Chase rocked slowly back and forth. "Trey told me about it."

"I can imagine what he said." Irritation crept into her voice.

"Was it the truth?" The words held a challenge that didn't match the conversational level of his voice.

Laura avoided a direct answer. "The truth is rarely black and white. I would certainly have thought less of Boone if he hadn't objected to abusive language that was used in addressing me."

"True." The pace of his rocking never changed.

"You don't think I should marry him, do you?" The tilt of her chin signaled her readiness for an argument.

"It doesn't matter what I think, Laura," Chase replied evenly. "The only thing that matters is what you want."

"There are worse faults a man can have," she insisted.

"I expect there are." He rocked a few more times. "Just out of curiosity, if you had to describe your fiancé to someone, what would you say about him?"

The unexpected question had Laura scrambling for a quick answer. "I don't know. I suppose I would say that he's the son of Max Rutledge from Texas—"

Chase didn't let her get any further. "That's an interesting way to begin. When most women talk about the men they plan to marry, they go on about how wonderful they are, how thoughtful and caring, or how funny and warm. They're usually slow to mention who they are related to. It seems to me you only have one question you need to answer—whether it's Boone Rutledge you're marrying or the son of Max Rutledge. If it's the latter, it doesn't matter what happened last night."

His words were like a slap in the face. Laura desperately wanted to hit back. It was infuriating to realize she couldn't, because there was a little too much truth in his statement.

"But whatever you do," Chase added, "just don't close your eyes to what you might be getting into."

"I know exactly what I'm doing." But she wasn't sure if she resented his suggestion that she didn't or that she was making a mistake marrying Boone.

"Good." He reached over and patted her hand, then settled back in the rocker. "Speak of the devil, here comes Sebastian now."

Turning, Laura saw Sebastian sauntering toward the veranda, his hands casually thrust in his pockets, the sun at his back, its rays igniting the russet lights in his hair. A pain twisted through her. Refusing to acknowledge it, she pushed out of the rocking chair.

"I think I'll go see if Boone has finished with his business calls," she said in parting and crossed to the front door, reaching it as Sebastian started up the veranda steps.

Laura was halfway across the entryway when the housekeeper appeared in the dining room arch and halted at the sight of Laura. "That's good timing," Allie declared. "I was just coming out to get you. Jack Weldon's on the phone. He asked to talk to you."

Laura frowned. "I don't know anyone named Jack Weldon."

Allie MacGuire waved a hand. "Sure you do. He's Harry's son, the one that took over the bar when Harry passed."

Laura's frown deepened. "Did he say what he wanted?" She asked as the front door opened behind her and Sebastian entered.

"Not really. He mentioned something about the Mitchell woman." Allie's shoulders lifted in a vague shrug. "Do you want to talk to him, or shall I tell him you aren't available?"

Sebastian answered for her, "She'll take the call."

"I'll make that decision, thank you," Laura flared at him.

Completely unmoved by her show of temper, Sebastian replied calmly, "Mitchell was still at the bar last night when Trey and I left. No doubt he was far from sober when he finally went home. We told her to go to Harry's. Remember?" Laura wanted to deny that it was any concern of hers, but the image of the woman's bruised and battered face came sharply back to her. Sensing the beginnings of agreement, he repeated to the housekeeper, "She'll take the call."

"I'll use the extension in the living room," Laura said by way of acknowledgement and moved in that direction, conscious of Sebastian shadowing her. She tried to ignore the physical awareness she had of him, without success.

In the living room she walked straight to the phone, picked up the receiver, and turned, angling her position to bring Sebastian into view. "This is Laura Calder."

"Miss Calder, this is Jack Weldon . . . from Harry's." There was uncertainty in his voice. "I'm sorry to bother you so early, but . . . Mitchell's wife and kids are here. I don't know how to say this, but . . . she claims you told her to come to my place."

Laura's mouth curved in a humorless smile at the blatant skepticism in his statement. "Yes, I did."

Before she could ask if Gail Mitchell was all right, Jack Weldon said in a shocked tone of voice, "Sorry, I never realized you knew her."

"Well, I do. Is she okay?" Laura asked while Sebastian watched her, intent on every word she said.

"She says she is, but her face doesn't look it. That's why I'm calling. She can't stay here," he rushed on. "I feel sorry for her; really, I do. That husband of hers is no prize. But I've got a business to run, and it ain't a shelter for battered women. She just flat can't stay here."

"Where's Mitchell?" Sebastian prompted.

Laura nodded and asked, "Where's her husband? Do you know?"

"No. She claims he came home roarin' drunk around, oh, thirty minutes ago. She said she quick locked all the doors, and while he was banging and swearing at the back, she and the kids snuck out the front." There was a small pause. "Somewhere she got the idea in her head she could hide out here until he slept the worst of it off." He didn't come right out and ask whether Laura had told her that, but the implication was there. "But she just can't. I don't mean to sound hard-hearted, but she's got to leave. You know as well as I do what a troublemaker that Mitchell is. Sooner or later he's gonna find out she came here, and when he does, that's gonna make him mad. I know you meant well when you told her to come here, but—"

"What's the problem?" Sebastian asked in quiet demand, his question coming over the top of the bar owner's words.

"Just a minute," Laura said into the phone, then clamped a hand over the mouthpiece to answer Sebastian. "She took the kids out the front when Mitchell was trying to get in the back door. The owner of the bar isn't going to let her stay there. He's afraid Mitchell will make trouble for him," she said, eliminating the lengthy attempts at justification that had been sandwiched between the owner's expressions of concern.

"Tell him to keep her there until I arrive," Sebastian said.

"But where will you take her?"

"To the nearest hotel—wherever that may be," he answered with a droll smile. Then he was moving toward the front door.

As she removed her hand from the mouthpiece, Laura made a split-second decision. "We'll be there as soon as we can. In the meantime fix them some breakfast. I'll pay for it when I get there." She hung up. By the time she noticed Boone standing in the doorway to the den, her mind was already made up. She called after Sebastian, "Wait, I'm coming with you."

"Where are you going?" Boone demanded, the darkness of displeasure in his expression.

"To town." Her footsteps never slowed or altered their straight course to the entryway.

Boone blocked her path. "You aren't going anywhere with Dunshill."

Laura knew all the ways and words to get around his objection and bolster his already sizable ego at the same time. Strangely, she had absolutely no desire to do so.

"I don't take orders, Boone. Not from you or your father or anybody." She took advantage of his momentary shock to shoulder her way past him.

Laura was halfway to the door before Boone managed to recover some of his former bluster. "Dammit, Laura," he began.

But she was already walking out the door. In long, stiff strides, he crossed to the door and stepped onto the columned veranda, catching only a glimpse of Laura as she slipped into the passenger seat of Sebastian's rental car.

A rocking chair made its slow back-and-forth movement in his side vision. Turning, Boone saw the elder Calder and vented some of his irritation.

"Why is she going off with him? She knows he's after her money. What's gotten into her?"

"Hard to say. When Laura gets high-headed like that, she's hard to rein down."

Lips thinning into a tight line, Boone made no reply and simply stared at the car reversing away from The Homestead.

Dust plumed behind the compact sedan as it sped along the main graveled road that led to the ranch's east gate. Morning sunlight poured through the windshield. Laura flipped the visor down to block its glare and wished for her sunglasses.

"You realize the nearest motel is miles from here," she told Sebastian somewhat caustically. "You can't just take her there and leave her. How will she get back? You're kidding yourself if you think she'll even agree to leave Blue Moon."

"I'm open to an alternative suggestion," Sebastian replied with the lazy ease that was so typical of him. It was an attitude Laura usually found appealing, but in the mood she was in this morning, she found it annoying. She kept her gaze transfixed on the straight road ahead of them.

"I wish I had my cell phone. Then I could call Tara. Dy-Corp has several houses in town that are sitting empty. I'm sure she could arrange for Gail and the children to stay in one of them temporarily. I'll call her when we get to Harry's."

"A house in town would mean the children would have to stay inside to prevent Mitchell from seeing them," Sebastian remarked.

"It wouldn't be any different at a motel."

"Most that I have seen have swimming pools."

"You're determined to get her out of town, aren't you?" Laura turned a challenging look on him.

"It would be better," Sebastian replied evenly.

"Why are you doing any of this?" she demanded. "Boone thinks it's all an attempt to impress me by showing how caring and compassionate you can be."

"Are you impressed?" He glanced at her, eyes atwinkle.

Laura refused to give in to his considerable charm. "I am never impressed by stupidity. Trying to help a woman who's married to a wife-beater is a waste of time. It never seems to matter how many times he pounds on her, she always believes him when he promises it won't happen again. And it always does," she said with exasperation. "She claims she loves him. Maybe she's in love with the man she wants him to be, but she is definitely not in love with the man who knocks her around. So why do they keep going back? Is it guilt? Do they honestly believe they've done something to cause this? Is it fear? Do they think they can't make it on their own? If the man died, they'd find a way. They wouldn't have any choice."

"I suspect there is always more than one factor at work." The calm pitch of his voice never changed.

"How do you know?" Laura eyed him with sharpened interest,

then said sarcastically, "Are you a champion of battered women back in England?"

A smile tugged at a corner of his mouth. "Do I detect a trace of bitterness? You and Boone must have had words last night. Naturally, you have no wish to speak sharply to the love of your life, not when I make such a handy whipping boy."

"You're very good at taking the conversation off in some other direction to avoid answering questions," Laura stated. "But it isn't going to work this time."

"I see that." He nodded thoughtfully and let a silence fall.

"So answer me," she said impatiently.

"The truth?" Sebastian countered with a quick, sideways glance. "I only ask because, in the past when I've spoken the truth, you've chosen not to believe me."

"You're doing it again, Sebastian, and I refuse to be side-tracked."

"The reason isn't really mine to tell," Sebastian replied somewhat cryptically. "Helen is the one you should ask."

"Your sister?" Laura frowned in surprise. "Are you saying she was abused?"

"Surely you don't believe it happens only to women in the lower scale of society?" he queried. "I suspect it's equally prevalent in the so-called privileged class, where it's often kept as a dark secret, perhaps out of pride or shame."

"You're serious." Laura digested that fact, then said, "But your sister seemed like such an intelligent and sensible woman."

"It's a conundrum, isn't it?" Sebastian replied. "Fortunately she had a friend who recognized all the hallmarks of an abusive relationship and held a hand out without ever becoming judgmental."

Laura remembered his own lack of criticism in dealing with Gail Mitchell. "I was pretty rough with Gail," she recalled.

"But you never pulled your hand back." There was a tenderness in the look he gave her that warmed Laura all the way through.

Suddenly all the inner turmoil was gone—the odd anger and edginess. In its place was a kind of heady calm. Sebastian drove through the east gate and turned onto the two-lane highway, heading north to Blue Moon.

An easy silence settled between them for a long run of miles. Rooftops jutted into the horizon ahead of them, their uneven angles close to the highway, making a jagged line against the sky. Standing two stories tall, close to the highway, Harry's was easy to identify from the rest.

Prompted by its nearness, Laura remarked idly, "I hope Mitchell was too drunk to go looking for his wife and kids when he discovered they weren't in the house. If he showed up at Harry's, I'm not sure Weldon would try to interfere—or call the police."

"I suspect your assumptions are accurate." Sebastian didn't bother to reduce the car's speed until they were closer to town.

To Laura's relief, the parking lot at Harry's was empty of vehicles. With a turn of the steering wheel, Sebastian swung the car into the driveway and stopped directly in front of the entrance. As Laura stepped out of the car, she happened to glance across the highway. The vehicle parked beside the pump island sported a light bar on its roof and a county sheriff's insignia on its door. Her attention instantly shifted to the uniformed officer making his way to the store at an easy walk. Even though his back was to her, Laura recognized him instantly.

"There's Logan across the way," she said to Sebastian, comforted by the knowledge that Logan was close by if they needed him.

As Sebastian turned to look, a bell jingled, signaling the opening of the door to Harry's. The squat owner, Jack Weldon, stepped into the open doorway.

"It's about time you got here," he declared, clearly agitated. "You'd better drive around back. Mitchell's across the street at Fedderson's."

Surprise held Laura motionless for a split second. As she swung around to look, two short, explosive pops rang out. Ranch-raised, she recognized the sound of gunshots. Even as fear leaped within her, she saw Logan pivot drunkenly away from the door he held open, his knees buckling, a dark stain on the front of his uniform.

"No!" The scream came from her own throat when he crumpled to the ground, though Laura was unaware of it.

On legs that felt strangely wooden and slow, she ran toward her fallen uncle. Sebastian caught and held her before she ever reached the highway. As she struggled to twist loose, the whole of her attention was riveted on Logan, lying motionless. She was only vaguely aware of the man who bolted from the store and scrambled to a pickup parked near its entrance.

Not until she heard the slam of the pickup and the engine roar to life did Laura take notice of the light blue pickup. As the truck peeled onto the highway, she got a good look at the driver; it was Mitchell.

Sebastian abruptly released her and took off for Fedderson's. Laura ran after him, her heart hammering, fear clutching at her chest. Sebastian was the first to reach Logan's side. He lay in a limp heap, blood saturating the front of his shirt.

Sebastian took one look at him and ordered, "Call for help. Quick."

With her own eyes confirming the need for haste, Laura hurried inside, teeth clenched against the sobs in her throat. She saw no sign of the owner, Marsha Kelly, as she ran to the counter and the telephone that sat atop it. When she reached over to pick up the receiver, Laura saw the woman lying unconscious on the floor behind the narrow counter, a trickle of blood coming from a small cut on her left temple.

Spurred by the sight, Laura climbed over the counter, scooped up the receiver and rapidly punched the emergency number. "This is Laura Calder," she said the instant she received an answer and crouched next to Marsha Kelly, searching for and finding a strong, steady pulse. "I'm at Fedderson's in Blue Moon. Logan"— she caught the beginnings of panic in her voice and clamped off her emotions, recognizing the need for cool, clear thinking— "Sheriff Echohawk's been shot, at least once in the chest, and Marsha Kelly is unconscious. I saw Gary Mitchell leave here in an old Chevy pickup, light blue in color. I didn't get the license plate number. But I'm sure he's the one who shot Logan. Send an ambulance, fast."

"We have one on the way."

There were more questions to which Laura could provide few answers. Through it all she kept an eye on the glass door and the partially obstructed view it offered of Sebastian crouched over Logan. After receiving a parting caution to touch as little as possible, thus preserving any evidence at the crime scene, Laura hung up, checked again on Marsha, then made her way around the counter to the front door, using a hip to push it open.

"The ambulance is on its way," she said as Sebastian stood and turned to meet her, the red of blood on his hands and his clothes.

For an instant, he made no reply. "I'm sorry," he said at last. Laura didn't have to ask what he meant; she could tell from his solemn expression and the look of deep compassion in his eyes.

Still the disbelief came. "No." She shook her head. "He can't be dead. Not Logan."

Needing to confirm it for herself, she started to push past him, but Sebastian caught her by the arms. "He's gone, Laura. You can't bring him back. No one can."

She stiffened, wanting to deny it, but her throat knotted up, hot and painful. When Sebastian folded her silently into his arms, Laura didn't resist. Just for a moment, she let her head dip against his chest, accepting his attempt to comfort, but she couldn't stop the whirl of thoughts in her mind.

One was foremost among them. "I've got to call home."

Wrapped in an emotionless calm, she turned out of his arms and went back inside the store. When she stepped behind the counter, there was a low moan from the woman on the floor. Laura bent down to her.

"Marsha, it's Laura Calder. Can you hear me?"

"My head," she mumbled, raising a hand to her temple.

"Just lie still," Laura ordered. "There's an ambulance on the way." The words only reminded her that Logan would have no need for it.

The woman was still too dazed to offer any objection. Still, Laura kept an eye on her as she straightened and picked up the phone again. She automatically started to dial The Homestead, then remembered her mother would be at the ranch office, and punched in the digits to her personal extension.

"Mom, it's Laura," she said the minute her mother answered. She thought she sounded calm, but something in her voice must have given her away.

"What's wrong?" her mother demanded with instant concern.

"It's Logan. He's been shot." Laura heard the quick intake of breath on the other end of the line, and something squeezed her own heart. "He's dead, Mom."

There was a moment of shocked silence, followed by a slightly addled burst of questions. "How? Why? Where are you?"

Laura briefly described the events that took place, ending with, "Aunt Cat." Her voice tightened up. "She'll have to be told." And there was Quint, too, so far away.

"I'll go to her right away. Laura," she began on a worried and questioning note.

"I'll be fine, Mom," she assured her, knowing that at the moment all she felt was numbness.

Chapter Eighteen

It was ten minutes later when Laura heard the first siren, and another twenty minutes before the ambulance arrived. By then Marsha Kelly had fully regained consciousness and told Laura and Sebastian how Mitchell had walked up to the counter with a sixpack of beer and wanted to charge it.

"He claimed he had an account here. I don't know where he got that idea, because he's never had one. But he kept insisting that he did. I could tell he'd been drinking," she recalled. "And he just kept getting angrier. It didn't do any good to argue with him. Finally I told him if he didn't leave, I'd call the police. I was reaching for the phone and—I remember seeing him swing the sixpack at me. After that, it's all blank."

Nothing was missing from the register's cash drawer, but the handgun she always kept under the counter was gone. Laura could only surmise that after Mitchell knocked the woman out, he saw Logan, grabbed the gun from behind the counter, and fired in a blind panic.

As soon as the crime scene was secured, the patrol officers turned their attention to Laura and Sebastian. There were questions to be answered and statements given. More than an hour passed before they were free to leave.

News of the shooting had spread quickly, drawing the curious. Laura was conscious of their eyes on her as she slid into the passenger seat of Sebastian's rental car, but she was beyond caring. A dullness encased her.

As they turned onto the highway, she had a brief view of the stretcher being loaded into the ambulance and the body bag that lay on it.

"My father died when I was small. I always imagined, though, that he would have been like Logan if he had lived." Her voice thickened. "It's hard to believe he's really gone."

A solitary tear slipped down her cheek. Sebastian saw it; there was only one. Laura Calder wasn't the kind of woman to wear her emotions. Behind all that chic sophistication, she was essentially a private woman.

Saying nothing, Sebastian reached across the seat and placed a hand over hers. Laura was surprised by the comfort she drew from such a simple gesture. With a coaxing tug of her hand and a signaling nod, Sebastian invited her to sit next to him. Laura obliged, discovering that she wanted the warmth of human contact. He curved an arm around her shoulders and fitted her against his side.

They rode like that all the way back to the Triple C headquarters, neither speaking; it wasn't a time for words. The grasslands of the Calder range rolled away from them, and the sun shone brightly in the immense sky. It seemed that nothing had changed, yet for each of them, some things had changed forever.

Journey's end came when they reached the big white, columned house that stood alone on its island knoll. Three other vehicles were already parked in front of it. And they were only the beginning, Laura knew; there would be many more before the day was over. Some people would come before they went to her aunt's house at the Circle Six, and others afterward.

When Sebastian parked near the veranda steps and climbed

out, Laura was slow to move. By the time she slid across the seat, he had the passenger door open for her. Weighted by some invisible heaviness, she stepped from the car. Sebastian lightly rested his hand on the ridge of her shoulder as they made their way around the car to the front steps. The front door opened, and Boone came out, long strides carrying him quickly across the veranda and down the steps.

Sebastian's hand fell away from her shoulder as Boone's arms reached to gather Laura into his embrace. "I'm sorry about your uncle, Laura," he said, holding her tightly to him. "I wish I had been there."

"There was nothing you could have done. No one could have. It happened too fast." It was the same thing Laura had told herself a dozen times since it had happened.

"Just the same, I wish I had been there." Boone kept her wrapped tightly to his side as he guided her up the steps.

She was halfway to the top before she realized Sebastian wasn't following them. Halting, she turned and saw him walking back to the car.

"Where are you going, Sebastian?" She said, frowning.

He opened the car door and turned to face her. "It's even more important now that Mrs. Mitchell and the children have a safe place to stay."

Laura had forgotten all about the Mitchell woman. Somehow, she wasn't surprised that Sebastian hadn't.

"Let's go inside," Boone urged. "Your grandfather wants to see you."

Once more she started up the steps, accompanied by the sound of the rental car reversing away from The Homestead. Already Laura was conscious of the vacuum that was created by Sebastian's departure.

Trey met her in the entryway when she walked in. There was no touching, no hugging. Such expressions of sorrow weren't necessary between them.

"Are you all right?" Trey studied her with a twin's sensitivity.

"I'm fine. What about Quint?" Laura asked, voicing the concern that was foremost in her mind. "Has he been told yet?"

Trey nodded. "Mom called him shortly after she talked to you. She chartered a private jet to fly him back. He should land some time early afternoon."

A slight smile lifted the edges of her mouth, but it had nothing to do with Quint's imminent arrival. "That's how she knew."

A frown flickered across Trey's forehead. "Who are you talking about."

"I always call her Mother," Laura explained. "But when I phoned about Logan, I said, 'Mom, this is Laura.' And she knew right away that something was wrong. I didn't understand how she knew . . . until now. I haven't called her Mom in years."

"She doesn't miss much," Trey said.

"Where's Gramps?"

"In the den with Laredo. He decided to wait until Quint gets here before he goes over to Aunt Cat's."

Without so much as a glance at Boone, Laura accompanied her brother to the den. It wasn't a deliberate snub. She simply forgot he was there.

It was shortly after two o'clock when the chartered jet carrying Quint landed at the Triple C's private airfield. Trey and Laura waited on the concrete apron while the aircraft completed its shutdown procedures. The hot wind gusted, blowing dust across the hangar area and whipping Laura's long blond hair. She held it out of her eyes as the cabin's hatch door swung open and one of the pilots lowered the steps. Then Quint took his place in the opening.

As one, she and Trey moved to the bottom of the steps to meet him. Encumbered by the walking cast on his leg, Quint made a slow descent from the plane. Seeing him, Laura was haunted by the strong resemblance to his father, both sharing the same blue-black hair, sharp cheekbones, and smoke gray eyes. Only this time, Quint's eyes were shadowed with the deep pain of grief.

Tightly jawed, Trey was the first to speak. "Dammit, Quint, I wish . . ." But the right words wouldn't come.

Quint eliminated the need for them. "You don't have to say it. I know how you both feel. It isn't something you can put into words."

A small smile curved Laura's mouth. "You always manage to make things easier for others, Quint," she said and kissed his cheek.

No further reference was made to Logan's death until they were on their way to The Homestead. Then Quint turned to Laura. "Aunt Jessy said you were there."

She had known all along that he would want to know the details. Aware that his interest was both personal and professional, Laura told him about the shooting and its aftermath as well as the circumstances surrounding it.

When she finished, Quint didn't say anything for several long seconds. Finally, as he stared out the window at the grassy plains, he said, "I can't remember a time when my dad wasn't aware of everything going on around him, whether off-duty or on. I'd be willing to bet he saw the truck parked outside and knew this Mitchell guy was in there. But he wasn't expecting trouble when he walked up to that door—at least not the shooting kind. He was in uniform, though. That's probably all Mitchell saw."

A silence followed, weighted by a mix of undirected anger, regrets, and grief. It lasted the rest of the way to The Homestead.

Boone was in the entry hall when they walked in. "We haven't met before," he said to Quint, extending a hand in greeting. "I'm Boone Rutledge, Laura's fiancé."

"I've heard about you," Quint replied, but in a tone that had Laura studying the impassive set of his features as he briefly gripped Boone's hand. "I'm sorry we had to meet under these circumstances."

"So am I," Boone stated, as Quint leaned on his cane for balance.

"If you'll excuse me, I need to see my grandfather." He pushed off the cane, taking that first step around Boone before he moved aside.

Boone fell in beside Laura, accompanying her as she followed Quint to the den, the walking cast giving him an uneven, hobbling gait. When they arrived, Chase had already moved around to the front of the big desk. Quint walked up to him. The moment he was within reach, Chase pulled him close.

Laura watched the emotional meeting, only vaguely conscious of Boone's arm possessively along her shoulders. For a long minute the two men embraced, heads bowed into each other, each hugging the other tightly. Laura had always been aware of the special bond that existed between the two, but it had never been more evident than now.

When they separated, Quint's cheeks were wet with tears, but Laura found nothing unmanly about the sight of them.

"It should have been me, son." The husky tremor in her grandfather's voice had Laura blinking back tears of her own.

Quint shook his head. "You're wrong if you think it wouldn't hurt as much to lose you."

The front door opened, but Laura paid little attention to it. People had been stopping by for most of the day, ranch hands and neighbors alike. Then something triggered an awareness within her. Perhaps it was something familiar in the tread of those footsteps that pulled her glance to the doorway, but she knew it would be Sebastian even before he walked in.

His eyes cut a path straight to her, and something quickened within her at the contact. Almost with irritation, she felt Boone's fingers tighten their grip on her upper arm.

Her grandfather was the first to openly recognize Sebastian. "There you are, Sebastian. I don't believe you've met my eldest grandson, Quint Echohawk."

With that smooth grace of his, Sebastian stepped forward. "I regret I haven't had the pleasure."

"This is Sebastian Dunshill from England, Quint," he said, finishing the introduction.

Quint smiled as they shook hands. "Trey's talked about you."

Sebastian responded with a droll slant to his mouth. "Yes, your cousin has been most intelligent in his efforts to teach me the cowboy way—without much success, I'm afraid."

"Mrs. Mitchell and the children," Laura began, unable to suppress her curiosity any longer.

"They are tucked away in a safe place," Sebastian assured her. "And I stopped in town to inform the police where they could be found when it becomes necessary."

"I take it Mitchell hasn't been caught yet," Quint guessed, his features hardening a little.

"Not to my knowledge," Sebastian answered. "Roadblocks have been established on all the major arteries around Blue Moon, and helicopters are making a sweep of the side roads. I expect it's only a matter of time before he will be apprehended."

"With any luck, he's drunk all the beer he took," Trey said. "and they'll find him passed out on some back road."

"There's no point standing around here speculating about it," Chase stated. "It's time we headed for the Circle Six. I don't have to tell you, Quint, how anxious your mother is to have you home. She's going to need to lean on you a lot these next few days."

Quint nodded. "I know."

They started for the door together, one young and one old, but each requiring the balancing support of a cane.

"Are you going over to your aunt's?" Boone asked.

"For a while," Laura replied.

"Then I'll come with you."

"If you want." She was cool to him, but it was the way she felt.

He remained smotheringly close to her as they passed Sebastian and followed the others into the hall. Laura was tempted to say something, but this was neither the time nor the place to make a scene.

In the entryway she stopped to collect her purse from the side table. "I'll drive the Suburban, Trey. That cast on Quint's leg will make it too crowded for all of us to ride together."

Trey never had a chance to answer her as the front door burst open and Mitchell lurched into the house, all wild-eyed and holding a gun. Half-drunk, he reeled to a stop when he saw them. The barrel of the gun made an arcing sweep of all of them.

"Where are they?" he demanded, then spotted Boone and advanced toward him. "You took 'em, didn't you? I'll give you two seconds t'tell me what you did with m'wife an' kids!"

"You're crazy." Boone's gaze jumped from the gun to Mitchell's angry face and back again.

"What d'ya expect when someone steals a man's wife an' kids from him?" the man raged. "Damn right it'll make ya' crazy— crazy enough to use this"—he brandished the gun—"if you don't tell me where they are."

In that moment Laura knew he meant it. Fear struck deep in the pit of her stomach, shooting adrenaline through her system.

"You are addressing the wrong gentleman, Mr. Mitchell." Sebastian's voice rang clear and strong far to the right. Laura swung her gaze to him, stunned to find him there. "I am the one who took your wife and children to a place of safekeeping."

Mitchell whirled in his direction, and, to Laura's horror, Sebastian stepped forward, separating himself from the others. "You did?" Mitchell looked at him none too certainly. "Then where are they?"

"See here, young man." Chase hobbled forward, his cane lifting.

"Gramps, no," Laura protested, terrified that he intended to foolishly shake it at Mitchell like a man scolding a naughty child.

Instead he swept it upward with lightning swiftness, striking the underside of Mitchell's gun hand and evoking a yowl of pain. At almost the same instant Laredo launched himself at Mitchell, tackling him from the side and driving him to the floor.

With amazing calm, Sebastian planted a foot on Mitchell's

wrist and twisted the gun from his grasp. By then, Trey and Boone had joined forces with Laredo to pin Mitchell to the floor.

In the blink of an eye, it seemed, the threat was over. Relief skittered through Laura as she turned an amazed look on her elderly grandfather. He was once more leaning on his cane and smiling at Quint.

"You have to use whatever weapon you have, son."

Quint responded with an amused shake of his head and glanced at Laura. "You'd better call the police."

Less than twenty minutes later a state patrol helicopter landed in the Triple C ranch yard. Its arrival was soon followed by a squad of police cars. In short order Mitchell was handcuffed and escorted off the premises, and the usual round of questioning and statements followed.

Trey and Laredo accompanied the last of the officers onto the veranda while everyone else remained in the den. Boone sat beside Laura on the leather sofa, his arm draped along the back of it behind her head. Quint and Chase occupied the two wingbacked chairs in front of the desk. Tall and lean, Sebastian stood at the window, observing the departure of the last officials and looking as unflappable as he had been through it all.

He turned from the window, his glance briefly making contact with her. Laura was conscious of the instant rise of her heartbeat. She realized it was a normal reaction to him, one that had existed from the outset.

"I think we can safely conclude this business is over," Sebastian declared to no one in particular.

Uncrossing her legs, Laura rose from the sofa and carried her empty coffee cup to the service tray on the desk.

"You do realize that you took a terrible risk speaking up like that." She eyed him with more than a little interest.

"But a calculated one," Sebastian replied with customary insouciance. "After all, if I was the one who knew the location of his wife and children, it was unlikely he would shoot me."

"As drunk as he was, he could have pulled the trigger without even knowing it," Laura countered.

"As I said, it was a calculated risk." His eyes had a warmly amused gleam to them.

Boone pushed off the leather couch, his jaws rigid with anger. "Was it part of your calculation to put this entire family in jeopardy?" he demanded. "None of this would have happened if you hadn't stuck your nose into something that wasn't any of your business. You've caused this family enough trouble, Dunshill. It's time you packed your bags and went back to England. And I mean right now."

In that instant, any lingering doubts vanished as Laura turned a cool look on Boone, her chin lifting. "You are only half right, Boone."

"What do you mean, half right?" he said with a frown.

"You are the one who needs to pack your bags and leave this house. Immediately." There wasn't an ounce of heat in her voice, only an icy determination.

"What are you talking about, Laura?" His expression was all shock and confusion. "We're going to be married."

"We were. But not any more." She twisted the engagement ring off her finger. "Here. You can take this with you." Laura flipped it to him with a touch of disdain.

The stunned look on his face as he caught the ring was almost laughable. "You're upset, Laura," he protested in a dazed fashion. "You don't know what you're doing."

"I always know exactly what I'm doing, Boone," Laura corrected, while Sebastian looked on, struggling to hold back a smile. "You have about as much style as one of your Texas barbeques. And I certainly don't want anyone as cunning and ruthless as Max Rutledge for a father-in-law. I don't care how much money he has; marriage to you would still be a step down. Now, leave."

Chase spoke up, "I hope he doesn't go. I would enjoy having him thrown out."

Boone glared at them, for a moment angry beyond words.

"You'll regret this," he pushed the words through clenched teeth and stalked out of the den, roughly shouldering Laredo aside when he met him and Trey in the doorway.

"What's got into him?" Laredo hooked a thumb over his shoulder in the direction Boone had taken.

"Laura just told him to get lost," Quint replied with a quietly approving smile.

"It's about time," Laredo muttered.

The grin Trey gave her was big and wide. "I guess that means we won't be hearing wedding bells around here any time soon."

"I wouldn't be too sure about that," Laura replied with a trace of smugness.

As she had known he would, Sebastian abandoned his post by the window and crossed to her side, snaring her waist with his hand. "I believe that last remark requires some clarification," he stated, addressing the others. "If you will excuse us, Laura and I will go somewhere and discuss this in private."

"By all means, do," Chase urged.

Nothing had ever felt so right as the light pressure of Sebastian's arm around her as he ushered her out of the den and into the living. But it was nothing compared to the swelling of pure joy within when he turned her into his arms and Laura met his ardent gaze and the suggestion of a twinkle it possessed.

"Have we finally gotten past the money issue?" The husky pitch of his voice was like a caress.

"I wouldn't say we've gotten past it exactly," Laura demurred with a touch of coyness.

An eyebrow arched in silent challenge. "Then what would you say?"

She slid her hands up to his shoulders and loosely clasped her fingers behind his neck. "That I've decided to marry you in spite of it"—Laura paused, a tiny smile showing—"*After* you sign a prenuptial agreement, of course."

A smile grooved the corners of his mouth. "Of course."

Laura touched a finger to the faint smattering of freckles across the bridge of his nose. "I do hope you don't pass any of these freckles on to our daughters. It would be nice if our sons had them, though."

"Regrettably, that's something over which I have no control, Lady Crawford," Sebastian countered lightly, even as desire darkened his eyes.

"I do like the sound of that," Laura confessed.

"And I look forward to calling you that for the rest of our lives."

"I do love you, Lord Crawford." She made the fervent declaration as she pulled his head down to kiss him and share all the fullness of her love.

Epilogue

Snowflakes fell thick and fast from the cloud blanket that covered the Triple C. Now and then a blustery north wind sent them swirling against The Homestead's windows, creating shifting patterns of gray and white. Try as they might, the cold and the snow couldn't penetrate the towering white house that stood so proud and tall on the knoll overlooking the ranch headquarters.

Lights gleamed from its windows in defiance of the premature darkness the November storm had brought to the afternoon. In the den, flames crackled and leaped over the stack of split logs in the fireplace, the heat from it bringing an extra warmth to the room.

Chase dozed in a wingbacked chair next to the fire, halfway between wakefulness and sleep. A heavy sweater hung loosely from his stooped shoulders, the added layer of clothing an attempt to warm his old bones. Dimly he felt the brush of something across his legs and stirred. His drowsy eyes were slow to identify the petitely built woman standing by his chair. For a moment her features swam in and out of focus, but the striking green of her eyes and the shining darkness of her hair, only faintly threaded with gray, registered immediately. Joy swelled within him and a tightness gripped his throat at the sight of his beloved Maggie.

As he reached out to her, she spoke. "Sorry, I didn't mean to disturb you, Dad."

Dad. His hand fell back onto the armrest, the illusion shattered. Chase worked to conceal the bitter disappointment he felt at the discovery it was his daughter Cat standing before him and not his late wife.

He used gruffness to hide any lingering ache in his voice. "I wasn't sleeping."

"Of course not." Cat smiled in dry disbelief and bent to tuck the edges of a heavy blanket around his legs.

The action prompted him to notice the new weight of it on his leg. "What's this about?" Chase demanded, the sight of it making him feel like an invalid.

"I don't want you getting chilled."

"So you're going to roast me instead?" His glance was sharp with reproof.

"Now you know what the doctor said, Dad." Her voice had that indulgent tone parents used when speaking to their children, further irritating him.

"The man's a quack," Chase grumbled. "He claimed I had pneumonia, but it was nothing but a damned cold."

The instant the diagnosis had been made Cat had appointed herself as his personal nurse and moved into The Homestead to care for him. Although Cat had never said so, Chase knew the move was to be a permanent one. Living in the ranch house she had once shared with Logan had proved to be too painful and too lonely. Truthfully, Chase welcomed her presence even if she fussed over him too much.

"It doesn't matter whether it was pneumonia or a common cold, we still can't risk a relapse," Cat insisted, "not with the wedding coming up next week. You know how determined Laura is that you be the one who gives her away."

At the mention of Laura, Chase suddenly noticed the lack of

chattering voices and other sounds of the flurry of pre-wedding activity that had filled The Homestead these last few days. "Where is Laura?"

"Upstairs with Tara and the seamstress. They're finishing up the final fitting."

He frowned. "How come you aren't up there with them?"

"I was. I just came down to check on you," Cat replied with a kind of studied nonchalance and drifted over to the window as if drawn by the thickening curtain of white flakes. "The snow's coming down a lot heavier. I hope the roads aren't slick."

Chase knew at once that the remark was more than just an idle one and guessed, "Quint went over to the Circle Six, did he?"

Cat hesitated fractionally, then nodded. "He wanted to check on the cattle—make sure there was enough hay out for them. I thought he'd be back by now," she added with a faint note of worry.

The day after his father's funeral Quint had handed in his letter of resignation. Chase wasn't surprised by his decision. The boy had always had a strong sense of duty, and there wasn't any doubt that Cat had needed him desperately in those first months following Logan's death.

"Quint's never been the kind to take unnecessary risks." Chase said to allay her concern. "If the roads are bad, he'll just stay at the ranch." After a slight pause, he added. "It's natural to worry about him. All parents worry about their children, whether they're four years old or forty. But you can't continue to lean on Quint. It isn't healthy for either of you."

"I know," Cat admitted on a faint sigh.

Chase was about to say more when an upstairs door opened and the house echoed with the sound of multiple footsteps and feminine chatter. He listened to it flow down the staircase and arched an amused glance at his daughter.

"With Laura in the house, the quiet couldn't last." He knew he'd miss the noise when she moved to England.

"How true," Cat agreed and moved away from the window.

"A snowy afternoon like this seems to call for a cup of hot cocoa. Would you like me to fix you one?"

"I'd rather have coffee." Chase replied.

"I'll bring you a cup." She crossed to the doorway and paused there, her attention transfixed on something in the living room. "Laura," she murmured, the single word conveying a wealth of utter appreciation and approval.

"Is Gramps in the den?" The familiar voice of his granddaughter reached his ears.

Chase spoke up before Cat could answer. "I'm here."

"Close your eyes, Gramps. I have something I want to show you," Laura said.

The beginnings of a small smile edged the corners of his mouth. "I think it might be hard to see it if I close my eyes."

"Very cute," Laura chided with affection. "Just cover your eyes and I'll tell you when you can look. Let me know when he's ready, Aunt Cat," she added.

Realizing that Laura was determined to have it her way, as usual, Chase chose to indulge her whim and placed a hand over his eyes. Almost immediately light footsteps approached the den's entrance, accompanied by the soft rustle of fabric.

"You can look now, Gramps."

He lowered his hand and beheld the vision of his granddaughter poised in the doorway and dressed in a wedding gown of white satin. Its line was simple but incredibly elegant, with long, flowing sleeves and an artful studding of pearls. She was all beauty and grace, a sight that caused a swelling of pride in his chest.

"I wanted you to see me in the gown I'll be wearing at our ceremony in Scotland," Laura exclaimed, careful not to make any direct reference to the fact that he wouldn't be present. It was the consensus that the trip would be too long and hard for him at his advance age. "What do you think? Do you like it?"

"It's beautiful, of course, but"—Chase frowned—"are you saying you have two wedding gowns?"

"Really Gramps, I can't have Sebastian seeing me in the same one twice. It just isn't done," Laura chided. "Besides, since the wedding will take place in Skibo Castle, I thought I should wear something with a slightly medieval look."

"Having two gowns is as foolish as having two weddings," he grumped. "One should be good enough."

"Now, Gramps, we've been through all that." With an indulgent smile, she glided across the room to his chair and sat sideways on the arm of it, facing him. "It simply wasn't feasible for Sebastian's family and friends to fly over here for the wedding. There wouldn't have been enough room to put them all up." She lightly smoothed his coarse gray hair. "And nearly every Calder bride has been married right here in the den. I couldn't very well break that tradition, now could I?"

"No, you couldn't do that. You are, after all, a Calder." A calmness settled over him. And Chase knew that long after he was gone, the Calder tradition would continue. That tradition of passion and pain, loving and losing, trial and triumph would never die. It was the Calder way.